HIS EVERYTHING

A Dark Bratva Mafia Romance

BY:

JENNY D

Disclaimer:

This book is a work of fiction. Names characters, places, and incidents are products of the author's imagination or are used fictitiously and are not to be construed as real. Any resemblance to actual events, locales, organizations, or people, living or dead, is entirely coincidental.

This book is dedicated to

Emilie

My friend and fellow author without her, this series would have never happened. Thank you girl

for all the crazy ideas that sent my mind into overload.

I appreciate you.

And to my Husband who always supports the crazy amount of time I spend reading and writing

Love you.

Trigger Warnings

He falls first

OTT Obsession

Forced Drug Use

Abduction

Human Trafficking

non-Con Sexual intercourse

Descriptions of torture

unaliving

- **Cussing**
- **Spicy Scenes**
- **Spankings**
- **Non-Con Blood Play**
- **Somnophilia**
- **Talk of suicide**
- **Suicide attempts**
- **Torture**
- **and probably more that I can't think of so be warned**

Please pay attention to these triggers your mental health matters!!

Moving to the Big City

Luna

Finally, I managed to get away from that backward nowheresville town I grew up in. Red Lodge Montana with its population of 1700 people it's a dead end life. One I have fought very hard to get out of. When you grow up in such a small town and you're adopted, everyone knows it.

I mean, sure my adoptive parents were nice enough. They ensured that I had proper food and all the necessary things. But everyone knew I wasn't like them and they made sure I knew it too. So after both of my adoptive parents died in a car accident last year, I decided to take what money I had saved up and the money I got from selling the house and I finally left.

I wanted to go to New York City and live a fabulous life. That is until I found out how much it costs to live there. So that went out the window really fast. So now I'm moving to Brooklyn in a small one bedroom apartment. It's not glorious or even pretty. It's dark and crappy looking. But that's just fine. At least it's mine.

I interviewed for a job before I got here at a bar called The Whispering Russian that was looking to hire a mixologist. Thank god I had enough experience to even be considered. I applied for it and had a few interviews over the phone and then my last one was this morning after I arrived. Of course, they had to make sure I knew enough to even work there. It's a pretty nice place right along the Riegelmann Boardwalk. I wouldn't go so far as to say it's classy, but it isn't a hole in the wall either.

I wasn't expecting for it to be so beautiful there though because just a block or two over it looks like all the buildings could use some repairs. Here on the boardwalk, though, you don't see anyone sleeping in the alleys or out front of the businesses. I would think they would rather be over here where it's nice and near the ocean. Then to be in some dark wet alley. But what do I know? I've never been homeless. Just unwanted. It's a feeling I know well. I've never had any real friends and I don't have any family, so moving away just seemed like a no brainer. Sure I could have moved somewhere nicer I am sure, but where better to get life experience than right here in Brooklyn?

I have a few days before I start at The Whispering Russian. I've decided to use that time to learn my way around and get situated. I've always loved the night, and the boardwalk is the perfect place to sit and look at the ocean.

Demetrius

Another day, another dollar. Today I have been keeping an eye on some activity I heard about over by Brighton 7th Street. I haven't seen anything as of yet but that doesn't mean there isn't anything. Instead, I decided to collect protection dues myself since I am here. Yes, I know that it's under the brigadier, but not everything can be blood and guts.

The people here need to know that it's not just the enforcers that are around. Everyone needs to see that I'm here. That I'm watching. Word will spread and maybe that will be enough for the Cartel to decide coming here and starting trouble isn't a good idea. After leaving the Russian guide of New York; yes that's the name of the business. Yes, I know it's a bit redundant. I step back out onto Brighton 7th Street and head for the other businesses we get protection dues from.

That's when I see her. An angel in the flesh. The most beautiful woman I have ever seen in my life and that's saying something since Russia has some of the most beautiful women in the world. She is looking at the apartment building in front of her with wide eyed wander. There is no way this innocent woman should be in this part of town. Ever. I can't help but watch her. If I can see her innocence, so can every other scum sucker on this street. She is in an old beat up Chevrolet that is rusted with faded paint. It looks like it should be in the junkyard, not parked on the side of the street.

As I look at her, my brain starts committing her to memory because I know she is mine. The way she moves. How her hair blows in the wind. The sway of her hips. I don't even want another man to look in her direction. If it was up to me, I would pluck all of their eyes out just for glancing at her beauty. She is mine to look at and I will have her.

She has the most beautiful black hair I think I have ever seen in my life. It's straight but thick. She has high cheekbones and beautiful almond-shaped eyes. Her dark hair makes her tanned skin look even more flawless, and she has some meat on her bones. I'm a hot-blooded Russian man and I need a real woman. A woman who can take a pounding. Literally. Not these twigs that don't eat. They always feel like they will break if I grab them too hard. But not her. She looks like she would be able to handle me. She walks across the street toward the building, leaving all of her things unattended. I shake my head at her naivety as I cross the street to make sure her things are still there when she returns. Otherwise, it will all be gone as soon as she enters the building.

I can see them all eying it up, but seeing me is enough to make them turn and walk away. Only one dared to try to the rest got the point when I broke his arms the moment he tried to reach for anything. I looked around the street and pointed at the truck.

"Did you see the woman who got out of this truck? She is off limits. Understood?"

I didn't need an answer to know they understood. Even the man at my feet who is crying nods and tries to scramble away. I can't help but laugh at the fool as he tries to get up. It's hard to get up without your arms and it's also very amusing to watch. But even as funny as it is, he can't be here when she returns, so I help his ass up and toss him down the road.

No one on this road will bother her and if they do now, they know I will be the last thing they see. I step back into the shadows and wait for my angel to reappear. It also gives me a chance to watch this street more often. Because my innocent little angel has no idea how unsafe this place is. But she has nothing to worry about. Her devil is here to see that she is safe.

First Glance

Luna

I get out of my old beat up truck and look at the size of these buildings. Holy shit, they are so tall they block out the sun. I have no idea how long it will take me to get used to this or even if I ever will. I got into the city late last night and I just got done with my final interview. Now I need to sign the lease for my small apartment and move in. I dropped by right before my interview just to see it. It's not much to look at, but the price is right.

I'll need to go and buy some white paint. I don't think that I could live there with those dingy walls. If they are at least clean, I can pretend that this is a nicer place than it is. No matter what, it's better than being in that hole in the wall town.

I take a deep breath and let it out. Squaring my shoulders. I walk across the road to take care of business. The property manager is a really skinny, dirty looking guy. I don't care how he looks, but he really is a scuzz ball. I almost don't want to go in to sign the lease because I will be in a room alone with him. He just gives me the creeps. I have no idea how he does it but everything he says, even if it should sound innocent and normal. Still comes out like a sexual innuendo.

That and he can't seem to figure out where my face is, since he is always staring at my chest. The man is just a pig. He doesn't even try to hide it. But I have to do this. I don't have much of a choice. It was live here or in a place so bad that the homeless were everywhere and the streets were dirty. So I will have to deal with the leering man who I hope is harmless; even if he is gross.

I knock on his door, and I hear him yell from inside. I can't tell what he said though because his TV is loud.

"I'm sorry to bother you, but it's Luna Lewis here to get the apartment on the sixth floor?" I yell through the door.

The door swings open and there he was in all his nasty glory. Leering at me.

"Oh yes, I remember you. Come on in. I have the paperwork here." He says, staring at my chest again.

I look up and down the hall, hoping someone, anyone, would see me entering his apartment. But the hall is empty. I take a deep breath and step into his apartment. It's not the best situation, but if he was stealing women, I would hope he would have been caught already. He hasn't really done anything ... yet. That makes me feel scared, but he gives off a vibe that is just unnerving. It went quickly. I signed the lease, gave him the money, and he gave me the keys. I walked back out quicker than I did when I went in.

When I stepped back out onto the sidewalk, the first thing I noticed was how quiet it was. If this were Montana, I would be looking for a tumbleweed or something to roll down the road. I shrug. It seems odd, but that's good if this is a quiet road. That means it's safer than I thought it was. I grab a few bags of my stuff and head up to my new apartment. I don't have much so it will be an easy move in day.

I look up at the building again before I walk back in. I am going to be really high in the air. I'm not scared of heights, but this will be the first time I have ever been higher than the second floor. I step forward to go toward my new home. The moment I take a step, I feel like I am being watched. I turn around and scan the road, but I don't see anyone.

I shrug 'O well, I must be imagining things.'

Even after making a few trips back and forth to my truck every time I step out of the door, I feel like I am being watched. It has to be because I'm new here. I must just be nervous about being in the city. I'm not used to so many people. Before I walk back into the building the last time, I scan the sidewalks again and I still don't see anyone. I shake my head and head back into the building.

Two Days Later

Over the last two days, I cleaned and painted the apartment. So it now at least looks clean and bright. I've met a few people around the neighborhood and so far everyone has been really nice. I was expecting that people would be rude. It is the one thing you hear the most about New Yorkers.

When I was at the small corner store down the road, I saw what was probably the most beautiful man I have ever seen before. I swear he could be a model. For such a large man, he moved like a ballerina. Smooth and graceful. But completely in control and masculine. He was speaking to the shopkeeper in what sounded like Russian. The man nodded at him and glanced in my direction and then back at the man when he growled.

Yea, I said growled and I don't think it should have turned me on the way it did. It made me shiver. When I got in line behind the gorgeous Russian, I really got to see just how large he truly was. Compared to him, I look like a child. When he turned to leave, I swear I almost fainted when our eyes met. His dark hair is cut short on the sides and longer on the top. He has to be over six feet tall easily, with broad shoulders and muscles for days. I grew up with farm boys that thought were big boys, but he makes them all look like small little boys.

When he looks at me, I can't even breathe. He flicks his eyes down to mine, nods, and walks out the door. I let my breath out slowly after the door closed. Wow, he is very intense. But damn, that's a tree I wouldn't mind climbing. Danger rolls off of him in waves and damn if I don't like me a bad boy. I can feel the wetness pooling between my legs.

Jesus, what's wrong with me? That's the kind of man I should avoid. But standing here as I watch him walk away, my body practically vibrates with need. The need to just reach out and touch him is so strong I have to force myself not to follow him. I shake my head to clear the thoughts and move up to pay for the stuff I need. Once I walk out of the little corner store, I look around and see that same man speaking to another shopkeeper. They both look very serious.

The shopkeeper sees me looking and smiles. The large man turns and looks at me. Once our eyes lock, it's all I can do to look away. The man has very intense eyes. But even from this distance, I can see a flicker of something I don't recognize. I break eye contact and quickly turn to head away.

What was I thinking looking at a man like that in the eyes? Violence and control radiate off of him. A barely there control. But I can't help the attraction I feel for him. I've always liked the bad boy type. I mean, who doesn't? But looking at this man is like watching a stranger walk down the road with an Uzi. You know there is trouble coming, but you can't take your eyes off of him.

She's Mine

Demetrius

That was much closer than I would have liked. It was very hard to walk away from her. I could feel her eyes on me when she watched me walk out of the market. Did she like what she saw? Are her feelings the same as mine? I doubt it. I already know I am crazy. But the moment I saw her, I knew. She is mine.

I can't stop thinking about her and the way she makes me feel. I haven't felt anything in so long that it's a shock to my system. She is incredibly beautiful. It was almost overwhelming. I tried to push those feelings to the back of my mind. I shouldn't have this much interest in her. I am too violent of a man to just walk up to such an innocent woman.

Every cell in my body wanted to go back and throw her over my shoulder like a caveman and just walk off with her.

Being so close to her made my whole body tense up with anticipation, and yet I felt strangely calm at the same time. It was almost as if I knew that everything was going to be alright. No matter what, I will protect her. Follow her and make sure she is safe from this world, even if I can't claim her as my own. It's crazy for me. I never had a woman make me feel that way before. Especially not with just a glance. I can feel the pull to her even now. But I know I can't claim her. Not in my line of work. It would just put her in even more danger.

I've thought about her for the past few days. Her thick, straight hair and her eyes that I have been seeing even in my dreams. The thought of someone even approaching her makes me tighten my hands into fists. Ready to destroy anyone who thinks they can have a chance with her. No, she is mine. It doesn't matter how long it takes.

I am going to make her mine. Even though I know I shouldn't. I have never been a man to not take what I want. She is just so fucking beautiful. Everything about her screams purity and innocence. When she walked out of the market, I felt her eyes on me again. The moment she looked in my direction, I could feel the tingle on my skin. I tried to fight the magnetic pull of her eyes, but my obsession wouldn't allow that. I had to look at her. My woman.

I shouldn't be thinking like this. Being second in command of the

Bratva would put her in danger. That's why I have to just watch her. Keep my distance. But fuck, I want to touch her so badly. She is perfection. Her dark tan skin is flawless, and her hips sway perfectly as she walks. It makes my mouth water and my cock hard. I swear that ass swaying has me in a trance as I watch her walk away. It's something I could watch all day long.

I need to walk away before I make a mistake. I try to think of all the reasons I need to behave. But none of them matter to me right now. My obsession with her is overriding any sane thought. I am the right-hand man of the leader of the largest organized crime syndicate in Brighton Beach. I have the reputation of being a monster and a murderer. I know she doesn't know who I am, but it's better for her that way. If she found out what I have done. What would she think then?

I would kill a hundred men to protect her. But I'm not sure I can protect her from me. My obsession with her is growing stronger the more I watch my little angel. I know I shouldn't be watching her, but I can't help myself. I cross the street and walk on the opposite side of the road from her. The conversation with the other shopkeeper is long forgotten.

I am watching her now. She has all of my attention. She is looking around a shop like she is interested. The shopkeeper is flirting with her. I can tell. I know I shouldn't be watching, but I can't seem to look away. He smiles at her and says something, and now I want to remove his tongue. How dare he speak to my angel?

My entire body tenses up when she smiles back at him. She is mine. I want to walk over there and remove his eyes for staring at my woman. To remove his tongue for speaking to her. His dick for even thinking he could flirt with what is mine. He can't have her.

I feel that tension build again while I watch her. My body is vibrating with rage. It's making me feel out of control. I should just let it go. Walk away. There are so many other women. Why is this one affecting me this way? I can't seem to stop. I have been watching her since I first saw her. I have to make sure she is okay and that no one is threatening her. That she is safe. Protected.

I watch her walk out of the shop. She looks so innocent and beautiful. She is smiling. That smile could probably stop the whole world if she aimed it at the right person. The shopkeeper is following her out the door. He is talking to her, but she cuts him off.

"I am sorry, but I have a lot to do today." She says with a soft accent. I can hear her even from where I am standing across the street.

The shopkeeper tries to keep talking to her, but she walks off instead of answering him. I stride across the street and step into the shop, dragging him with me. He knows who I am. This is a Russian owned store. His eyes are wide when I shove him into the back.

"Don't ever speak to her again. Don't even look at her." I growl out in Russian.

"I didn't know. I am sorry."

"Stay away from her," I say.

"I won't talk to her again. I swear."

"I will be watching," I say, scowling at him.

He nods and I leave him standing there.

He is lucky today. I don't have time for this. I need to keep an eye on her. She seems to be oblivious to the danger that surrounds her. Monsters like me surround her. I have to keep her safe. I can still see her walking down the street. I continue to follow her as she continues down the street. I have watched her go to a couple of different stores, and she has a few bags from shopping. I continue to watch her until she steps off the street and goes up the steps of the apartment building she lives in.

I follow her as close as I dare and wait till I hear her steps fade. I open the door to the apartment building and follow her in. I have to make sure she gets into her apartment safely. I don't want anyone hurting her.

This is a dangerous building with no security. I watch which floor the light stops at on the elevator. Looking around the entryway, I see the manager's door. I walk over and knock on the door. When he opens it, I look at him with cool eyes.

"Your new tenant Luna. What is her apartment number?"

"Oh, interested are you? That, for sure, is one hot piece of ass." I scowl at him and narrow my eyes at him. But he stupidly keeps rambling. This American doesn't seem to understand who I am. But he will soon find out. "I tried once already, but she seems like a prude. Not that I am giving up. I know she wants it. She is just playing hard to get."

I have no control over my hand when it wraps around his throat. I pick him up off the floor by his neck and walk into his apartment. Kicking the door shut behind me. His eyes are wide as he scratches at my hands, trying to get me to put him down. The monster in me is enjoying watching his face go red. The panic on his face. He kicks at my legs and I drop him to the floor.

"Never talk about my woman again. Never even think about her again. Don't even look at her." I growl out, my accent thicker to madder I get. "You understand me?"

He nods his head quickly while he scrambles backward, trying to gain some distance between us.

"Shit, yes!! Who the fuck are you?" he gasps, trying to catch his breath.

I grin at him, even though I am sure it looks more rabid than anything. "Demetrius Sokolov."

I see the realization dawn on his face. He doesn't even try to hide his fear.

"Oh fuck, fuck, fuck. I'm sorry I didn't know," he screams out. "She's your woman? I swear I didn't know." He says, all in a rush.

"She is a sweet, innocent girl. And here you were thinking of taking her like she could be yours?" I say in a mocking tone. Bending down to get face to face with him. "Never try to approach her again or it will be the last thing you do. I have no problem making that promise to you."

"Fuck ok, I get it."

"Now that we have an understanding. What apartment." I say, standing back.

"She lives on the 6th floor apartment 615. I swear I won't ever say anything to her again, just don't kill me."

I lean over and pat him on his cheek like the obedient dog he is. "Just make sure no one else bothers her and this will be the end of this ... little incident. But if I find out, you are bothering her." I give him a meaningful look.

"You won't. I won't bother her again. I swear."

"Make sure you don't,"

I leave the apartment manager and head to the elevator. I go to the 6th floor. I step off the elevator without making a sound. I am here for my own reasons. I don't want to be noticed. I need to make sure she is secure up here. I walk to her door. I can hear her in the apartment as she flitted around. This door is so flimsy it won't protect anyone. I will have to fix this. My angel needs more than this flimsy wood to protect her while she is here. She deserves so much better than this shitty place. But for now, it will have to do. I will make it safer.

I put a tiny camera on the ceiling across from her door and pulled up the app. I always carry a few cameras. You never know when you might need them. I adjust it so I can see her door perfectly. I need to be sure she is safe even when I am not around. I will send some men tomorrow to replace the door and locks. That way, I know she will be safe. The whole world wants her as far as I am concerned. She doesn't seem to know how beautiful she is or how much danger she is in.

I ride the elevator back down and pound on the scumbag's door again. "I will be sending men to replace her door tomorrow. I want you to tell her if she asks that the building is making some improvements. Understand? Don't try anything funny I am watching."

I show him the screen of my phone. He nods vigorously. I turn and walk out of the building. Now that I have a camera on her, I can go about my business until she leaves the apartment again. Then I will put a few inside of her apartment as well. She is mine. I must make sure that she is always safe. I want to make sure she has everything she needs and wants. I know I have a lot of work to do before I can make her mine. But I will make sure that happens.

I will be watching over her until the day I die, regardless of anything else. I already know this to be true.

The Whispering Russian

Luna

Tonight is my first night at The Whispering Russian. I'm more nervous than I thought I would be. The uniforms aren't super revealing but then again; they aren't not revealing either. They have these super tight shirts and booty shorts. At least they are black and it will be kind of dark in there. Otherwise, I might not look so great. I'm not exactly a stick figure, so I keep tugging at the shirt as I walk down the boardwalk. I feel like a fat Pocahontas in this getup. I frown when I see myself in the window of the bar.

I look up at the building and take it all in. Today, I have an early shift to get trained and learn where things are when it's not busy. I keep getting this feeling of being watched, but every time I look around, I don't see anyone. Before I walk in the door, I glance at myself in the window again. I could have sworn I saw someone duck between two smaller buildings. I must really be paranoid. No one would follow me. Look at me, for fuck's sake. I wrap my arms around my midsection and head inside to start my first day. As soon as I walk through the door, security stops me. He looks me up and down.

"New here?" he says in a heavy Russian accent.

His appearance is not bad, but he looks like a mountain in a suit that has clearly been tailored to fit him, despite being too large for it. I suppose it makes sense that he would be Russian. I mean, the name is The Whispering Russian.

"Yeah, my name's Luna. This is my first day."

He points to the steps. "I'm Anton. Go see the boss. First door. Top of steps." He says in broken English.

I nod "Thanks."

I can feel his eyes on me as I walk away. It's not a creepy feeling, but I can tell he is looking at my ass in these shorts. Not sure I would call them shorts. They are closer to those girl boxers if you ask me. I slowly climb the stairs. The other day, they didn't interview me up here. Hopefully, the boss is the lady that hired me. This uniform is already uncomfortable, but I need the job. I'll just have to get used to it, I guess. I let out a deep breath to steel myself. I shake out my arms, trying to loosen up. I raise my hand and knock on the door.

I hear a male voice with a Russian accent holler for me to come in. The moment I open the door, my stomach tenses. I feel uneasy. The man sitting there isn't a bad looking man. He is actually gorgeous in a very unconventional way. He just has this vibe about him that makes me uneasy. His dark hair is very short, almost shaved on the sides and very short on the top, almost like a buzz cut, but a little longer than the sides. The most noticeable detail is the scar that goes through his eye and down his cheek. His eye is still there, but he still reminds me of a Bond villain.

I stand right inside of the door, afraid to move away from it. My instincts are telling me I should run, but I can't. I need this job. When he finally looks up, he doesn't hide the fact that he seems to like what he sees.

I clear my throat to try to say something. "Um, I'm Luna. I was told I started today."

He smiles at me. At least I think it's a smile. It's very unnerving no matter what it is. He pulls a cigarette out and lights it, blowing the smoke in my direction.

"Come closer. Let me see you better. You are here to be a dancer?"

He has a Russian accent, but it isn't as thick as the security guard.

My eyes widen, and I shake my head. "No, I'm the new bartender."

He slowly drags his eyes over me again. "Are you sure? I think I would love to see you take your clothes off."

"No sir. I am here only to be a bartender."

Shit. When I call him sir, he gets turned on and desire fills his eyes. I can even see him palming himself behind the desk. I need to get out of here. But if he is the boss. I can't just run. My new landlord gave me the creeps, but this guy seems truly dangerous and creepy.

"Fine. Sit." I don't really want to sit, but here I am. He presses a button on his desk. "Get Becky in here."

I look everywhere but at him while I wring my hands in my lap. I really want to get out of here. After what seems like forever, I hear the office door open.

"Viktor, you wanted me?" When I hear her voice, I can't help the feeling of relief that washes over me. "Oh, there you are Luna. I was looking for you."

"Take your new hire." He motions with his hands. I practically jump from the chair and hurry toward the woman who hired me. "I will be seeing you, Luna."

I can't tell if that's just a normal thing for him to say or a threat, but I don't want to stay long enough to find out. I turn to look at him, and the leering look he gives me makes me cringe. Which makes him smile. I quickly wave and practically throw myself out of the open door. Becky pats my back and guides me toward the back of the bar, toward the kitchens.

She looks around and then in a whisper says, "Maybe try to avoid Viktor?"

"Yeah, I think I will. That was intense."

"Yes, well, make sure you don't say anything about him to anyone. He is ..." she looks around again "a powerful man. Just maybe avoid him as much as possible. He generally leaves us alone."

I nod and wring my hands. Maybe this isn't the job for me. But where else would I find a job on such short notice? I am truly stuck for now. How bad could it be? I'm not even sure I want to know. I will just have to do my best to avoid him.

"It will be ok. Let's get you sorted."

The rest of the day flies by and thankfully, I don't see Viktor again. Everyone I work with seems great so far, and the job is everything I was hoping it would be. She tested my knowledge of drinks. A few I needed refreshers for and there were a few I had never heard of before. She said were popular because of the Russian clients, but that most would just ask for vodka. Before I left for the day, I stepped into the back to clock out and there was Viktor standing waiting for me.

I stopped dead in my tracks and glanced around. Great, once more we are alone. Maybe this won't be so bad. Maybe he is just here to see how my first day went. I slowly approach the time clock.

"Hello again," I manage to squeak out.

"I came to see how your first day was." He touches my shoulder and it sends a wave of repulsion through my body.

I try to hide the fear that he causes, but I don't think I catch it in time because he sneers at me.

"It was good, thanks." I almost whisper. I grab my time card and clock out. "I need to get home." I turn to leave when he speaks again.

"When is your next day?"

"Um, in two days. I work my first night."

He looks me up and down, smiles, and walks off. I let my shoulders sag with relief before turning and hurrying out. Maybe I am overreacting and he is just being a good boss. I mean, they do have exotic dancers here on the weekend. I'm sure he could get one of them much easier than messing with me. I just need to get home so I can change and relax.

Tonight is the first full moon since I left home. I think I'll go home and take a nap so that I can come out onto the boardwalk and watch the moon as it comes up. This will be the first time I will ever get to watch it over water that isn't a lake and I can't wait.

I can't wait to watch the sunset at the beach and the moon rising over the water. I bet it will be the most beautiful thing I have ever seen. I still have the feeling that I am being watched, but I really just think it's because there are people everywhere. I mean even I people watch sometimes. So it just must be that.

The sunsets here are amazing! I am so excited to see the first one over the ocean. The sky is red with the setting sun and the waves crash into each other as they try to reach shore. I can still feel eyes on me, but it's not as intense now. As the sun goes down, fewer and fewer people are around. It's like everyone has gone home for dinner or something. That's when I notice the man in black standing on the beach, watching me.

He's tall, with dark hair and eyes, and a handsome face... he kind of gives me the creeps, so I move back toward the boardwalk to watch the moon rise over the water. He follows me. When I turn around, he grabs my arm and pulls me close to him. I scream and push his hand away.

He laughs and says, "Don't worry baby, you'll get used to having men touch you."

I look around, and there is no one on the boardwalk at all. I'm alone. I'm scared and confused. Why did he grab me? Who is he? What does he want from me? My heart races and I start to panic. Shit stupid Luna, this isn't back home. What. are. you. thinking.

"Let go of me!" I yell.

He smiles and pushes me against the pier and holds me there. His hand runs up my shirt and grabs one of my breasts through my bra. I struggle, but he has me pinned.

"Stop!" I say, trying to push him away.

"You will do." He sneers at me as I struggle.

"No! Let me go!" I yell.

His fingers pinch my nipples, and I cry out. He kisses me and bites my lip.

"Please stop..." I beg.

Suddenly, he is just gone. I'm so surprised that at first, it doesn't even register. I turn my head and see the large Russian man again. The one from the corner store the other day.

"Go." He says to me in a dark, dangerous voice.

I didn't need to be told twice I take off running. What was I thinking? This isn't Montana. Oh, my god if it wasn't for him I would have been ... I can't even think about it. I sob as I run.

Dead Man

Demetrius

When I entered the bar earlier, Anton stopped me to tell me there was a new hire. Some American girl. That got my attention, so I asked a few more questions and found out that Luna had gotten a job here at The Whispering Russian. It's a good and bad situation. Easier for me to watch her. But harder to keep her from my brother. I know he will notice my obsession with her if I stick around here every time she works. It will cause even more issues if he shows an interest in her.

I had a small, quiet conversation with Anton about her. He understands he is to keep an eye on her when I am not around. He may be on my brother's payroll, but he has always been loyal to me. When we were younger, his family ran into some trouble and I helped them. He has been loyal to only me since then.

I had just come from my brother's office when I got the notification that she was leaving her apartment. I quickly moved in her direction. I spotted her coming toward me, so I ducked into an alleyway and watched her from there as she passed me. She looks so beautiful with the sun setting behind her. Her black hair flowing around her face, making her look like some kind of nymph from a fairytale. It takes all my self-control not to go after her.

She shouldn't be out here at night. I growl deep in my throat as I watch her walk. She continues to walk along the boardwalk and I follow. She looks around but doesn't seem to notice that I am there. I shake my head at how oblivious she is. I am a mountain. I always stand out like a sore thumb everywhere I go. She is too busy taking it all in. I spot a man that is watching her before she does. I stand and watch her as she heads toward the beach. Right toward him. What the fuck is she thinking?!

Someday I will punish her for this. She is putting herself in danger. Finally, she notices the man and starts to head back toward me quickly. Not that she knows she is heading for me. She seems to of realized the danger she put herself in but it's already too late. I can see the panic on her face. I stand and watch her. Waiting for the right time to intervene.

The man moves in on her and I feel the fury take over. He has just fucked up. He will regret the day he laid a finger on her. She's mine.

I see him grab her and that's the end of any self control I might have been holding onto. I watched as she tried to fight him off. My brave angel doesn't just give up. She is a fighter. I'm already in motion. I'm going to rip him limb from limb. She says something to him, but I am too lost in rage to hear what it was.

I yank him from her and the only thing can growl out is, "Go" She shouldn't see what I am about to do to him.

I have him up off the ground by his neck as she turns to run off. I pull his hair back and bare my teeth to his face. "Do you want to die tonight?" I growl out at him.

I know she is safe when I hear her footsteps fade. I am still furious as I look around the empty boardwalk. I throw him and he crashes to the ground. I kick him until he stops moving. I pull him under the pier. Put my gun to his head and sneer in his face when his eyes open.

"Never touch what belongs to me." I pull the trigger and drop his body into the sand.

I know I should have kept him alive for information. But my need to protect her overruled any and all thought. Now I don't know if this was random or if she has people watching her. But since this guy's brains are all over the beach.... I guess it's too late to worry about that now.

I look around once more before walking out. She needs to stay inside where it's safe. I don't have time for this shit. I pull out my phone. I call Anton to clean up the mess and dispose of the body.

“Oh, and Anton.”

"Da?"

"I need the door to Luna's apartment replaced yesterday. I will need someone to fix the locks and install some cameras in the apartment. As far as she needs to know, the door is an improvement the building is making. Hide the cameras. Don't let her see you do it." I look around. "Oh, and Anton. Keep this between us."

"Of course."

I hang up and head toward Luna's building to make sure someone else didn't follow her. I get a notification as soon as she enters her apartment. Good. I'm going to put out some feelers. She may need a guard to follow her. I should have thought ahead. My obsession has put her in danger.

I am the one who has put her in this position. I'm the one who let my dick make decisions for me. I should have just walked away. But I want her. No, I need her. But not at the risk of her life. I will make sure no one else touches her. She will be safe now. I will make some changes and make sure she is safe.

I call Anton again, "I want you to put feelers out. Find out if she has people after her."

"Da."

"I don't want them to know what she is to me."

"Yes, we will find them."

"Don't underestimate anything, Anton. Tell me anything you hear."

"Da."

I look around again to make sure I don't see anyone suspicious watching her building.

"Keep this between us, Anton. Don't mention anything to the Pakhan."

"Da, of course. You know where my loyalty lies."

"I have a feeling she is in danger. I need to protect her. Someone just tried to take her. I can't allow this." I can feel my chest tightening as I say this.

"Of course. I will take care of it."

I hang up and walk around her neighborhood to make sure no one is lurking. That mother fucker thought he could touch what is mine.

Close Call

Luna

I ran straight home. When I got into my apartment, I slammed the door shut and locked it. Then I walked around the apartment, pacing back and forth. Oh my god, what was I thinking? If it wasn't for that man, I would... I swallowed hard at the realization of how close I just came to being just another statistic.

I am shaking from head to toe. I can still hear that guy's voice as he told me I would get used to men touching me. I don't even know who that man was. I am so freaked out that I just sit in the dark, trying to calm my nerves. My phone rings and I jump. I don't recognize the number, but I answer it, anyway.

"Hello?"

"Are you ok?" I hear a deep Russian voice ask me.

"Who is this?"

"I need to know you are safe."

It takes a minute to realize that the man who saved me is on the phone. He sounds angry, and he has a thick Russian accent. "I'm ok."

"Don't walk around after dark. It's not safe. Do you understand?"

"Yes. Thank you so much." I sob.

"No more thank you's Luna. This is my job now. I'm going to put some men on you. You won't see them, but they will be there. They will protect you. You are mine, and I don't want anyone touching you."

"What? What do you mean, I don't even know you?" I whisper.

"I know, but I can't stop thinking about you." He says in a voice that sounds almost pained.

"Please..." I whimper into the phone.

He growls. "Luna. You are mine. This isn't a game. If someone was to touch you. To touch what is mine. It will be the end for them. No one will touch you. They will know. I will kill them if they do. This is my promise to you. No one will hurt you. Do you understand?"

I feel fear and excitement at his words. I've never had anyone say they would protect me, much less kill for me. He scares me a little but also makes me feel safe. It's confusing, but I just nod. Then I realize he can't see that we are on the phone.

"Yes.." I whisper.

"You belong to me."

"But I don't even know you."

He laughs. "I will fix this."

"Ok..." I whisper.

"Don't talk to strangers, Luna."

He hangs up, and I stare at the phone. But he is a stranger. What have I gotten myself into? I know I shouldn't talk to him, but what if someone really is after me? Who else would save me the way he did? Maybe I can trust him. I hope he isn't lying. I know I shouldn't be feeling aroused right now. I should be scared, cowering in a corner, crying.

But seeing the way his whole body seemed even bigger than before when he ripped that man from me like he weighed nothing. It does things to me. I never thought something like that would. Then he called me his, and he knew my name. But I know nothing about him. Who is he and how did he know my phone number? I just don't understand any of this.

I shake my head and try to clear it. I go to take a shower to calm myself down. I have thoughts of my big, mysterious Russian protector while the water flows over my body. I don't know what's wrong with me. But I can't seem to push the thoughts away. The sight of him big and looming. Threatening and powerful.

I can feel my heartbeat in my pussy. I have never felt this way about anyone. I am by no means a virgin, but this man makes my body come alive in a way that I never knew was possible. I wonder if he will really be able to protect me. I can't help but wonder if his cock is as big as the rest of him. I slide my hands to my breasts and run my fingers over my nipples.

The water cascades over my breasts and runs down my stomach and legs to my feet. I run my fingers down the inside of my thighs and imagine it is his fingers touching me. I pinch my nipple, imagining it's his fingers on my body.

I glide my fingers toward my pussy, running my fingers over the outside of my pussy lips, and press hard. I moan out. I pull my hand back and start again. I am so wet, my body is on fire. I touch my pussy and dip my fingers into my wet heat.

"Oh god..." I whimper.

I start to move my fingers faster on my clit. I bite down on my lip to hold in the moans.

"Fuck..." I whisper.

I press harder on my clit and slip a finger inside myself. I can't believe how wet I am for a man I don't even know. I slide my finger in and out of myself, faster and faster. I Imagine him looming over me, sucking my nipple into his mouth as he takes me. He is so fucking big that his huge body dwarfs mine. His hands are holding me down while he takes me roughly. His huge cock sliding in and out of my pussy.

"Fuck me." I pant.

Moving my fingers in and out of me faster, I pinch my clit with my other hand. I can't hold back any longer. I let out a scream as I came all over my fingers. I ride out the waves of my orgasm as they course through my body. My whole body feels like it is floating.

When I come back to my senses, I quickly rinse off and climb out. I don't know why I did that, but I need to think clearly. This isn't normal. I have never felt like this about anyone. Much less a man who knows who I am, but I know nothing about him. I don't even know his name. I wonder if he is still watching me.

Maybe he won't like what he sees. Maybe he will tell me not to do that again. Oh god, what if he knows? That somehow makes me horny all over again. The thought of him watching me somehow as I touch myself. I lay on my bed and get my battery operated boyfriend out. If there is ever a time I need him, it's now. The thought of this large Russian has me going out of my mind.

I am too aroused to even sleep. I hear his voice in my head. He saved me, protected me, and called me his. That is something that shouldn't turn me on this much, but it does. I can feel how slick I am between my thighs. I think about him as I slip a hand back between my legs and cup my pussy in my hand.

I feel so hot. My whole body is tingling with arousal. My pussy is so wet that I can feel it dripping down my in between my ass cheeks. I reach and rub my clit and moan out loud. My head is filled with thoughts of his powerful hands holding me down while he pounds into me. Completely dominating me. His dick is so massive that it stretches me out. Causing a little pain with the pleasure. I push my dildo inside myself and move it in and out quickly.

I know he has to be big. Bigger than my dildo. But the thought of him inside me has me gasping out in pleasure.

"... Oh fuck, fuck me." I cry out.

I start to feel my orgasm build and I work myself up to a peak. I can feel my body tensing as my orgasm starts to build into something I have never felt before.

"Yes, oh fuck..." I pant.

"Fuck yes... that's it. Come for me, Luna. I'm going to fuck you so hard you'll never forget it." I hear him say in his deep voice in my head.

His voice fills my head as I lose myself in pleasure. Now that I have heard him speak to me, his voice is all that I hear. The growl of his words sends chills through me. His deep accented voice is even better in person than it is over the phone. I know he is not here, and he is not touching me, but I still have an orgasm stronger than I have ever had before.

I collapse back against the bed with my hands covering my face. I can't believe what I just did. That was one of the best orgasms I have ever had in my life and it was just to thoughts of him. What would happen if it was really him? He saved me and I used him to get myself off. What the hell is wrong with me? I was almost raped, or worse than that. I'm ashamed of myself for fantasizing about a man I don't even know while I could have been raped or worse.

"God, Luna, get your act together. Start thinking straight. You don't even know him." I whisper to myself.

I lay on the bed for a long time, thinking. I fall asleep, but my dreams are filled with the image of my Russian protector.

Viktor

Luna

Two days later

Two days after the man tried to grab me, some large Russians showed up at my apartment with a new door and some locks. They said the apartment building was making sure all the tenants had new doors for security purposes. But I know it had to be my protector. I'm not stupid. They aren't talking to anyone else and I only see one door.

He had his men come and fix everything. While they were there, I knew the apartment would be safe, so I headed out to the corner store quickly. By the time I returned, they had already completed the work. Only one man was there holding my new set of keys to give me.

The first two days after that incident, I stayed in my apartment. I've hardly left. Today I have my first night shift training. I know it's going to be much more stressful. But I love what I do so I am sure it will all be ok.

I know he said he would have someone guarding me and that I wouldn't see them. But I literally don't think there is anyone. Maybe he was just talking. I hope he does though, because I have to walk to work at dusk. After what happened, it makes me almost panic.

I walk around the neighborhood to get a feel for what's happening. I'm looking around for anyone who looks suspicious. I'm on edge. I make my way to The Whispering Russian on the boardwalk and hurry in. Security greets me at the door. I recognize Anton from my first day.

"Hello, Miss Luna. You are well?"

"Hello, Anton. Yes, thank you."

We both nodded as I continued on. I heard the other man say something in Russian. It seemed like Anton's voice had dropped to a growl when he answered the man. There was almost a look of surprise on his face. The men didn't look at each other again. But I could tell whatever he said to the man had something to do with me.

The bar is really busy tonight. It's going to be a long night but I am actually glad to be here. I love how busy everything is. I know it's going to be very stressful and I can't help but scan the room, hoping to see my Russian protector. I know they have security here, but I can't help it. Somehow, this stranger makes me feel safe. I don't really know anyone here yet. But somehow I know he will keep me safe.

I do my rounds as the night goes on. I am not used to the long night shifts yet, so I am starting to drag. The night shift is much harder and longer. But I do have some fun as the night continues. It seems the Russians like a woman with meat on their bones because I think they have hit me on more tonight than I have been in my entire life.

Around two in the morning after last call. I feel his eyes on me. I look up and there he is, standing up on the second floor, leaning on the railing, watching me. He gives me a smile and walks away.

I try to look up for him as I go about cleaning up and restocking. But I don't see him anymore. I head into the back to grab a few bottles of liquor that need to be restocked as well.

I feel someone grab me from behind and pull me close. "You are a sexy little thing. Can you feel how much you are turning me on?" The man says into my ear, pushing his hips forward so that his erection rubs on my ass.

"Let go of me!" I struggle, but he has me pinned in his arms. I can hear the music and voices around me as he starts to put his hand up the leg of my shorts.

"No! Please! I said no." I recognize his voice now. It's Viktor.

"You're not gonna tell me no tonight, bitch." He says as he presses his hand against my pussy through my panties. "No one tells me no."

He pulls me into the storage room and shoves me up against the wall. He yanks at my shorts and starts to pull down my panties. "I have been watching you all night. I need to fuck you."

I scream and the door opens. It's Anton. I can see the look of concern on his face before he quickly wipes it off.

"Viktor, we have a problem. Demetrius called." He says urgently.

Viktor turns to him. "What kind of fucking problem?"

"I am not sure." He says a few things in Russian that I don't understand. But his eyes keep flicking back and forth from Viktor to me.

"Fine. Some other time sweet thing. You haven't escaped me. I always get what I want."

I am shaking in fear as he leaves. I pull up my pants and sink down to the floor, letting out a strangled sob. I work to straighten myself up. I just want to leave. I needed this job, but I'm unsure if I can handle this. Anton closed the door after Viktor left. I could see the anger on his face. When I step out of the backroom Anton is still standing there waiting for me.

"Are you ok?" He says to me with concern.

I nod. "Yes. I just need to go." I say, looking away from him. "Thank you for what you did. I know he is your boss."

He doesn't say anything as he walks with me to the front door.

"I will see you home safe. But first I must make a phone call. You don't leave my side."

He takes his phone out of his pocket and puts it to his ear. He is speaking rapid fire Russian to a man on the other end of the line. I have no idea what he's saying, but it sounds serious. When he hangs up, he tells me to follow him. He pulls out a gun and checks it. Then tucks it back into the holster.

"Ladies first. I take you home."

I look up at him with fear. "You don't have to. I will be ok."

He shakes his head no and continues to follow me. He never takes his eyes off the surrounding area as we walk away from the bar. I'm glad to be away from there. It's not that Viktor is bad looking. I don't know what I don't like about him.

He just gives me the creeps and then, after trying to force himself on me. I'm not sure I can go back there. I didn't even bother clocking out or saying goodbye to anyone. But I really need the job. I still have a little money left. Maybe I should just look for something else.

"Thank you for taking care of me," I say quietly to Anton.

He nods but says nothing. When we get to my apartment building, he nods. "Good night, Luna." He says before turning to walk back down the street.

I'll Kill Him

Demetrius

That mother fucker. If I could kill him for this, I would. He put his hands on my Luna. Tried to rape her. If not for Anton calling me as soon as he saw Viktor follow her into the backroom. I am sure he would have raped her without a second thought. My Luna is strong. She was trying to fight him off as best she could.

I am sure Viktor will be the first one I take care of when this is all over. I won't allow anyone to touch my angel. His days are numbered. He is becoming unhinged. This means I will have to be around the bar more than I was planning. I have to make sure he doesn't have the opportunity to get her alone without me being there.

I am just starting to walk away from the building when I see them. They are watching my angel's building. I recognize them from the pictures that Anton sent me when he spotted them. They are here for her. But they aren't going to get to her without a fight.

I know she is safe at home. Anton walked her there himself to make sure she was ok. He told me she put on a brave face but that she was clearly upset. I watch them from the shadows. They are definitely watching the building. I get my phone out of my pocket.

"Anton"

"Da"

"They are here again. Gather a few of the guys you know are loyal to me and come here."

"On way boss."

"Also, thank you for earlier. I would have killed him had he done anything further to her."

"Is no problem. You would do the same."

I grin and look back at the two men watching the building. I am ready for this to end. I am tired of waiting for my opportunity to see my angel again. I need her. I can't stop thinking about her. But first, we will take care of these men. It's clear that the other day was no random incident. Someone wants her. It's time to find out who.

I wait for my men. We surround them and take them down one by one. I knock the last one out. I need answers. I turn back toward the apartment.

"Take this one to my safe house for questioning. I will call in the cleanup crew for the others."

Anton nods at me.

"Make sure he doesn't get away," I say with a frosty glare.

I call the clean up crew and head to my safe house to get some answers. I need to know who is trying to take my Angel. I won't have it.

Luna

I got home around 3:30 am. I am exhausted. I lock my door and make a cup of tea. I want to take a bath but I just don't have the energy. I pull on my PJ pants and a T-shirt and sit down on my small couch. I can't sleep. I keep thinking of Viktor and what he was about to do to me. If Anton hadn't walked in. I'm not sure what would have happened. Well, that's not true. I know exactly what would have happened. I am beyond thankful to him. I am just so scared.

I didn't want to say anything to Anton because Viktor is his boss, but the look on his face was clear. He was angry, but not surprised by what was happening. I'm not sure why he looked so angry, but I am glad he seems to like me enough to keep an eye on me. I couldn't let him see how scared I was. So I put on a brave face and walked home with him.

In reality, I was terrified and, if I am being honest, in shock.

I must have fallen asleep on the couch because I was startled awake by the crashing sound of a window breaking. I sit up with a start. My heart is pounding so hard I can feel it in my throat. The hair on the back of my neck is standing up and I am shaking in fear. I am not sure what's happening, but I am frozen with fear. A big man comes from my bedroom. He is wearing a mask. I scream and jump up to try to get out the door.

The man is too fast, and he grabs me and pushes me against the wall.

"Be quiet!" he yells.

I can't. I scream again. I'm so scared. I'm trying to get away from him, but he is too strong and I can't move.

"I said be quiet!" he yells again as he puts his hand over my mouth.

I scream against his hand, but he won't take it away. The next thing I hear is a shot. I look around and he has a gun pointed at my head. Did his gun discharge? I start to shake. I want to throw up. He looks at me with anger. I can't take my eyes off him. I don't want to die.

"No! Please..." I cry.

It's muffled by his hand, and I can feel my tears pooling and running around it.

"You are coming with me." He says in a low voice.

He starts dragging me toward the door. His hand is still over my mouth to keep me from screaming. The tears are streaming down my face and I am trying so hard to get away from him. It's still dark outside, but we are going to be spotted. There are still people on the streets. But there is no one coming. Everyone that was on the street disappeared quickly. I scream louder as he pulls me into an alleyway. I look around and see that there is no one there. But I see a large white van parked in the next alley over. He drags me to it.

He pushes me into the van and shuts the door. I look around and see three men all wearing ski masks. I have no idea who they are or what's happening. One laughs when I scream again. The next thing I feel is the prick of a needle, and then everything slowly goes dark around me.

GONE

Demetrius

After an hour of torturing this mother fucker we finally get some answers. They are gathering women for a human trafficking ring. He won't tell us which one. But I am just getting started when my phone starts giving notifications from Luna's apartment. When I pull out my phone, the captive starts laughing.

Rage rolls over me when I watch a man with a mask on walk through Luna's apartment. I see the fear in her eyes and on her face when she screams. I cannot look away when the man shoves her up against the wall. Then pulls out a gun and a flash from the muzzle. He puts it to her head. I see her eyes widen when she realizes exactly what's going on.

He takes her right out her front door. I hear Anton on his phone giving orders to the men we left there. But I am unable to stop watching as he leaves the building with her. I commit every minute detail about him to memory. I am shaking with rage when they leave my sight down a dark alley. I will kill him and everyone he cares about. I will slaughter them all.

I walk over to the prisoner. I grab his hair and yank it back so he is looking at me. "You know who I am." I sneer at him. "This is the last chance you get to tell me what I need to know. You can die slow or you can die fast. It's your choice, but I will get my answers even if I have to call in Sergio."

I can tell he knows the name. Sergio knows so many torture techniques and he enjoys it so much. He always gets the answers we want. I prefer to do it myself, but if the information is crucial, it might require the help of more than one person. Sergio's name usually only comes up in interrogation sessions.

"No! I'll tell you what I know. It's not much."

I smile and release his hair. "That's good. Talk."

"I'm a nobody. I just got a call and said to take three men and go to that apartment and wait for a chick with tan skin and long black hair."

"That's Luna."

"Yeah her."

"What about her?" I growl at him.

"We were supposed to grab her and take her to the contact. But you got us first. I can tell you where. I'll give you the location." He says, almost crying.

"What's his name?" I sneer at him.

"I don't know his name. They just call him The General."

"Why?"

He shakes his head and doesn't answer.

I grab his hair again and pull him back to look at me. "You don't have to die slow. I can end this now. I am going to give you another chance."

He nods his head frantically.

"Who is The General?"

"He is a monster. He has been collecting women for months. He chooses ones who have no family. That no one will miss. He avoids Russian women says it's too much trouble. I swear that's all I know."

"What does he look like? Who does he work for?" I growl.

"I don't know. He has people that handle anything face to face. A man answers the phone, and he gives me instructions. I have never met him."

"Tell me how to find him!" I yell in his face.

He just keeps shaking his head. I get my gun out and shoot him in the leg. He screams in pain. I then grab him by his hair and hold a knife to his crotch.

"Talk!" I snarl at him.

He is shaking in terror. He talks, but he says very little about anything that is helpful. The man who answered the phone told him he had to take her because they wanted her. She is an orphan and has no friends. No one will miss her. Well, surprise mother fucker. I will. Luna belongs to me. I am her family. She needs no one else.

He has no idea where they will be taking her. I will have to find another way. I am not sure who The General is working for but I will find him and he will die. He will die for touching what is mine.

"Anton, find out information about this man, The General. Find her!" I yell at him as I stand up.

"Yes, boss."

I shove my blade into the man's throat and watch as he gargles and chokes on his own blood. He is dead. I feel nothing. I am just a shell. I need to get her back. They can't have her. I will kill them all.

I roar in rage. I need to find her.

"How do I find her?" I whisper to myself.

I started making calls and calling in favors. I will do what I need to in order to find her. Viktor be damned. Anton leaves the room to make some calls of his own.

Luna

When I come to, I am handcuffed to a bed and I have no clothes on. Where are my clothes? Oh, my god what's going on? That's when it comes back to me. There was a man who grabbed me from my apartment.

Oh no. There are two men sitting next to me, and they both sneer at me when I open my eyes. One is older, maybe mid-forties, with dark hair and blue eyes. The other is younger, probably about thirty, with blond hair and green eyes. Neither one looks friendly.

They ask if I remember anything and I tell them I don't know what happened.

"Where am I? How did I get here? Let me go!" I scream "Please please, I'm not worth anything. Please."

They laugh. I'm pretty sure this isn't going to end well.

"Oh, you have plenty of worth as a warm hole to be filled and then sold. You will make plenty of money."

The older man stands. I scream as loud as I can and try to get away from him.

"I'm going to take her while she can still fight. I like em feisty."

The younger man is laughing as he watches me struggle. The much larger man removes his clothing while looking at me and climbs on the small bed with me.

"That's right sweetheart, fight me, make it better for me. I love it when they fight."

He shoves his hard cock into me. I scream. Fuck, it hurts. It feels like he is ripping me apart. I try thrashing and scratching, but I am handcuffed and tied to the bed. At one point, I managed to bite him. The whole time he and the younger man just laugh and seem to enjoy my pain. He puts his hand over my mouth and fucks me harder. It hurts. Oh my god, it hurts so badly. I bite down on his palm and draw blood, but I don't let go of him. His other hand slaps me across the face so hard I see stars.

"I knew you would be worth it."

I'm screaming and crying when he comes in me. Thank god I have an IUD. The last thing I would want is a child born of this. I sob and turned my head away. I am so humiliated I don't even want to look at the glee on his face. The enjoyment of my pain.

“Your turn.” He tells the younger man as he gets off of the small bed.

He smiles and climbs on top of me and instantly pushes inside me. I don’t know how long any of this lasts, but I stop fighting and just let him do what he is going to do. It’s not like I can fight back, anyway. They have me handcuffed and tied to this bed. All I can do is cry. How worthless is that? How did I end up here? I sob quietly as he moans and comes in me. He smiles down at me like this was just a fun time.

“Damn, I wish I could afford you. That's some good pussy. I bet that ass is still a virgin.” He licks his lips and I look at the wall, sobbing to myself.

They leave the room and come back with a tray full of syringes.

"This is going to hurt," the older man says and puts the needle in my arm.

My body convulses, and I scream again. Even though my legs are tied to the bed, I try to kick him. But the younger one grabs my legs and holds them still. He injects more drugs into my arm and punches me in the stomach. I am screaming and crying, but he doesn't care. As the drugs hit my system, I stare at the ceiling, the strange feeling pulling me out of the situation I am in.

He tells me I need to calm down because he needs to put an IV in my arm. I keep trying to struggle, even though I don't really think I am doing much of anything. The younger man walks to the other side of the small bed I am lying on and grabs my face. He pushes me onto the bed hard and grabs at my soft flesh.

He grabs my breast and squeezes. "Get used to this. There will be plenty of men interested in trying you out. Especially after I tell them how good of a time, you gave us. A real fighter."

I go still when I hear other women screaming and crying. There are deep voices moaning all around me. I can hear men rutting behind the curtains that surround me. I start sobbing more when I hear the other women that are here screaming and crying. Some are fighting. I can hear it all. The sounds of the sex. The violence. The pain. My head starts to swim and I start to feel euphoric. My eyes are heavy and they want to close. I need to fight it, but I don't think I can.

"That's right, let the drugs take effect. It will make all of this easier for everyone. You might even get to enjoy it if you are lucky." They leave the room.

I'm shocked and horrified as I listen to the sounds of pain and pleasure coming from every direction. The older man comes back into the room and pours water into my mouth. I choke and spit it out. He takes the cup away and leaves again.

I'm alone now except for the screams of women and the moans of men. I try to get up, but I am handcuffed to the bed. Everything hurts. I lay there crying. I wonder how long I have been here. No one will even miss me. I have no one. No friends. No family. At the bar, they will think I just decided to not keep the job. Maybe Anton will notice or my Russian protector. I wish he was here to save me. It's the only comforting thought I have.

I have to hold out hope that I will get out of here. There are no windows, just what looks like hanging lights in a makeshift hallway. My head swims more as the feeling of the drugs take effect. I start to drift off and I hear a woman scream. She yells and cries and then it goes quiet. Did they kill her? I'm fighting so hard to stay awake to not let this drug take me away. But I am fighting a losing battle.

I lay there in terror, sobbing, as I started to nod. I hear footsteps walking down the corridor. I try yanking at my handcuffs, but I can't move. I can hardly function. I try to move my legs but I can't.

A man enters the room, and I stare at him with fear and confusion. He smiles and says, "Hello little lady, we've been waiting for you."

The man is tall with silver hair, and he is wearing a very expensive suit. I have no idea who he is or why he would be waiting for me. But no matter how hard I fight, I can't keep my eyes open.

Someone Help Me

Luna

When I wake up again. I feel like I am floating above myself. I can see my body lying on the bed, but it's like I am not in it. I see slight cuts on my breasts and trickles of blood on my skin. I feel like I am in a dream. I try to sit up, but I can't.

My body won't respond. I am trapped in my mind. I am in a dark place and I cannot escape. Handcuffed and tied to this bed. I try to turn my head toward the wall. To take my mind somewhere else, anywhere else. Please. please don't do this to me.

I feel the man's fingers inside me and I cry out. Then he is on the bed, pushing into me with no mercy. He moves faster and harder and I cry out again. I feel my body shake and convulse in pleasure. I hate that my body is feeling pleasure because of what this stranger; this monster is doing to me.

I can feel the warmth as it moves through me. Every touch lights up my skin. My body asking for more. While my mind screams no. I feel like my body is betraying me when I orgasm. I hear the man grunt over top of me. I feel his come warm and sticky on my thighs. Someone anyone please help me. I don't want to be here. Please.

"That was nice, wasn't it, baby? I'm glad you enjoyed yourself. Those drugs are first rate, aren't they? We'll have to do this more often. Maybe you'll be a good girl and give me a blowjob after I fuck you next time."

I feel him moving away from me, and I try to move my body away from him. Just to hide to do anything. But I can't move. I can't even open my eyes. I hear the curtain opening and closing. I hear a woman's voice. I can't even open my eyes enough to see who is talking.

I hear the girl in the area next to me crying and the man's voice that just left my bed as he speaks to her. Another man enters my area. I am too drugged and weak to even move. What did they give me? I want to run and hide. I'm so dazed I can feel my body wanting to nod out again. But I can feel every sensation. The air as it moves across my skin. The touch of his hands on my body. I can feel the bile in my throat.

"Just relax and enjoy it, baby. Don't fight it. This is going to be the best day of your life. You'll never forget this. And don't worry, I won't hurt you. I promise. I'll take good care of you."

I hear the man walk towards me, and I try to scream. Nothing comes out. I hear him unzip his pants and I try to move my body again. I can't. I am paralyzed because of the drugs and fear. I try to focus on anything but the man approaching me. I close my eyes and try to block out the world. I feel cold metal on my skin and then the feeling of it slicing through my skin. It hurts more than anything I have ever felt. My skin feels so incredibly sensitive. I scream at the pain it causes.

Please, please make this stop. Please, what did I do to deserve this? Someone help me. I can feel the knife as it makes slight cuts into my skin and then the warmth of his tongue when he licks the blood from my skin. His tongue on my skin makes me shudder, regardless of if I want it to or not. I can feel the tears as they roll down my cheeks. What did I do to deserve this?

I feel his hands on my thighs and the blade as he rubs it across my skin.

“So beautiful. You have all of this perfect skin for me to mark up.”

I feel the blade on my nipple as he makes a cut on my breast. I can feel the rumble of his mouth when he moans and licks my skin. I can feel my body betraying me as it gets aroused. Please don’t. I don’t want this to feel good.

How can it be unwanted and my body still reacts to it with pleasure? Please, please don't respond. But I can already feel my pussy getting wet. It has to be something they gave me. He reaches in between my legs and cups me, moving his fingers over my sensitive pussy.

"No," I try to scream, but it just comes out as a hoarse whisper.

"What was that? Did you just tell me no?" I now know that was the wrong thing to say because now he looks very excited. Too excited.

"Please, please don't." I can't even cry anymore. I've cried so much that not even the IV can keep me hydrated. If that's even what it is for.

"Oh, don't you worry, dear." He sneers, "I'm going to take good care of you. We are going to have so much fun."

I shake my head no, but I feel it when he climbs onto this bed and gets in between my legs. I feel him notch up and push into me. I try to scream out in protest, but I can't. All I can do is lay here and take it. I turn my head and try to go to a faraway place, but my body betrays me and I come harder than I ever have before.

I feel the liquid as it pours from my body. What's wrong with me? How can I get off while being raped? I cry softly as he climbs off of me and licks my face. I feel his come leaking from my body. In between my legs feels raw.

"Oh, we are going to have so much fun. Look how much you

enjoyed yourself."

I hear him moving around as he puts his clothes back on and then the curtain opening and closing.

No, No, No

Luna

It seems like forever before anyone else comes into my area, and I'm thankful for it. I have no idea where I am or what is happening. My head is swimming and sometimes it spins. I can hear the other girls screaming and crying. Some are begging and pleading for their lives. Others are whimpering. I try to hold back my own tears, but I can't. I am terrified. Someone, please save me.

I keep nodding in and out. By the feeling of my body, men have been coming and going for a while. While I'm not even conscious. A man walks in wearing an expensive suit. He takes off his suit jacket and lays it across the chair and begins to unbutton his cuff links.

"Oh, you look so delicious. I bet you taste better than any of these other whores."

"Please don't hurt me," I plead. "Let me go. Please." I slur when I speak. I can hardly concentrate. I don't want this.

He laughs and says, "I won't hurt you, honey. Just relax and enjoy." He reaches for my breast and I try to move away. He laughs. "Don't be afraid, I'll be gentle. Now, spread those lovely legs and show me what a good little whore you are. Stop fighting this. It's going to happen, anyway."

I want to fight, but I can't move much. The drugs in my system make my head spin when I try to move away from him. I close my knees the best that I can, but he just pulls them apart and climbs on me.

"You're mine for right now, little one. I'll have some fun with you first and then try someone else."

He touches me, and I cry out in pain. I feel something cold and wet on my skin and I cry out again. He laughs again. "Don't worry, baby, it's just lubricant. It will make things go smoother."

He rubs it on my pussy, and I try to pull away. He grabs my hair and pulls my head back. He licks me and I try to scream, but he pushes his cock inside me and I that's the last thing I remember.

Despite waking up, I'm still unable to focus. I feel a sticky sensation from the come between my legs. No one is with me at the moment, but in between my legs hurts and feels overly used. I can hear more sobs coming from all around me. One girl is screaming for her mother as a man tells her to yell louder. I hear her scream and the sounds of someone being hit.

One woman screams so loud I think someone must be really hurting her. I hear a gurgle and then nothing. I don't understand what is going on. Did someone just get killed? My mind just wonders away from all the thoughts. I can't seem to concentrate.

I don't know how long it's been since they drugged and brought me here. I feel sick and dizzy. My skin hurts. Everything hurts and I still can't move. But my head is a little clearer. Not that I want it to be. I don't want to remember this.

The curtain opens, and another man walks in. He is wearing a white lab coat and has a stethoscope around his neck. He takes off the jacket and tosses it aside. I recognize him immediately. He is the man who kidnapped me.

"Hi princess, I thought you might be awake," he says, sneering at me.

"Why?" I whisper.

"You had too much fun last night. You're going to be a bit sore today. But don't worry, this will help." He pulls out a needle and sticks it into the IV the older man put in my arm. "We have many buyers lined up for you. So just relax and be a good girl while they test the merchandise."

"Why are you doing this? What did I do to you?" I cry.

"You didn't do anything wrong, sweetheart. It's just business. There are so many buyers for someone like you that I bet you make more money than any of the other girls. Enjoy your new life." He laughs as he leaves the room.

I cry harder as I stare at the ceiling.

Demetrius

I have been scouring the city looking for my angel. I promised I would keep her safe. Now she is gone. She has disappeared without a trace. I do, however, have a lead on who The General might be. The word is it could be Gabriel from the cartel. But there are a few who believe he is part of the Italian Mafia. It would make sense if it was Gabriel. He has one of the largest human trafficking rings around. She may never come out again if Gabriel has taken and confined her in one of his warehouses. I'm ready to burn this entire city down. If I don't find her, it will be a bloodbath.

I have to find her. I will find her. She is mine. I don't even know if she will come out the same as she was. I don't care. I still want her. Four days have passed since someone took her and I still haven't found her. I called Sergio in to get as much out of that piece of shit we capture outside of her building as I could.

He says she is in a private area and that they give them heroin and ecstasy. She might not even remember what happened. That would be a blessing if you ask me. Additionally, he revealed that they had already planned for multiple men to take advantage of her prior to her abduction.

I know how these places work. My poor angel. The things they are doing to her. I feel like I might break apart at any moment. I am a monster, but she is my light in the darkness. Now that I have seen a glimpse of that light. I have to have it. I can't lose her. I will burn this city to the ground. The streets will turn into a bloodbath.

"You look like you are thinking of burning this city down," Anton says to me in Russian.

"You know me so well," I tell him.

He sits across from me at the table and drinks a glass of whiskey. "I will help you burn it all to the ground if you want. She is a very sweet girl."

"Thank you, Anton."

"What can I do to help?" He asks me.

"The cartel has to be behind this. If she abducted and moved into one of his human trafficking rings, this would be their type of place. I'll need you to help me find out which warehouse they took her to. If I have to, I will buy her back. Money is no object."

"We will find her, Demetrius." Anton pours another shot of whiskey into his glass.

He may not be blood but I have been around him enough to know his tells. He is worried and upset.

"Find her Anton. I want her back. No matter what happens."

I don't wait for him to reply before I walk out of the room. I need to blow off some steam. I have some men to torture information out of.

I go downstairs to find the man who kidnapped her. They tied him up in my basement. I passed his photo out to my men from the cameras. He took off his mask after exiting her building. I take off my tie and step closer to him rolling up my shirt sleeves.

"Where is she? Where did you take her? Tell me and you might live." I wrap the tie around his throat and squeeze.

"She is our most popular girl. I won't tell you anything." He gasps trying to breathe.

I squeeze tighter until his face is turning blue and he stops struggling.

"You can tell me where to find her or you can tell me where to find your grave."

I grab a knife from the table and hold it against his throat.

"Where are you taking the girls? Where is the girl that I am looking for?" I demand.

He glares at me with hate in his eyes. I push the knife down harder.

"Okay. Okay. We are taking the women to a warehouse down on the docks. Can't miss it." He coughs as I release the pressure on his throat. "The auction will be in two days."

I stare at him for a minute wondering if I should believe him. Even if he is lying this is the most I have found out. I slit his throat and watch the look on his face. At least that was satisfying to watch.

I take a deep breath. I'm getting angrier and angrier and I need to calm down. I have to keep a clear head so that I can get my angel out of there. I have to come up with a plan. If this is Gabriel's place then I know what kind of merchandise they are going to be selling. I hate these things we almost had them all shut down until Viktor took over as the Pakhan. That slimy fucker. The Bratva has been moving away from anything to do with women and children. I shake my head and wipe the blood off of my hands. I will save my angel even if I have to kill them all.

Please Just Stop

Luna

I wake to a bunch of weight on me. I hear a man grunting and can feel his cock as it moves in and out of me. I can't even fight back as he pushes himself in and out of me. My hands and feet are bound. I can't see anything. I just feel the weight of him on top of me.

"Please stop," I beg over and over, but he doesn't stop. He seems to enjoy my pleading.

He shoves a gag in my mouth when I try to scream. He is groaning with pleasure. "You like this, don't you? I know you do. Look how your body is responding to me. You are going

to get used to this. You are going to be used like this every day. You feel so good."

I have never felt so helpless or so violated. I have to just lay here while he continues to pound into me. I feel the tears running down my face. It hurts, it feels like he is going to break me. He is fucking me so hard. He just keeps going and the pain between my legs gets worse. It hurts and yet it feels so good. I fight the pleasure and I feel disgusted with myself. How can my body betray me like this? But all he cares about is his pleasure.

I hear him grunting and I can feel my release shudder through my body. I cry at my body's betrayal. He keeps going for what seems like forever until finally; he moans with his release. I can feel his hot come spurting into me. Coating my insides. I can't do anything but continue to cry. I feel so little, so degraded and used.

"This is going to be your life now. You belong to us now, and you will do exactly what we say. Tomorrow we will sell you. But tonight we get to break you in."

He gets up and leaves me alone for a moment and I hope it's over. I can feel his come dripping down my legs. I feel my anger. It's like a raging volcano, but I know it will do me no good. My body is shaking from the drugs and the trauma. I keep nodding in and out, no matter how hard I try to stay conscious. I wish they would just kill me. Just please kill me and get it over done. I don't want to live. This isn't a life I would wish on my worst enemy.

I hear the curtain move again. I want to scream. I'm naked and helpless. What has happened to my life?

Two men come in, both of them are tall and handsome. One man has blond hair, and the other has dark hair. The blond one is looking at me and smiling. Panic sets in. I've never had two men before. I'm already hurting. My body can't take much more.

"We are going to play with you now."

I try to cry out, but the gag muffling my voice. The blond man ungags me.

"This will be the first of many pleasures you will receive. We are not your friends and we are not going to give you anything. But we will take everything from you. You belong to us for now and we are going to use you for our pleasure. And you are going to take it. We are breaking you in for the auction. So please fight and scream. We enjoy it."

"Noooo" I say. I can't let this happen. They both just laugh at me.

The blond man uncuffs my hands while the dark-haired one holds me down. I try to struggle, but it is no use. I'm too drugged, and the man holding me down is huge. They are too big to fight.

"You can't do this," I slur out, trying to push him away. I squirm and wiggle the best I can, trying to get away.

"That's where you are wrong," he says and he kisses me hard and demanding.

The blond haired man lets go of my hands after releasing them from the cuffs. I try to push the dark haired man off of me, but it only makes him push down harder on my body. I can feel his hard cock against my naked body.

I scream as he pushes himself into my tight little hole. He smiles and puts his hand over my mouth to keep me quiet. He is so big, and he fills me completely and I can feel it rip. It hurts, but the dark haired man doesn't stop moving. He keeps pushing into me. The pain between my legs is intense. I'm trying to fight him. I dig my nails into his chest and yank them down his body as hard as I can. But he just moans and pounds into me harder. Fuck. No, oh my god, this hurts.

"Yes, fight back. Thats so good."

I sob in defeat. There is nothing I can do. I just lay there and take it. I have no choice. I just lay there as the two men have their way with my body. I don't even attempt to fight back, in the hopes that their enjoyment is minimized. The dark haired man moves faster and faster and then I can feel him come inside of me. He takes his hand away and his hot seed dribbles out of my hole. I can feel the come dripping down my thighs.

The dark haired man smiles at me as he wipes some of the come from my leg and sucks it off his finger. I can't believe he just did that. It's disgusting. I don't even know how many other men have been there before him. They will sell me off to the highest bidder. That's the harsh reality of my situation. I am just a possession. Someone took away my life. I try to sink into a place in my head where I am just not here mentally anymore. I try to think of the large Russian man who protected me. He said he wouldn't let any harm to come to me, but here I am. I sob.

"My turn," the blond man says as he moves over me.

The dark haired one pins my hands above my head.

"Let's see what this little thing can do," he says as he puts his cock in front of my lips.

I try to move my head away, but he just holds my wrists and makes me take his cock in my mouth. I bite him as hard as I can. I have no hope of avoiding the blow that I receive. I can taste the blood in my mouth. My head instantly hurts, and so does my eye.

"If you do that again, I will kill you, bitch. Learn your place."

He shoves his cock back in my mouth. Why am I such a coward? I don't even care about myself anymore. I just want them to go away. I don't want this. I never wanted this. He shoves his cock so far into my mouth I gag. Unable to breathe, I panic and he sneers at me.

I feel the pain between my legs as the blond man takes me. He fucks me hard and rough. His dick is so big that I feel like I'm going to break. He has no regard for my feelings. He just wants to have fun with my body and use it for his own pleasure. He fucks me repeatedly and I can't do anything. I feel his seed spill inside of me. I hear him groan as he comes. I don't even care that they are here with me. I just lay there and take it. I'm empty and broken. Maybe they will just kill me. Maybe I should bite him again just so he does kill me. Then my suffering will be over. But I am a coward. I don't really want to die.

The dark haired man takes his cock out of my mouth and says, "My turn again."

He is still hard. I've never seen such a huge cock before. I can see the veins on it. It is huge. I try to fight back, but the other man just holds me still and presses my wrists down even more. He moves one hand away from my wrists and puts it between my legs. He starts rubbing my clit, making my body respond with pleasure.

I feel so helpless as the dark haired man spreads my lips and pushes his cock into me once more. The blond man pushes into my mouth and I taste myself on his cock. I feel him stretching my throat out. I gag and try to breathe. He is choking me. I want to scream, but he has his dick in my mouth. I can't breathe. He just holds himself there in my throat and groans. I start to panic as I feel the pressure in my head from not getting enough oxygen.

The blond man looks at me. "You're going to learn how to suck this," he says as he pulls his cock out of me and I gasp for air. Coughing. He pushes his cock back against my mouth and says, "You are going to do what I tell you. I can see it in your eyes. You want this."

He presses his hand against the back of my head and forces me to take his cock into my mouth. He starts to fuck my face as I choke on his cock. The pain in my jaw and my throat is excruciating. I try to breathe anytime I can. I taste him when he comes inside my mouth, the warm salty fluid on my tongue. I want to throw up and spit it all on him. But he rams so far into the back of my throat that I am forced to swallow it. I feel so humiliated. There is so much come I can feel it dripping on my face. On my body. In between my legs.

I just lay there as the man moves his cock away from my mouth. "That's a good girl." I am glad that is over. I just want to breathe. I wanted to survive before, but now I just wish they would kill me.

"My turn again," the blond man says as he moves back over me. He pushes himself into my wet pussy and fucks me. I feel him pushing into me over and over again. He keeps going until he finally comes.

After he finishes, I can sense the warmth emanating from my body. The dark haired one moved back between my legs and spreads my pussy open with his fingers. He puts his cock inside me again and fucks me hard. I feel so weak. I wish I could just disappear. I don't even try to fight back anymore. I just let them have their way.

I am lying here on the bed, naked, and they are using my body as they please. They both continue to take turns on me. I have no idea how long this all goes on. I nod in and out. There is literately nothing I can do about it. I'm just a slave now. Not good for anything else but to be used. I don't care anymore. I just stare at the wall as if I'm not even there. My mind goes to another time and place. To my Russian protector. I can still picture his face in my drugged out haze. How safe I felt when he yanked that man off of me. I don't even know how long ago that was. It feels like a lifetime ago as these men just abuse my body over and over.

I can feel them come inside me. I feel so used and abused. My body is a mess. They shattered my mind. I am a broken woman. No matter what I do, my mind isn't able to handle the things that are happening to me. It doesn't matter what I try to think about or imagine. I can't escape. I try as hard as I can to concentrate on my Russian. I know he isn't mine. I'm sure he hasn't even looked for me. Of course he hasn't I'm no one. He definitely won't want me now. I'm used and broken.

The dark haired one leaves and comes back with a cloth and wipes the come from in between my legs. He shoves some pill in my mouth and they leave.

I Will Find You

Demetrius

It's been almost a week, and I have been scouring all of Brooklyn for Luna without any luck. That fucking piece of shit kidnapper must have been telling the truth about her whereabouts. My brother has been keeping an eye on my movements, but I don't give a fuck. Nothing is as important as she is. Nothing. I am going crazy imagining what is happening to her. My nightmares keep me awake. The sounds of her screams. The look in her eyes, the fear on her face.

I can't sleep while I know she is being beaten and used. Every time I do manage to sleep, I dream she is helpless somewhere and I can't get to her. Beaten and raped, left for dead. Alone. I promised I would protect her. The most basic of things and I couldn't even manage that.

When I got to her apartment in my rage, I killed the guard who was supposed to be watching her. Fuck him. He couldn't do the one thing I ordered him to do. She is gone.

I hear a phone ring in the distance and Anton's voice coming closer. I am in my Office. It's completely demolished. The only thing left intact in here is the chair I am sitting on. It's all that has kept me from burning the city to the ground to find her. If she isn't found soon, I will start a bloodbath in this city until I find the person who has her.

Anton walks into my office and looks around, then looks at me.

"Da." He says into his phone and then hangs up. "We found the exact location of Luna."

"Where is she?"

"Inside of Gabriel's compound. Like that piece of shit said."

I know the things that slimy scum sucker does. He traffics women selling them at an auction to the highest bidder. But before that, they use them in the worse ways. Making sure they break them before they go up for sale. They are going to pump her full of narcotics, making her extremely strung out.

"The Pakhan has ordered you to attend the auction. To ensure there are no Russian women being sold," he says in Russian.

"She is not a fucking thing to be sold. I am getting her out of there!" I yell at him.

My temper is flaring and I'm about to snap.

"The Pakhan wants you to go. This could be a better idea than war. Unless you want a war with the cartel. You will have to hope she is there and you can buy her back. I am sorry, boss, there is no other way." He says sadly.

I begin to pace the room and think. My head is stuck in killing them all mode. I would rather go in there, guns blazing. I want to kill them all. It's better to be near her. It will make it easier to get her out if I am there. Maybe she will recognize me. Fuck!

"Fine. We will be at the auction tomorrow. But you are coming with me to help me stay in control. I might kill them all when I see what they have done."

"I will arrange it all."

I nod "I will be in the gym."

I walk from the room. I need to kill someone, but this will have to do. I manage to lift for all of thirty minutes before I rage and destroy that room too. I don't care. I'm so close to just exploding. If I thought I could burn down his compound and not harm Luna ... it would be on fire already.

Luna

I wake up with a pounding headache and cramps. The pain is pretty bad. I can hear the other girls still screaming and crying. I try to open my eyes, but it feels like someone is holding my eyelids closed. I can feel the man that is on top of me moaning and grunting. I can smell others on him when he pulls out and leaves the area. I hear a girl crying and begging. Pleading to be let go. I want to help her. I want to save them. I want to run away and hide.

I hear the curtain move again, and I try to move my body. Another man enters my area. I feel so wet and sticky in between my legs. I am so drugged I don't know what has been going on. How long have I been here? I feel dirty and gross. The man walks over to my bed and I hear his clothes hit the floor. Oh, no, not again. PLEASE! I scream in my mind.

I try to get away, but I can't. I am completely helpless. I have no control over my body. I can't even move. I hear the man moan and say, "Oh yeah, that's it, baby. That's it."

He grabs my hips and thrusts into me. Pounding into me without mercy or thought. Just a hole to use. Just someone to hurt. He grunts and shoves himself into me so hard it hurts me deep inside. When he removes himself from me, I feel the warmth of his come drip down the inside of my thigh. I am so humiliated and disgusted. How many times this has happened? Every time I wake up, there is another man on me, using me. My legs hurt and my pussy aches. I nod out again, letting the peaceful bliss of the drugs take me away. My last coherent thought is how I hope they accidentally give me too much.

When I wake again, there is a man untying my feet from the bed. They have removed the IV from my arm. But I am still too drugged to think straight. He moves up and unlocks the cuffs from my wrist. I try to move my arms, but I can't. I hear the curtain open and the man says, "Time for you to clean up and get ready."

I feel him grab my hand and pull me up. He helps me stand and I fall against him. He puts his arms around me and lifts me onto my feet. He yanks me to the bathroom and tosses me in.

"Clean up and put those on," he sneers at me. Unlike the others, this one has a slight Latino accent. He slams the door and I hear the bolt slide into place.

I try to wipe myself clean with the washcloth he gave me. I can hardly lean against the wall. I am covered in sweat and come. I cry as I try to clean everything off of me. I don't even know how I got so filthy. I have been in and out of a drugged haze the entire time I have been here. I can't believe what has happened to me. How I could be so stupid as to think my Russian protector would find me? I know in my head we didn't even know each other. That there is no way he would even know I was gone.

I feel despair when I think about this being my life. I don't even know how long it's been. Where I am or even who took me. I don't even know how many times strangers have used me for their pleasure. I would wake up to find different men using my body. I sob. How could I even think he would find me and save me? How did this happen? If he did find me, I am so disgusting there is no way he will ever want me. I don't even know how many men have used my body.

I dry off the best I can and put on what looks like lace. It is very tight and shows my curves. What do I do now? I feel like I should be trying to run away from this place. But I know I can't. I can't run and I can't fight. I'm so drugged that even dressing is hard. I have no idea what is going to happen next. I try to calm myself and remember to breathe.

The door opens, and he yanks me out and ties me in a line with other women who are dressed much the same way as I am. I remember someone talking about an auction and testing the merchandise. Is that what we are? Merchandise. I can't help but cry. I am so scared and confused. What will happen to me now?

The Auction

Luna

I am led through the building and down a hallway. I can hear the other girls crying and begging for their lives. Some of them look worse than I do. Many of them have been beaten. Many of them have cuts from men using knives on them, the same as me. I try to keep my head down and pretend I am invisible. If I make myself small, maybe they won't notice me. Fat chance, but I can always hope. My head is still foggy, but it's not as bad as it was.

I hear a helicopter in the distance getting closer as we stand here. I don't understand why there would be a helicopter

here. Except for the fact in the back of my head, I know exactly why. I can hear someone yelling. I can't tell if it is a man or a woman. I can't make out the words or the sounds over the helicopter.

They stopped us at a door, and the man unlocked it. I watch the other girls scream and beg as they are led out through the door. Eventually, we are all led onto a stage one by one. The lights are so bright I have to squint when they lead me onto it. I try to look away, but I can't.

I feel my heart racing and my breath coming fast. I try to hold back tears, but I can't. In a state of panic, all I can feel is the man's hand on my hip as he leads me to the center of the stage. I look up and see a crowd of people. I can't make out faces, but I see lots of cameras. I see the man in the expensive suit and I see the older man beside him. They both smile at me.

The man who has the expensive suit on licks his lips and I know I am in real trouble. Not like I'm not already fucked, but if I end up with that guy, I know I am truly going to be in pain the rest of my life.

"Here is our next girl. Apparently, she is a favorite," he says. "As you can see, we have a special treat for you. We have a new girl here today and the talk is that she is fantastic. A real fighter."

An older man laughs and says, "I have already tested her and damn, she feels so good."

I hear the man laugh and I know I am dead meat. Another tear rolls down my cheek.

"Now let's begin. Our item up for bid is a beautiful young lady named Luna. She is twenty-one years old. Her family has asked me to find her a husband," He laughs at his own stupid joke. I hear the crowd laugh in return. "I have a few offers already, but I thought I'd see what we can get for her. So, gentlemen, please welcome our newest member of the club."

I try to stumble away from him. I feel the man's hands grab me and pull me toward him. I feel the man's hand on my back and the cold metal of a gun against my skin. He pushes me forward toward the crowd of men and I stumble. I hear the crowd laughing and cheering.

"Ok, let's start the bidding at ten thousand dollars."

My head is spinning and I feel so dizzy. I can't even think straight. I don't want to be sold. I am so scared. I try to fight. To do anything I can to get away. But a man grabs my arm and I feel the burn of the drugs as they hit my system. I almost instantly feel like I am floating.

"Come on, guys, she is a real fighter."

"Twenty thousand." I hear someone yell. I glance over and it's the man in the expensive suit.

I look around in a daze and see a man standing in the crowd. There are people talking and a conversation? I think? But I can't pay attention to that now. I am fighting to not nod out right here where I stand. I need to know what is going to happen to me.

"Thirty thousand." Another voice calls. It sounds like he has a slight accent.

The man who has me on the stage turns toward the man standing at the back.

"Thirty-five thousand," the man in the expensive suit yells

I remember him and I know I really don't want to go there. He is one of them who used a knife on me. I see a very large man standing with his arms folded across his chest. He is wearing a black suit. His face looks scary and stern. I can't see what he looks like because of the lights in front of me. But even in the shadows, I can see he is scowling at the man in the expensive suit.

The auction guy yells out. "Thirty-five thousand. Do I have anyone else?"

I hear him laugh and yell. "Fifty thousand"

I look up toward the accented voice that says that. It sounds so familiar. I look to his left and even the other man seems familiar. Am I imagining him here? Have the drugs started giving me hallucinations? My heart beats faster. Is he really here? I sway on my feet.

"Oh wow, we are getting a good price tonight. Fifty thousand dollars," he yells as he pushes me toward the large man with the accent. Is it my protector? Please let it be him. I hope I am not imagining this.

The man looks over at me and his face goes dark with rage.

Broken but Alive

Demetrius

I hate these awful auctions. Treating women like they are animals. But I will not let Salvatore get her. I can't. He is a true monster. Whatever I might be, he is worse. He has been collecting women and selling them off like they are property after he uses them if they survive. It's sickening and disgusting.

I stand in the back and wait for my chance to get Luna out of here. I watched as they led the girls onto the stage one by one. They all look scared and hurt. My heart hurts to see them. But when I see Luna walk onto the stage, I feel so much anger and a blinding rage at what they have done to her. I can see cuts all over her delicate skin, and her face is bruised. Her beautiful hair is in tangles and I see the shame and fear on her face.

I hear Anton growl beside me when he sees her. He takes a step forward and I have to stop him from grabbing her off of that stage.

"Anton, not yet," I say, shaking my head, although I know exactly how he feels.

He looks at me and nods his head, but the look on his face is one of anger and fury. I look at Luna and she looks so scared. I can't help but feel even more fury as Salvatore and his lap dog make jeers at having raped my Luna. My angle. I have never been so angry in my entire life. If I wasn't so careful and in control of myself, I would have killed everyone here by now. I take deep breaths to calm myself.

I watch as the auctioneer pulls her forward, pressing a gun into her back. My eyes narrow in on him. "Let's start the bidding at ten thousand dollars."

"Twenty thousand," Salvatore yells

"Thirty thousand." Another voice calls.

I look at Anton. “It's important to remember who these men are. We can visit them later.”

He nods, and I see him jotting down names and descriptions.

"Thirty-five thousand," Salvatore calls out again.

I narrow my eyes at Salvatore. He will never get what is mine. I will kill him for this. It's just a matter of time. He will fuck up and be alone, and that is when I will strike. He will pay.

The auctioneer calls out, "Thirty-five thousand. Do I have anyone else?"

I smirk at him and give a sardonic laugh "Fifty thousand"

I can see the auctioneer's eyes light up. "Oh wow, we are getting a good price tonight. Fifty thousand dollars." he pushes her towards me and I see my opportunity.

I step toward her. I want her to see me, to know I am here for her. I need to show her I'm not going to leave her. She isn't alone. She looks up at me with those gorgeous brown eyes of hers. I am glad she can't see my face. Our eyes meet and I see the emotions that are there. She looks broken, and that kills me. I will kill them all for what they have done to my angel.

The lights are blinding me and I can't see anything. I can hear the crowd. I hear a voice getting loud and I know I am in trouble. Most of the voices are men yelling out numbers. I can't concentrate on what they are saying, but I know they are talking about me. Whatever they gave me is making me feel very disorientated.

I keep looking at the big man, who is now standing closer to the stage. No matter what, I just stare at him. He is holding my gaze. I feel a hand on my back and I am pushed forward. I stumble and fall to my knees. I feel hands grabbing my arms and legs. I try to kick, but I can't move. I feel the cold metal of a gun pressed against my head and I hold as still as I can.

I lay there trying to breathe. I am so drugged I hardly know what is going on. Why are these men grabbing me? How did I get near them?

"Let them touch you. They are paying good money," the man with the gun says into my ear.

I feel hands grab me and lift me up. I can feel the cold metal of a knife against my throat. I try to scream, but again I can't make a sound. I feel a man's hand on my breast and another on my thigh. I can hear jeers from the crowd. I try to fight, but I can't. I can't move. I can't even cry out. I feel the man's fingers inside of me and I feel my body react. I can't stop it. Here in front of this crowd, they are just pawing at me like I am a prized pig. Something for their enjoyment.

I hear a loud, deep voice yell something. The entire room went quiet. I hear the man with the gun breathing heavily.

"You heard what he said. Take your hands off of her."

I feel hands on my hips, and I am pulled to my feet. I look for the voice. He has stepped closer and I can see him a little better. It IS my Russian protector.

"Demetrius to what do we owe the honor of your presence?"

"I will take her."

"The bidding hasn't finished yet."

"Then get on with it."

I can hear the barely contained rage in his voice. His normally slight Russian accent is becoming thick as he speaks. The man yells that the bidding will start again. I scan the room, trying to find him. Finally, my eyes meet the man I called my protector. Demetrius is what he called him. It's the same man I was staring at.

He is tall and handsome. His eyes are piercing blue and his hair is short and neat. I see now that the other man is Anton, standing beside him. Somehow, it makes him look even bigger as he looms over every other man in this building.

"Fifty thousand dollars is where we were," he says.

I continue to watch him, unable to take my eyes off of him. Even in my drugged haze. I know I will be better off with him than with one of these ... rapists.

I hear the man with the gun say "Fifty thousand from the Bratva brigadier. Anyone else?"

"Fifty-five thousand," the man in the expensive suit yells and then winks at me.

The man with the gun turns to the man in the expensive suit.

Demetrius yells out, "Sixty thousand"

I look at the man in the expensive suit willing him not to bid, but he smiles at me and says, "Sixty five thousand. Don't look at me that way sweetheart, I'm not letting you get away that easily. I have plans for you. We have things to finish."

I feel my heart race and my breath catch in my throat. I look at Demetrius. He looks at the man with narrowed eyes. He must see the rage on his face because he winks at him, too.

I hear the auctioneer with the gun say "Sixty five thousand"

"Eighty thousand"

The man in the expensive suit raises his eyebrows and looks at him with what looks like a calculated look.

I hear the man with the gun say, "Eighty thousand from the Bratva brigadier. Any other bids?"

I look at the man in the expensive suit, and I feel a chill run through my body. I want Demetrius to win. At least I know him as my protector. He didn't come in and rape me. That I know of.

How did he find me? Has he been looking for me? Dare I hope he has been? But he won't want me anymore. So many men have used me. I don't even know how many.

You can't have her

Demetrius

This mother fucker needs to stay in his lane before I put my gun down his throat right here in front of everyone. He can not have her. She is mine.

"Eighty thousand," I growl out.

He will not take her. I will not allow it. I don't care who he is. I will win and then I am taking her home and spanking her ass for getting taken and sold. If this scum bag doesn't stop marking her up, I am going to rip his head off too. I observe her crumbling on the stage. My poor angel. I can't believe this is happening. I feel my blood boil and I growl low in my chest.

"Eighty five thousand," he says with a smirk

The fucking Italian mob wants to go to war tonight, I can tell. He knows I want her. By the look on her face and the fear, I see there. I can tell they have met. Salvatore is infamous for taking what he desires without any hesitation.

I hear the man with the gun say "Eighty five thousand. Do we have any other offers?"

I feel my mouth twist into a snarl and I look at Salvatore. I don't like him. I never have. I can't let this piece of shit take her. I will kill him first. Time to end this, I'm tired of games.

"One hundred thousand," I growl out.

I watch with satisfaction as the grin drops from Salvatore's expression. I know he has the money, but he won't spend that on something he knows he will end up killing.

"One hundred and one thousand," Salvatore yells

Salvatore grins and looks at me. I can see the lust in his eyes.

"One hundred and fifty thousand." I grin back at him. I cross my arms on my chest.

Let's see how far he's willing to take this. This is now a man's game. That smile isn't there any longer, and one of his men steps up behind him and said something in his ear. I see the frown appear on his face.

"Fine Demetrius, she is yours. You can have the whore I got to fuck her first, anyway."

The auctioneer looks pleased. "Going once." He looks around. "Going twice. Sold to the Bratva brigadier for one hundred and fifty thousand dollars. Enjoy your prize."

He shoves her toward me, and she stumbles, falling to the ground. I look at Luna and I can't help but feel sorry for her. She is so scared and confused. I can't stand the thought of her being treated like this. I have to take her now. I walk up onto the stage and pick her up bridal style.

I tell Anton in Russian to pay for her and meet me in the car. He looks at Luna and nods his head. He takes off his jacket and puts it over her.

"Demetrius, wait!" Salvatore yells. I look at him. I can see the anger in his eyes. "When you are done with her. I will buy her from you."

"You will not touch her. She is mine." I give him a long, icy stare. "She is protected now. You will never have her again. If you try, I will kill you. If you want to try, then that is on you."

I turn my back on him and walk away. She is so drugged she can hardly react to anything. I am surprised she could even stand up there. I can smell the other men on her as I take her from this place.

My poor angel. The first thing I need to do is bathe her. I carry her out of the club and into my car. I sit her down in the back seat and buckle her in. I get in beside her and wait for Anton to take us home.

"Where are we going?" Luna asks in a small, slurred voice.

"Home. We are going to get you cleaned up and fed."

I look at her, and I can see the fear in her eyes. I know she is afraid of me. She is terrified that I am going to hurt her. I would never do that to her, but I understand why she would look at me that way. I did just buy her.

I will punish her when she is bad and show her who her daddy is. But I will never force myself on her. I am not that kind of man. She is the light in my darkness and I will worship the ground she walks on. But first I need to help her. She needs to heal.

She shrinks back from me. I watch as she presses herself into the far corner of the backseat and tucks her head into her chest. I can tell she is terrified of me. I see a tear roll down her cheek.

My poor little girl. She is so hurt and fragile right now. She is in so much pain emotionally. I reach my hand out to her, but she flinches and shies away from my touch. I unbuckle her and pull her to my lap, anyway.

"Shhh angel, I have you now. I will take care of you. I will never hurt you, I promise. You are mine, and you will always be safe with me."

She cries into my chest. I wrap my arms around her and pull her to me. She is so drugged I can feel it as she starts to nod.

Luna

I was terrified when he walked up to the stage and picked me up like I weighed nothing. But the drugs are still in my system too much for me to even try to react. I feel fear and some of my thoughts are still flowing. But I am just along for the ride with little to no control.

When he sets me in his car, I'm so tired I can't keep my eyes open. I keep fighting the nod, but I know it's coming. I'm afraid to think about what I might wake up to. My head is swimming and everything is starting to go dark. He reaches for me, but I flinch away. I don't mean to. I see the hurt cross his beautiful face. It's just a reaction. He pulls me onto his lap.

"Shhh angel, I have you now. I will take care of you. I will never hurt you, I promise. You are mine, and you will always be safe with me."

I sob into his chest, seeking the warmth he is offering. After god knows how long of the coldness I have endured. I can feel myself starting to nod again.

But this time it feels different. Shit, did they overdose me? I think I am dying. I've always heard you know when you're about to die. I can hear my pulse beating in my ears. I can feel my body shutting down. Everything is going black.

I can't fight it anymore. I can feel the darkness closing in on me and I let it take me. It's like a cloud of comfort that envelopes me. I don't want to be here anymore. I let the darkness consume me. It's warm and comforting.

I just want to let go and be free now. I don't want to wake up. I don't want to remember. The pain and humiliation will be too much to bear. My body did things that I didn't want it to. Did I want it? I don't want to see the look on his face and feel the rejection of my big protector when he finds out how used and broken I am. I would rather die.

No one will ever love me again.

I let myself drift away. Everything is quiet and I can feel nothing but the dark. It's dark and safe.

The dark feels good. It's comforting. I always thought I would fear death. But I guess I was wrong about that, too. Letting go is the easiest choice I have ever made.

DON'T DIE ON ME

Demetrius

I look down at Luna as I hold her in my arms. Her eyes rolled back, and she began convulsing. Fuck. Where the fuck is that Narcan. That shot on the stage when she tried to fight. Fuck. They overdosed her. Do I have it in the car? I try to keep a supply when we come to these things. Please let some still be in the car.

"Don't die on me, Luna," I whisper softly to her. Silently panicking. I am the second in command of the Bratva. I don't panic. But fuck, I am panicking. Where the fuck is it?!

I can feel her heartbeat slowing and I pray to God that she is not too far gone already. Don't let my angel be gone.

"Please, no," I mutter under my breath. "Anton!! The Narcan!!"

I feel the car yank to the right as he slams on the brakes. I the door as he jumps out of the car. I'm watching Luna and I can't see her chest rising and falling. I can see the color leaving her cheeks. I hold her to my chest as if I am just willing her to take my life just so she lives. She has to live.

"Anton!!" I yell in a voice that doesn't even sound like my own.

The door swings open on Luna's side of the car and he shoves the needle at me.

"Here, boss."

I look at him, and I can see the panic in his eyes. I shake my head to clear my panic and I send up a prayer that this works. I take the Narcan and shoot it into her muscle. It's the longest 30 seconds of my life before she takes a gasping breath.

"Holy fuck, that was close, boss. They almost killed her. Mother fuckers!"

I nod my head and I can feel the rage under my skin. The fucking cartel needs to be run out of town. This shit is too much. It's barbaric even for the Bratva. My panic turns to a barely contained rage. They had better be glad she is my only priority right now or I might be tempted to go back and start a war.

"Fuck," I mumble and then I look at her. Her eyes are wide with fear, but she is alive. She is looking around wide away and full of panic. I just continue to hold her in my arms, cradling her to me.

"Why? Why didn't you just leave me alone? Just leave me to die. I'm ruined!" she cries. I can hear the despair in her voice and it breaks my fucking heart.

"Calm down angel. You're okay. I'm here. I've got you," I murmur softly to her. "No one will ever touch you like that again."

"Oh my god," she says, putting her hand over her mouth. She starts to sob uncontrollably. "Why didn't you just let me die? You're never going to want me! Not anymore! I'm used and broken!" she screams.

"Anton, get us home."

I hold her as she sobs in my arms. We drive in silence, and I try my best to comfort her until we reach my house. Anton pulls in and parks in my garage. He turns off the car and gets out, leaving us alone. I look down at her and I get out with her still in my arms.

She looks at me with a panicked look on her face. I can see her looking around, trying to figure out what to do. I brush the hair from her face while I continue to cradle her to me.

"Are you ok?" I ask softly. "Eventually, we will have to speak about what they did." I tell her.

She looks at me and shakes her head.

"No," she whispers.

I grab her chin and make her look at me.

"You will tell me what happened. You will tell me everything and then I will make them pay. Do you understand me, angel?"

She shakes her head again.

"I don't remember."

"I will let you get away with lying exactly once. You need to talk about this Luna."

"I can't," she screams, shaking her head.

"We will talk about this. You will tell me. You belong to me. We will discuss this, but for now. Let's get you cleaned up and fed. Then I will let you rest."

She looks at me, and I can see the fear in her eyes.

"I don't understand. I don't know what happened."

I look down at her. I will let this go for now. Her lies. But eventually, she will tell me and then I will deal with it. They will pay. I know what happens in those places. It's no secret that some men will go back and try the women out. See if they have enough spirit to make it worth it. Those fuckers. The rage I feel is almost unbearable and right behind that is a deep sadness that is now a part of my soul.

"Let's get you cleaned up. We'll eat and then you need to rest. Don't think I have forgotten about punishing you for lying not once, but twice."

"But..."

"Don't argue with me. I am not in the mood."

"You're not the boss of me!" she yells at me. "You can't tell me what to do!"

I set her down on her feet, making sure she can stand.

"I am, and I already have."

I slam the door behind us and lead her through the house. I can hear her stomping behind me. I'm taking her to our suite. It's like a fortress. No one will get to her. But she also won't be able to escape before she realizes I am the man for her. I will be her daddy and I will take care of her. I have her now there is no changing that. She will never get away from me now. Mine.

"It's time to get clean. We need to get all of this.." I motion to the dirt and those horrid clothes they put her in, "off of you. Bath or Shower?"

She looks up at me with big eyes. She is still so fucking innocent and cute. I feel my heart squeeze when she looks at me like that. It makes my dick hard to think of her in my house. In my bed. In my bathroom. But not now. She needs to heal. I have to build her trust. Get her use to my dominance.

"You choose," I tell her.

I can see the panic in her eyes. I wait patiently to see if she will answer me.

"Bath," she finally whispers.

I nod my head. "Come, then."

I walk away from her, heading through our living room and down the hallway, into what is now our room, to the en suite bathroom. It has an enormous bathtub. I started the water for her and put some oils in the water. I will take care of her and make sure she is always safe. She will learn to love me. She will never want anything again. I will give her everything, including my life if needed.

I remove the lace from her body, which is covered in blood, vomit, and who knows what else. She turns and looks at me as the garment drops from her body. She is beautiful. She stands before me in all of her naked glory and I feel my mouth water at the sight of her. She is delicate and fragile. Even with all the cuts and bruises that mar her beautiful skin. I will build her back up and earn her trust. I will protect her until my last breath.

She steps into the bathtub and sinks down into the water. Her shoulders relax a little. I pour a few more drops of the oils into the water and I can smell the vanilla.

"Scoot up," I command her as I shed my clothes.

I get into the water behind her and pull her onto my lap. Although she is initially tense, she eventually realizes that I won't make any unwanted advances.

"Come here, let me wash you."

She looks up at me and nods her head and moves to get comfortable. I can feel her trembling when she sits on my lap in the water. I know she needs some time to deal with her reality and her trauma. But she is mine. I have known it for a while even if she didn't. I spent a lot of time looking for her. She will get used to it in time.

I'm so hard right now. There is no way to hide the fact that I am aroused by her. The feeling of her ass on my cock in the water makes me want to groan. But that's the last thing she needs right now. I need to hold on to the rigid control that I've imposed on myself my whole life.

She needs to know I have restraint. That I won't make her do anything she doesn't want. I wait until she calms down a little. Using soap and a washcloth, I start to clean her up. After I washed her hair twice, I drained the water and ran fresh. She crossed her arms over her breasts, trying to cover up, but I move them. I don't let her cover up. She will have to get used to me. I have to prove to her that even naked; I have restraint. We will be together for a very long time.

"No need to be shy Luna," I whisper to her. "I have already seen you. I won't force myself on you."

I reach between her legs and I can feel how wet she is for me. She moans softly.

"What do we have here?" I purr to her.

I run my fingers through her wet folds. She gasps.

"You're so wet. For me."

She moans as I slide my fingers inside of her. I rub her clit with my thumb as she grinds on my fingers. Still so responsive to me. Even after everything she has been through. She has to feel the connection between us.

"Yes. That's it, Luna. Fuck my fingers. Just relax. This is about you and what you want."

"Fuck!" she screams when she explodes around my fingers.

I pull out and bring my fingers to my mouth. Savoring what taste I can. It's heaven.

"You taste so good," I groan while sucking my fingers.

She gasps as she watches me. While she looks at me I can see the fire in her eyes. I need to reteach her that not all men are only out to take. I want to give her everything. I can only hope she doesn't freak out. So far she seems receptive to me. I am not sure if that's because she had kind of known me before or because I hadn't hurt her. Only time will tell. But for now, she needs to sleep.

"Come with me Luna," I tell her.

She gets out and I dry her off with a big fluffy towel, being careful of the cuts I can see marring her beautiful skin. It makes me see red and I want to kill those bastards. I will kill those bastards. They will learn not to touch what belongs to me. Once she is dry, I take her by the hand and lead her into the bedroom.

"Lay down Luna. On your belly."

She does as I ask, and I feel a wave of satisfaction course through me. I take the ointment that is on the bedside table and I apply it liberally to her back and any mark I see on her.

"Relax," I say when she squirms and tenses up.

She stills and lets me continue. I take special care when I put some on her pussy. I don't want to spook her, but I also want her to heal. I want to worship this woman. Let her know that she's mine. I never thought I would ever feel this for someone. I want her to be happy. I want to make her happy, to take care of her in every way possible.

"Roll over so I can get the rest of you."

After I finish, I pull back the covers and tell her to climb in. She does and I turn off the light. I slide in next to her. I try to pull her to me, but she fights it.

"Don't run from me Luna," I say to her in the darkness.

I can hear her heart race as she lies next to me. I feel her head move as she shakes her head. I smile to myself.

"Good girl."

I fall asleep long after she does to the sound of her breathing. Her head cradled to my chest. My arms wrapped tightly around her body.

LITTLE GIRL

Demetrius

I'm woken up by the sound of Luna screaming. I jump up, ready to kill someone. I scan the room and see Luna standing in the corner. She is naked and crying, huddled in a ball. I slowly cross to her with my hands up.

"Luna, what is wrong?" I ask her.

She looks at me, and I can see the tears in her eyes.

"I don't want to be here. I don't want to be your slave. Please ... please don't hurt me."

I look at her, and I see the fear in her eyes.

"I know you don't and you aren't. But you are mine and

you will obey me or I will punish you. Do you understand me? I will take care of you and I promise to never do anything you don't want. But you will listen and I will help you. We can get through this together"

She nods her head.

"Good girl. Now come to me."

She slowly stands and comes to me. I scoop her up in my arms and take her back to bed.

"Lie down and get comfortable."

She lays down on the bed and I can see her trembling. I'm not sure if she is scared of me. But I know she will learn I am never going to hurt her. If it wasn't too much for her, I would tell her everything, but I can't. Not yet. It would be too much for her. I will tell her when she is ready. I will tell her why she has to stay here. More importantly, I will have to share the complexity of who I am.

I climb in beside her and pull her to me. I lay her head on my chest and hold her tight against me. I stroke her hair and rub her back. Giving her the comfort I know she needs.

"It's all right. You are safe now. I will always protect you. Was it a nightmare?"

She nods. My poor angel. I kiss the top of her head and I can hear her sniffling.

"I'm sorry," she whispers.

"You have nothing to be sorry for. You went through a lot, and when you are ready, you will tell me all about it. Those men will pay for what they did to you. I swear it." I kiss her on the top of her head and I can feel her body relax.

"Thank you for getting me out of there," she says. "I was so scared I would end up with that man in the suit."

"Of course I did. I could never leave you in a place like that. I would have never let that monster Salvatore have you, even if it took everything I own."

I hold her close.

"What were you doing there?"

"I was looking for you."

I smile when I feel her relax a little in my arms.

"How did you find me?"

"I saw you get taken. Anton and I have been scouring all of Brooklyn for you. Finally, a contact called with information about a woman who matched your description. I went to get you back."

Mostly true. She doesn't need to know we tortured a few people until we finally found someone who knew anything. I know she is going to have questions that I can't answer yet. I also know that eventually, she is going to lash out. I will let her get away with it for now. But she will learn quickly that it won't fly after I spank her ass red. For now, she has a better version of how we found her, and it will have to be enough.

***

Luna

"What's your name? Is it really Demetrius? I heard them say it."

"Demetrius Sokolov and you are Luna Lewis from Red Lodge Montana"

How does he know that I am from Montana? What does he do that he has an invitation to an auction for humans? A place where they treat us like less than people. Was he there to buy women? No, he said he was there for me.

But it is obvious he has been to a place like that before. He has been good to me so far, but if I push him too far, will he abuse me as well? I know he paid more money for me than I have ever seen. Am I going to have the opportunity to leave? Do I want to leave?

He doesn't seem to be the type of man to beat me or use me sexually. I would think if he was going to, it would have happened already. He was my protector before this. I think he wants something different from me. I can feel some sort of connection with him. But there is no way he will ever want me after he finds out what happened to me.

But ... if he knew what that place was and what happened there. Wouldn't he already have a really good idea of that? Yet he saved me anyway. Yes, I know he bought me, but I'm going to choose to say he saved me.

"Thank you for rescuing me," I whisper

"I'm not sure I would call it rescuing. You still belong to me. But I will never abuse you. I promise to always take care of you. But if you misbehave, I will spank that gorgeous ass."

I can feel my cheeks turning red. Why do I even feel like I might want him to? I've just been used over and over by random strangers. But the thought of this large Russian spanking me makes me want to squirm with need.

"Why? Haven't I been abused enough?"

"I would never abuse you. But as your daddy, I need to discipline you and teach you."

"My daddy?" Jesus, this man is trying to kill me here. He opens his mouth and the deep timber of his voice is enough to warm me up. Then he speaks about spanking me and being my daddy. "What the hell are you talking about?" I scream, trying to move away from him.

"I told you I'm going to take care of you. But I am your daddy and I will spank you when you need it."

"What if I don't want to call you daddy?"

I move off of the bed and he just looks at me passively. This is all too much. I am still a prisoner, only now the man is saying he will take care of me? What the fuck. I look around the room. I'm still skittish. There is nowhere for me to run. I need to get out of here. I want my life back. I run over to the bedroom door, but it doesn't open. The knob turns, but the door won't budge. I look at Demetrius, who just looks at me with a calm expression on his face.

"You can't escape. I own you."

"Fuck you," I growl at him.

I knew the moment I said it; I went too far. His face went passive, and he looked at me with cold, dead eyes.

"I think I will keep you here. You will learn to respect me and follow my rules. You will obey me. I will take care of you and you will be my little girl. But if you don't obey me, then I will punish you."

"I want clothes right now. Why am I naked?" I screamed at him. Starting to panic.

"Because you were in danger and I had to remove you from that situation. I will provide you with clothes when you earn them. You can only wear them when I tell you to."

"No, I don't want any of your shit. I want to go home!"

I don't want to be here. I want my life back. I want to pretend none of this happened. I back myself into the corner and huddle down, covering as much of myself as I can. I don't want to be touched. I don't want to be talked to. I don't want to be seen. I don't want to be heard. I want to disappear.

"Stop that," he snaps at me.

"Don't touch me," I say louder.

"I'm not going to hurt you. I will never hurt you. I will take care of you. I will love you. I will show you how a real man treats a woman."

"You're a fucking rapist! I hate you!" I scream at him.

"I'm not a rapist. I'm going to take care of you."

"I don't want you to be my daddy!" I scream at him.

"I think you do. Judging by what happened, you need someone to watch out for you."

"I don't want you to be my daddy! I'm not a child!" I scream at him.

"Then stop acting like one. You're not a child anymore. You're a grown woman. You will do as I say." He growls, "You will be my girl." I look at him and I can see the anger in his eyes. "You will be my girl. I will take care of you and protect you. Yes, that also means punishing you when you need it. But that also means showering you with affection as well."

I don't understand. This big Russian wants me? He owns me. It's not like I have a choice. I look at him and I see understanding in his eyes.

"I'm not going to hurt you. I will never hurt you. I will take care of you. Always. You will see Luna. I will prove it to you. Until then, you will stay in this room. You will eat when I tell you to. You will sleep when I tell you to. You will obey me. Do you understand me?"

"I will do what I want!"

I know I am being a bit much, but it's how I feel and if I am going to die or be abused, I might as well get it out of the way. I look up and he is watching me with a slightly amused look on his face.

"You will do what I say. You will obey me. If you don't, then I will punish you. Do you understand me? This is your only warning. The next time, I will pull you over my lap and turn your ass red. But understand with comes the fact that I will worship you like the goddess you are."

I focus all of my hatred on him. While he looks at me passively. He walks toward the door and puts his hand on a pad I didn't notice before. I hear the door's locks click. He opens the door and walks out of the room, naked. I hear the click of automatic locks as the door re-locks.

I run to the door and try pulling it open. I put my hand on the scanner. It blinks red and makes a buzzing noise. Fuck. I'm trapped in here. I grab the table and the lamps that are near me and throw them across the room and scream in fury. I break anything within reach. Screaming and crying. I walk back to the bed and sit down. I cover my head with a pillow and I cry. I'm tired of being treated like a child. I'm tired of being afraid. I'm tired of everything. I want to go home.

WATCH WHAT YOU SAY TO ME

Demetrius

I watch her on the monitors while she screams and destroys our room. She is so beautiful in her righteous rage. I can't believe she is mine. I feel like I should be kneeling before her while worshiping at her feet. I'm supposed to be her daddy. I should be taking care of her. I'm supposed to be showing her how a man takes care of a woman. I'm supposed to be loving her. I'm supposed to be kissing her. I'm supposed to be protecting her.

I want to go to her. I want to hold her and comfort her. I want to make things better. I want to kiss her and show her how much I love her. I want to be gentle and loving. But that isn't what she needs right now, and it's not the man I am. She needs structure and consequences. Her life is out of her control. I get that. I am giving her leeway to get accustomed. But if she keeps it up, I'm going to smack that beautiful ass.

I can tell she needs it. She would have been more receptive if I had been able to continue on the path I had been on. But that's not how things went. I walk into the closet, grab one of my suites, and start getting dressed for the day. I will instruct the kitchen staff on what to feed her and when. The cook will be the only one allowed in the room I have known her since I was a child. She traveled here with me from Russia and is one of the most loyal people I have on my staff. I can trust her.

I pull on a pair of black slacks and a white button-up shirt. I button my shirt, leaving the top three buttons undone. My jacket hangs from the chair in the corner. I grab it as I walk out of the room. I see Anton waiting for me.

"Anton, I have to go see the Pakhan. You will stay here and guard Luna. Only Anya is allowed in the room. I do not want you entering the room unless it is a life or death situation. You are to let Anya in and then close the door behind her. When she knocks, you can let her out again. Is that understood?"

"Yes, sir."

"Good. Now, I will be back soon."

"I will be here."

"Thank you."

I leave the suite walk down to the kitchen to speak with Anya, and then head to my brother's place. I have put him off as long as possible. I need to keep Luna a secret for now. I am sure he has heard I bought a woman last night. But for her own protection, I won't tell him her name. I hope he doesn't ask. He didn't seem to worry when she never showed back up to work. But I suppose after what he tried to do, it wasn't surprising.

The last thing I need is for him to find out about her. That could cost Luna her freedom or cause me to kill him. I'm leaning more toward me, killing him because she is mine. Pakhan or not. Brother or not, he can't have her. She is mine.

I walk into the kitchen set everything up with Anya, and then head out to my car.

I drive to my brother's house and park in the garage. Entering through the side door, I walk straight to his office and knock on the door.

"Come in." I hear him yell from inside.

I walk inside, and he stands up.

"You summoned me, Pakhan."

He looks me over. I know he won't see anything different. I have spent most of my life perfecting this cold exterior. It's difficult to break. But I hate when he gives me that knowing look.

"I wanted to speak to you about something important. I have a new business venture and I want you to go pick up my money from Salvatore."

"What kind of business venture?"

"It's a very lucrative one. I'm going into business with the Italians. You don't need to know all the details for now. They are looking to expand their reach in the United States. I want to see where this could go. I want you to help me with this endeavor."

"I will do what I can, Pakhan."

Being close to that motherfucker right now isn't a good idea, but I can't tell him no. I will have to do as I'm ordered.

He stares at me for a moment like he has something else to say.

"Have a seat, Demetrius"

I sit in the chair in front of his desk and cross my leg over my knee. I can tell by looking at him that he has already heard about last night. I wonder how much he knows. I look at him and I see him staring at me. I can't read his eyes or the look on his face.

"So, did you have something you wanted to tell me, Demetrius?"

"Nothing that I can think of, Pakhan."

I know better than to give up a piece of information to him. He might be my older brother and the Pakhan, but I know what he is capable of. I would rather not have to kill my brother today. But if he makes a move to take Luna from me, he will pay. I will make sure of that.

"I heard about a situation last night. I heard my younger brother and second in command bought the woman that Salvatore wanted. I also heard that she is a sex slave." I look at him and I can see the anger in his eyes. "Why?"

"I wanted her." I shrug.

"That didn't answer my question."

"It's all I have. I wanted her and he couldn't have her."

"Did you know he was trying to purchase the woman?"

"Yes, he was bidding against me."

"Are you trying to start a war over a whore?"

I narrow my eyes and stifle the growl in my chest. I can't let him see how much he pissed me off. I can't afford to lose my cool. I don't want to have to kill my brother today. So I can't let him know she means anything to me. I have to hide it better than this. But I will do whatever it takes to protect Luna.

"I am not interested in starting a war. But I will protect my investment."

"Your investment? What does that mean?"

"I purchased her for a reason. I will protect her until I see fit to sell her."

I hate this conversation already. I will never tire of my angel. She damn sure means more to me than that. But I can't let him know how much she already means to me. I have to try to make him believe once I'm done with her I will get rid of her. That's obviously not even a thought in my head. But I have no choice. I look at him and I see him staring at me. I don't like it. I feel like he can see me.

"I will do what I must to protect what is mine."

"I see. Perhaps you can bring her by and I can try her out as well. She must be a really great whore if the amount you paid is accurate, brother."

I can tell he is sizing me up. He is trying to get a reaction out of me and I can't give it to him. I want to jump up and beat him to death for even thinking of her that way. But I don't. I can't. I won't. She isn't well enough to deal with this kind of threat.

"I couldn't care less. Just remember, she is my property."

"Go meet Salvatore and collect what's mine."

He nods and I know I am dismissed. I stand up and walk out of the room. I don't look back. I don't want to see the look on his face. I don't want to see the anger in his eyes. I can tell he knows I would never let him near her. If he tries anything, he will learn what happens to those who try to steal from me.

I walk out of the house. Get into my car drive to the Italian restaurant and park in the lot.

I walk inside and see Salvatore sitting at the bar.

"Salvatore," I seethed coldly.

I can't stand this man. He is as slimy as they come. Word is he might be the next Don. I should kill him now before he can cause trouble. But I can't do that either. At least not yet. I sit down next to him.

He looks at me and smiles.

"Hello, Demetrius. How are you?"

I glare at him. "I'm fine."

"How is my little pet?"

I narrow my eyes at him. "She is not your fucking pet. She is mine. She is my property, not yours. Get over it."

"Ah yes, I forgot. She is your property. So you say. But I've had her already. Did she cry for you? Her blood tastes divine. I dream of her screams as I broke her." he does a chef's kiss. "Delicious. " I watched him shiver with pleasure.

He looks like he is relishing in the pain he caused her, and I want to break his neck right here. He knows he is pushing my buttons. One day soon he will push too hard, then I will kill him where he stands without a second thought.

"She is a very beautiful woman. I enjoyed her tremendously. I wonder what else she enjoys? Did she suck your cock? We had a date for that, but you interrupted my plans."

I can't believe he is talking about her like this to me, of all people. The balls on this guy. My hand is so close to pulling my gun out of my holster. My fingers are itching. All it would take is one bullet, and I would never have to hear his mouth again.

"I don't care what you enjoy. I don't care what you did with her. If you speak of her again, I will rip your dick off and feed it to you. Do you understand?" My Russian accent becomes more pronounced and my voice gets deeper.

His smile disappears, and he looks at me with disdain.

"I'm sorry Demetrius. Did I upset you?" He asks sarcastically.

"You should be. I will not tolerate disrespect from anyone. Especially you. You will show respect or I will end you." I sneer.

"I didn't realize we were playing games, Demetrius. I thought your Pakhan wanted to be partners."

"I am not him. Give me what I came for so I can leave."

"I'll give you what you want. But first," he smirks at me and moves closer, "have you tasted her yet? I didn't get that privilege either. She was already filled with come when I got there."

Who the fuck does he think he is? He might be the Don someday, but that day isn't today. Right now, he is insignificant to me. The only thing I need now is to kill him. He doesn't seem to be getting the; I will fucking kill you vibes.

"I don't have time for your games. I have work to do. Give me what I came for before I gut you." I growl at him.

He laughs. "Oh, I think you have plenty of time to play. I had plans for your pet."

I push my chair back and stand up to my full height. I don't have to puff my chest out. I know how big I am. I lean down and get in his face, gritting my teeth.

"I thought I told you to show me some fucking respect. Boy." I gritted out.

I grab him by the hair and slam his pretty boy face off of the bar. Then I hold it there. Smashing his face into the wood. I bend over and get in his face again and get to watch the blood drip from his mouth.

"Now, if you are done with the fucking games, give me what I came here for so I can fucking leave."

He looks at me with contempt and sneers. "Here."

I bounce his head off of the bar one more time just for the joy of it and stick the money in my suit coat pocket.

"Don't speak of her again or next time I'll fucking kill you." I sneer in his face.

I turn around walk out of the restaurant and get in my car. I have more important things to do than deal with this fucker.

I drove back to my brother's house and in front. I don't plan on staying any longer than to throw this envelope on his desk and leave. I enter through the front door and strolled straight to his office. Knocked on the door and waited for him to tell me to enter.

"Demetrius."

I toss the money on his desk. "Next time I suggest you send someone else or I might kill him."

"Watch how you speak to me, brother."

I narrow my eyes at him. "You know how to find me if you need me." I turn and walk out.

I walk out of the house and get into my car. I need to head back home to Luna. I know I shouldn't speak to him like that. It will only cause him to look into my situation more. He is the boss and I am his second. I just can't stop the anger that's coursing through me. I never liked that slimy bastard, anyway.

Now I would rather skin him alive. I can't do it yet. I have to wait and be patient. But one day that opportunity will come and when it does, he will regret fucking with me and touching my angel. He will pay.

Until then, he had better steer clear of me. After that meeting, I need to get back to her. My obsession is only growing. I have been on edge since I left the house. I need to have her back in my arms. To see her with my own eyes and know she is still ok.

Why Me?

Luna

After throwing my tantrum, I have to admit I feel much better. Since I had no clothes, I wrapped the sheet around me like a toga and called it good. Sitting here with nothing to do isn't good for my head. I keep getting flashbacks of things that were done to me when I would nod out. Things I don't want to remember. None of it is good. Most of it is too painful to even think about. My body still hurts, but whatever Demetrius put on it last night really helped with the pain and soreness.

This whole thing with him is confusing. I remember seeing him around Brighton Beach at the corner store by my apartment. But we never really spoke. Just that one phone call after he saved me. Obviously, I noticed how gorgeous he was. How could I not take notice?

But how does he know so much about me? I also don't know why he would want someone as broken as I am. Someone so used. He can have anyone he wants. So why me? After everything that happened in that warehouse, I'm half the woman I was. I don't even recognize myself. I don't know who I am anymore. I feel lost and broken.

Like I am losing my mind. I don't know what I want. The feelings he stirs in me make me even more confused. Last night in the bath he was so gentle with me. Even when he gave me an orgasm, it was soft and gentle. I think it was meant to help me trust that he wasn't going to treat me like a sex slave. There is no way he paid that much money for me and he is just. What? Going to take care of me? Does he expect nothing of me? Yeah right. That's not how life works.

I don't know what to think. I don't know what to do. I don't know how to act. All I know is that some part of me wants to be with him. I can't stop thinking about him. I hardly know him. I don't even know what it is he really does. But whatever it is, I can tell he is a powerful man. They said he was a Bratva brigadier, but I don't know what that is.

When he speaks, I can't help but want to obey. Authority rolls off of him in waves. I never even knew I was so attracted to it. But when he opens his mouth and talks about being my daddy, it makes my head spin. My body just reacts to him in a way I can't even put a finger on.

When the door opens abruptly, I jump up and gather myself at the top of the bed. A short, heavyset older woman enters the room with a tray of food.

"Come. Eat. Demetrius. He send this for you." She says in a very heavy Russian accent.

She turns and heads for the door again and I move quickly to stand with the sheet wrapped around me.

"Wait, please." She stops and turns, looking at me expectantly. "I'm sorry I am going crazy in here. Are you able to get me a book or anything?"

"I speak with Demetrius. When he gets back. TV? Is ok?"

"Oh, my god, yes! That would be great."

She nods and walks to the dresser and presses a button. A large TV extends from inside the wall while I watch it in amazement.

"Demetrius. He buys. Now eat. You hungry?"

"Yes, thank you."

She hands me the remote, nods, and knocks on the door. I hear the lock click and it is opened. She steps out and I hear her and the voice of a man speaking in Russian. The door closes and I hear the lock engage.

I turn the volume up and try to find something to watch. I can't focus. I am too nervous and scared. I feel like I am stuck in limbo. It doesn't seem like he has anything malicious planned for me. But how would I know? I can tell he is a dangerous man. I don't know what to do. I don't know where to start.

I turn on the hallmark channel. If I can't find a sweet romance there, then I'm screwed. My thoughts still keep wandering. I can't concentrate on anything. I grab the food the woman brought up for me and I pick at it.

It's all very good filled with fruits, sandwiches, coffee, and juice. But I just can't bring myself to eat, so I push it away. I break down crying for myself and all the girls that were there. I cry even harder, knowing I made it out, and they didn't. Who knows where they ended up or what's happening to them? The guilt is eating me alive. How am I supposed to live with this? Not only am I ruined and broken, but I couldn't help anyone. Including myself.

The tears won't stop. I wipe them off of my face and blow my nose. I sit on the bed and cry until I can't breathe. My stomach starts to twist with the loss and stress I feel. I run to the bathroom and throw up. I fall to my knees and sob uncontrollably on the bathroom floor. I hear the lock for the door click and the door opening. I hear Demetrius' voice call for me, but I am too broken to respond. He finds me laying on the floor in a sobbing mess of tears and vomit.

"Luna, here, let me get you up."

I lift my head and look at him. His eyes are full of concern.

"Are you okay?"

I shake my head.

"Please. You should have let me die."

"No. Never. Come here." He picks me up bridal style and holds me tight to his chest. "Never say that again or I promise you I will spank you hard enough that it truly hurts."

I wrap my arms around his neck and bury my face in his chest.

"I'm so sorry. I'm so sorry."

"Shh. It's okay. I forgive you. I know this is hard. Speak to me. Tell me what happened. Tell me what you need."

"Why me? Why did I make it out of there? What about everyone else?" I sob.

"Because you are strong. Because you fight. You have to know that you aren't alone. That you have me. I will always be here for you. You are my angel and have been since the very first time I saw you. I never want to hear you say about dying or taking your own life again. Do you understand me?"

I nod and cling to him when he sets me on his lap.

LET ME GO

Luna

A day later

I wake feeling like a raw nerve has been exposed. The shame is hitting me so hard that I can't take it. I feel it swallowing me whole. I don't want to live. Why couldn't he have just let me die? I shouldn't be here. I need to die. I can't face the memories of what happened. My thoughts are filled with shame and regret.

I am still naked and I feel exposed. I am sitting up against the headboard in Demetrius' room. The room he has locked me in to keep me "safe". I think I am still in shock and my body is in a lot of pain. My mind is cloudy and foggy and I feel numb. The only thing I can focus on is the fact that I was abducted and sold into human trafficking.

Drugged and raped too many times to count. And I can't remember anything except for a few faces of the men who held me captive and used my body. I can't remember anything else, and I am scared that they may have broken something in me. I should have died after he found me and saved me. Well bought me. They had overdosed me.

But no he had to fucking save me. I am a worthless piece of trash who should have been able to protect myself. I should have fought harder and screamed louder. Maybe someone would have helped me. I am so stupid, so weak. Why did he have to save me? I wanted to die, to leave this world and be free. I can't even think straight. My head hurts so badly.

The door opens, and Demetrius enters a doctor behind him. He sits on the edge of the bed and the doctor sits in a chair. "Luna, I am Doctor Matthews. Can you tell me where it hurts the most?"

I shake my head and curl into myself. "Leave me alone, I want to die," I whisper as tears fall down my face.

"Angel, we need to make sure you are ok. Let him check you over."

"NO!" I shout as I sit up. "Don't touch me! You should have let me die. You should have just let me leave this world. You should have left me to die. I want to die. I don't want to be here! I should have died! You should have let me go." I sob and I feel arms wrap around me and pull me close.

I smell his sweet, alluring scent and I cry even more. He shouldn't care for me. He shouldn't have saved me. He shouldn't be worried about me. I shouldn't be here. I feel a gun tucked into Demetrius' pants. I pull it out and point it at myself. Before he can react, I stand and move away from him. His face gets serious as he stands up. I point the gun at my head.

"Luna, you don't want to do this. You aren't thinking straight."

"No, no, I'm not thinking straight. You're right. I am thinking of leaving this world. I am thinking of leaving the shame, the memories, the hurt, the pain. You don't understand." I scream.

"Angel, please, I want to help. Let me help you."

"NO! I have so much shame! YOU DON"T UNDERSTAND! My body ..." I start to sob harder. "My body reacted to the horrible things they did to me! How could it like it! HOW! I was so disgusted with myself. I am dirty and ruined. They used me over and over. I was a sex toy for them! And my body liked it! I wanted it to stop. I wanted to die. But I orgasmed anyway. How could you save me? You should have let me die!"

"Luna, angel, come here. It's ok, you are safe now."

"No! I don't want to be here." I flip the safety off the gun.

He lunges at me. "NO!" I scream and pull the trigger.

He manages to shove my hand far enough away that the bullet just grazes me, but my finger is still on the trigger. I jump away from him. Somehow, the gun is still in my hand.

"Luna, calm down, please. Don't shoot again."

"You should have let me kill myself. Now I will never leave. I will always be dirty and useless." I place the gun against my temple. “Please let me go. I don’t want to suffer anymore.”

"Luna, please, we can work through this."

"I don't want to be here. I am not worthy to live."

"No, Luna, that is not true. You are worthy of living. Please put the gun down."

"I'm dirty and used. I liked it. How could I like it? I didn't want it. I swear I didn't want it. “ I sob. “How can I live with this shame? I have no purpose. Please let me go."

"No, I will not let you die. I am here to protect you and take care of you."

I have blood dripping down my face and he approaches me slowly with his hands up. I shake my head and step away from him.

"Luna, please listen. You were kidnapped, raped, and drugged. Those men, they are monsters. The way they treated you is an abomination. I swear I will avenge you and make them pay for what they did."

I am sobbing and shaking, and my arms are getting tired, but I keep the gun pointed at my head. He is close to me now, close enough that if he grabs the gun, I won't have a chance to pull the trigger.

"Please angel, come here." He holds his arms open and waits.

"I... I..." I fall to my knees and let the gun fall to the ground.

He walks over and kneels next to me. "Let the doctor help you Luna, please."

"I'm dirty, useless, and damaged. I don't deserve your kindness or protection."

"No, that's not true. You are perfect."

"I'm not, my body..."

"Luna, it's natural. You can't help your body's reactions."

"It's not normal, not for someone who was raped."

"It is. You can't stop the body's reaction, angel."

"Please let me go. Just let me go."

"I can't do that. I won't do that. I have to protect you. You are mine, and I protect what is mine."

"Why? Why would you want a dirty, used, useless, damaged woman?"

"You aren't any of those things. You are the most beautiful, sweet, caring woman I have ever met. I will get you justice and I will protect you. Please let the doctor help you."

"You will regret this. I don't want to be a burden."

"You could never be a burden. Not to me. Let the doctor help you."

"Ok," I whisper.

I am too weak to fight anymore, and maybe it's time I accept my fate.

He picks me up and carries me to the bed. The doctor stands there and watches. I know he wants to help, but I am too afraid and embarrassed. Demetrius holds me and kisses the top of my head. The doctor comes over to me.

He doesn't touch me, he just looks at me for a moment with calm, understanding eyes. "It is the body's natural reaction. There is nothing you could have done to stop it. There is no shame. Now please, let me examine you."

I nod and he touches my shoulder first, looking at the cuts and bruises. Then he checks my face.

"Luna, your face is healing nicely, and the stitches from the knife wounds will come out soon. I am going to give you something to help with the anxiety and the flashbacks. I need to look at where the bullet grazed your head. I am going to have to touch you, ok?"

I nod. He moves closer and touches my face. "Hmmm, the wound looks ok just small. The head bleeds a lot. You will be ok. Your body is showing signs of malnourishment. I am going to give you some vitamins and you need to make sure you are eating more."

He stands and walks to his bag. He pulls out a needle and fills it with medicine. I look at him with wide eyes and panic hits. My heart starts beating so fast I can hear the whooshing of blood in my ears.

"Shh, it's just a vitamin injection. It will help your body heal. Ok?"

I cry and try to move away, but Demetrius holds me there, whispering in my ear, calming me. The doctor comes back and wipes my arm and sticks the needle in.

"There we go. All done. Luna, you are going to be ok. It's a lot for your body to process. You need lots of rest, and you will probably have nightmares. We will deal with those as they come. For now, I am going to give you something for the pain."

He takes another needle out and I watch as he sticks it in my arm. "You might go through withdrawal from the drugs they were giving you. If it gets bad, I want you to call me back again. For now, this should help."

"Thank you."

He packs up his things and leaves the room.

Demetrius is still holding me while I am crying. I don't even know why, but he is rubbing my back and holding me close. I'm a useless waste of space. He needs to let me go.

"Please let me die. I can't be here. I can't live with the shame. Why couldn't you let me die?"

You're Breaking My Heart

Demetrius

It breaks my heart every time she says those words. It wasn't her fault. "Shh, you're ok. We will get through this. I promise."

"Shh, you're ok. We will get through this. I promise."

"It was my fault," she whispers.

"It wasn't your fault. You didn't ask for it, Luna. Nothing you did directly caused this to happen."

"I can't, I just can't. I don't want to live."

I hold her tighter and kiss the top of her head. "You are perfect Luna, and I am here for you. I will never let you go. I will always be here for you. It is not your fault, do you understand? Not. Your. Fault."

"You don't understand. They took me. They took me and drugged me and raped me and hurt me. You weren't there. You don't understand."

"No, angel, I understand better than you know. I got you from there, remember? You are perfect. I will take care of you and make them pay. They will all pay. I promise you. The torture they will receive will be worse than death. I will make sure of it. Now please, get some rest."

"Why? Why are you being so nice to me? You bought me."

"I did. But I was also already keeping an eye on you, remember? I had already decided to claim you as mine before this. This is just an opportunity."

"No, that can't be. You don't even know me."

"Angel, it is. I knew the moment I saw you, I needed you. Your sweet personality, the wonder in your eyes as you looked up at the tall buildings. I will always come for you."

"Please, please, let me die. I don't want this. You shouldn't care about a broken, used, useless woman."

"Stop it. Stop saying those things before I paddle your ass. I still might after you are doing better. Don't ever try to kill yourself again. Do you understand?"

"Why? Why would you want such a damaged woman?"

"You are not damaged. You are perfect. Please, please, believe me."

"No. No. Two men used me at the same time. I... I had..."

"Luna, it was natural. It is a natural reaction of the body."

"I'm so dirty."

"You are not. You are mine and you are perfect. This doesn't define you, angel. I promise I will do everything I can to help you through this."

"But the things they did..."

"Don't think about that. You are not dirty. You are not useless. You are mine. Let's get you cleaned up and we can cuddle. I will hold you all night if I need to."

I can't push her. She needs time. If anyone who knows me saw how I am with her, they wouldn't believe it. I rarely let anyone see the softer side of me. But something about her brings that out in me.

I stand with her and carry her to the bathroom. She doesn't fight or even really look at me. She is just here, and it really tugs at my heart to see her this way.

I sit her on the edge of the tub.

"Luna, angel, can you look at me?"

She slowly turns her head and looks at me. She is so sad. I lean in and kiss her.

"Please, trust me."

"I am so dirty."

"No. You are not. We can talk more in the morning. Ok? You need rest."

She nods and looks away. I turn on the water and help her undress. Once the water is warm, I help her into the bath.

"I... I can do it."

"I know. But I need to do it. I need to take care of you."

"Why?"

"Because angel. I have to show you that you are mine and you are precious. And I want to. I want to make sure you are ok. Are the stitches or the knife wounds hurting?"

"A little."

"I'll be gentle. I will put some ointment on them when we are done. Then I will wrap them."

"I can do it."

"Luna, angel. Let me. Let me take care of you. It's the least I can do."

"But I am dirty and used and damaged."

"Angel, you need to stop saying things that aren't true. Please, trust me. Let me prove to you that you are not those things."

"How? How can you prove that?"

"I am going to show you. I am going to take care of you. I am not a good man Luna. I hurt people in my line of work. I have killed many but with you. With you, I am a different person. Please let me."

"Ok. I don't understand, but ok."

I smile and take the soap. "We can get through this together. I will help you and protect you."

"I am not worthy."

"Angel, please."

She stops talking and lets me clean her up. Once she is cleaned, I rinse her off and dry her. My poor angel. I will kill them all. If anyone ever touches her again, I will kill them. She is so fragile. She needs help.

"Now, let's get the wounds covered. We don't want you to get an infection. Come, angel lay on the bed."

She does as she is told and lays down. Her beautiful body is scarred with bruises and cuts. The knife wounds are healing, but still look painful.

I put some antibacterial ointment on the wounds. Then wrap her in bandages.

"There. Now, let's get you something to eat."

She shakes her head and curls into a ball.

"Please, just a few bites. You have to eat. Let's get you some broth. Please."

"Ok," she says so softly I barely hear her.

I call down to the kitchen and have some sent up. I sit beside her on the bed and slowly spoon feed her. I want to take care of her. No, I need to take care of her. The anger I feel toward what happened to her is overwhelming me. It takes all my self-control not to scream and break things. I am going to rip those bastards apart. They will suffer so much before I kill them.

When she is finished, I pull her into my arms. "Let's get some sleep, okay? You are safe."

"Please, please, let me die."

I turn her toward me and cradle her to my chest. "Luna, please. I will get you justice. They will pay. I promise. We will go through this together. Please, angel. I need you. I need you to stay with me."

"I can't live. I don't want to be here."

I want to scream and shout and smack her ass for thinking this. But I know none of that will help. She needs to see that she is not what she thinks.

"You can. I will show you that you can. Together, we will get through this. I need you. We can help each other through this. You are the only one who can ever be the light to my darkness. My angel. Please, try for me."

"I will try, but it won't change the way I feel. I don't want to live. I don't deserve to live. Why would you want a dirty, used, useless woman who has no purpose?"

"Stop. That is not true. You do have a purpose. Your purpose is to be my angel, my lover, my queen. I can't live without you. Please, try. I need you, my angel. I don't want to hear that from your mouth again. You're mine. I want you. I need you. Please."

She shakes her head.

"Please, Luna, let me love you."

"I can't. How can you want me when I have been used?"

"You are not used. You are a person, not a car Luna. You were a victim. Please, Luna. Let me love you."

She shakes her head.

"Please, let me love you."

"You shouldn't. You should find a woman worthy of you."

"You are all I want. There is no one else."

"I don't know how."

"You do. Just trust me, angel."

"Please don't leave me."

"I won't. Ever."

I kiss her softly.

"Please, let me love you. I have never wanted anyone the way I need you."

"But why?"

"Because you are perfect for me."

She shakes her head but doesn't speak. I run my fingers through her hair and kiss her forehead. I wrap my arms around her tightly, holding her to me. I will kill them all. They will all die in the worse way imaginable. I will make them pay for this. She has probably never done anything to anyone in her life. She is pure. They forced her body to do things she can't handle, and her mind will have to heal. But it is not her fault.

I will keep telling her that until she believes it. I need her. I should probably feel strange about that, but I don't. I've never needed anyone like I need her. The pain and panic I felt the whole time I couldn't find her made me realize how obsessed I am with her. But now that she is in my arms, I have a chance to make it right.

"I will kill them all. I will torture and maim and kill every last one of them. No one will take you from me. They will pay. You will have your revenge."

She whimpers and shakes.

"Shh, shh, it's ok. It's ok."

I rock her back and forth and try to calm her.

“You will have your revenge. I promise.”

She cries herself to sleep with the help of the medicines doc gave her.

It breaks my heart to see her like this. I can't even begin to imagine what she went through. I know she has had a rough life being an orphan. But the men who took her, the ones who hurt her, they will pay. The ones who made her feel like she is worthless will pay.

I hold her close and fall asleep with her held tightly in my arms.

Too Quiet

Demetrius

The next day she still isn't talking much, and her face is pale and sad. She won't look at me and she doesn't eat much. I can feel how desperate she feels and the guilt she has. I just don't know what to do. I will give her time and help her. But I can't make her get better. She needs to see that she is strong. She is worthy. That what happened isn't her fault. She needs to learn that and to trust me.

She sits quietly in the corner of the room, staring out the window.

"Luna, please, say something."

She doesn't move or speak.

I sigh. I can't make her talk or open up. I wish I could. I can't imagine the things that were done to her. I am not a gentle man and I have killed many, but seeing her like this is too much.

"Angel, I have to go out. The door will be locked and Anton will be outside."

She still doesn't respond. I can't force her. But if she tries to hurt herself, I don't know what I will do. Anton, as always, will be here to guard her.

"If you need anything, you can ask him."

She doesn't respond.

I leave her sitting there and go to find Anton.

"You know where to find me."

"Yes, sir. Is there anything else you need?"

"Not at the moment. Keep her safe. If she tries to hurt herself, you have permission to restrain her and call me."

"Of course, sir."

I pat him on the shoulder and leave the house.

I have a few things to take care of and a few people to see.

First, I need to find out as much as I can about the men who were there when I found Luna. They will pay, and they will pay soon. I will make them suffer.

I get in my car and drive into town. The first thing I need to do is visit the club and get any information that might be floating around there. I need to know the names of the men. I will track them down.

Luna

I heard him, and I know I should answer. He has been nothing but kind to me. Even if I can't wear clothes. But honestly, that might be for the best. I am already looking at the sheet and wondering if I could make a noose out of it.

He is doing everything he can to take care of me and make me feel better. And I appreciate it, but I don't deserve him. I don't deserve anything. I can't even look at him because all I can think about is how much pain I am in. My body is healing, but my mind is broken. I just want it all to stop.

My thoughts are consumed by what happened. I can't escape the memories and the shame. Demetrius left a while ago. He has been gone longer than normal and I'm starting to get worried. I can't stand the thoughts that are rattling around in my head. I go from worrying about him to wondering when he won't want me anymore. Or when he will decide I am more trouble than I am worth. Maybe he will forget about me and just let me die. But he is trying to protect me. But maybe he will just decide I'm not worth it. I can't blame him.

How long will it be until he tires of me?

Maybe he has decided that I'm too damaged. Too used. No, he keeps telling me it wasn't my fault, but I know it was. I walk into the bathroom and go through the cupboards and drawers. There has to be a razor or something sharp.

"No, Luna. Don't." I say to myself.

But the thoughts keep coming. Maybe if I take a bunch of pills, he will leave me alone and not find me in time. He left the pills the doctor gave me in case I needed them. I don't want to do this, but the voices in my head won't stop. I can't take the way I feel. I crave that quiet darkness.

I grab the pills and fill a glass of water. I sit on the edge of the bed and start to take the pills one by one. But my hands are shaking and the tears are falling. My breathing is shallow and erratic.

I can't. I can't. I shouldn't. But I have to. It's the only way to escape the pain.

I have taken three pills, and I am working up the courage to take the others. My hands are still shaking. I take a deep breath and take a few more. There are ten left, just a few more to go. I take a deep breath and grab the rest of the pills.

"Please forgive me."

Just as I am about to take the pills, the door opens. It's the short Russian woman, she is looking at me with concern.

"Luna, you can't. You are not supposed to be touching the medicine. Demetrius will be so upset."

I shove the rest of them in my mouth and swallow them with the water.

"NO!" she shouts.

I look at her and smile.

"You will regret this," she says with a sad shake of her head.

I don't know if she is right. But if I am not here, I can't regret anything.

The pills are hitting my system, and I am getting sleepy.

"Don't tell him. Please."

"I have to. I don't have a choice. He will punish me if he finds out I didn't tell him."

"Please. Let me go. Let me die."

"I'm sorry. You can't die."

I hear her start banging on the door, calling out in Russian for Anton.

I lay down and let the darkness come. Please just let me drift off.

Because I Love You

Luna

I wake up to the sounds of beeping machines and muffled voices. It takes a few minutes before I realize that I am still alive. But then the panic sets in. Why? Why am I still alive?

The machines beep faster and faster.

"Luna. Shh, Luna, angel. You're ok. I'm here."

"Please, let me go. Please. I just want to die. I don't want to be here." I cry

"Angel. Shh. We can talk about this later. Right now, I am

just glad you are ok. I almost lost you. Do you understand? I can't lose you."

I shake my head.

"You can't leave me. You have to stay. You are mine. Mine to love, to hold, to take care of. You have to let me."

"No, please, I'm not worthy."

"Stop. Stop this right now! Stop it!"

I blink in surprise at his sudden angry outburst.

"I will not have you speaking this way. Not to yourself, not to me. Not to anyone. You are a strong, beautiful, perfect woman. Do you understand? I don't want to hear this shit ever again. You are not leaving me. You are mine. We can help each other. Be there for one another. You are perfect. You are mine. Say it. Say it Luna."

"No."

"Say it."

"I'm not yours."

"Say it. You are mine. SAY IT!"

"No."

"Yes. You are mine. I don't care if you fucking like it or not!" he yells, his voice becoming deeper and his Russian accent becoming more pronounced.

"No. I'm not. I will never be yours. I don't want to be yours. You shouldn't want me. I'm dirty, used, and broken."

"Stop." His voice is so deadly calm I look at him in shock. "I will not allow you to speak about yourself like this. Do you understand?"

I stare at him, unsure what to say.

"I...I can't."

"You will. Now say it Luna, say it right fucking now."

I shake my head.

"Luna. Angel, please."

"No, no, no. I won't. You shouldn't want me. You shouldn't."

"That's not for you to decide! YOU ARE MINE! YOU BELONG TO ME!" He shouts, his face going red.

"NO, NO, NO!"

"Yes, you are. You are mine. Say it."

"NO, NO, NO, NO."

"YES, YOU ARE!" He shouts back his eyes turning dark.

"I DON'T WANT TO BE."

"That's too fucking bad! You are mine and that's that!"

"No."

"Yes, you are. Say it."

"NO, NO, NO, NO, NO!"

He looks about ready to explode. "Well, they fucking pumped your stomach, and you almost died. And now I have to deal with your attitude. Fucking stubborn woman."

"Good. I want to die. Please let me go."

"Fuck that!"

He storms out of the room. I feel bad. I know I am his. I can feel it too. But I don't want to. I just want it all to end. Maybe now he will realize I am not worth the trouble. I can feel the connection we have. I felt it that day in the corner store. The instant attraction. I roll on my side and stare at the wall. I know he wants what's best for me. But I don't think he understands.

"You fucking stubborn woman."

"Go away."

"No. You are mine and that is that."

"No, no, no, no."

"Yes. You are, even if you won't admit it. What happened to you doesn't matter to me. Only you matter. Do you understand only you? Nothing else. So fucking stop. Stop pushing me away. You are mine. You need to learn your place. And if that means I have to punish you to teach you that, I will. I have been trying to be nice. But I am just watching you sink. I won't have it. I won't have you thinking you are dirty, useless, broken, or worthless. You are none of those things. Do you hear me? None. Of. Those. Things."

"I am."

His hand reaches out so fast I flinch. But he grabs my chin and forces me to look at him.

"Stop. This ends now. I can't help you if you don't let me. I can't show you what you mean to me if you insist you mean nothing. This is your last warning. STOP. You are mine. And that is final. Stop. Stop talking about yourself like that. Stop fighting me. Just stop."

As tears stream down my face, he embraces me. "Your mine. I don't care. I don't care angel. Nothing they forced on you was your fault. I don't care about that. I care about you. Only you."

He holds me tight as I cry.

"Please, I can't, please."

"Shhh, stop, please stop. I will help you. Let me."

"I'm not sure there is help for me."

"There is. Please. I have never wanted anything more. Please, let me. Just try. I know it's hard, but I will help you. Please."

"How?"

"By loving you. We will learn to live again. Together. You will be my queen. And I will protect and love you. Let me. Please. Just let me."

I sob and cling to him. I know I need him to. But how can he even want to love me after so many men touched me?

"Ok. I will try."

"That's my angel. That's all I ask. Just try. I have you. We will figure this all out. Together."

"Ok."

"Now, I am going to spank you. Then we are going to go back to the house. You are going to behave and accept the fact that you are mine."

"But..."

"NO. I am not playing Luna. You are mine and you are going to accept that. And if I have to paddle your ass every day to show you, then that is what I will do. I paddle your ass and all is forgiven a completely clean slate. No hanging onto this bull shit. Do you understand? No more feeling worthless or dirty. No more self-hate. I will not tolerate it. From now on, when you think about it, think about how I will feel when I have to punish you."

"But."

"NO! This is not open for debate. You are mine and you will learn your place. And if you want to fight me on it. That's fine. It will be a lesson for you. If you continue to fight, I will keep paddling you. Do you understand?"

"Why?"

"Because, my stubborn girl. I love you."

My heart stops. No. He can't. No one loves me.

"You can't."

"I do. I love you. Now, we can either do this the easy way or the hard way. Your choice. But I am done playing games. I am not going to let you sink into despair and depression. I have seen enough people do that, and I won't allow it to happen to you. Now, choose. Easy or hard?"

"Easy."

"Good, now I am going to spank you for trying to kill yourself. Do you understand?"

"But..."

The easy way or The hard way?

Demetrius

"Do you understand? No buts."

"Yes."

"Now, stand up."

"What? Why?"

"Because angel. I told you I was going to paddle your ass. Now do it."

I hope this is the right thing to do. But I have exhausted everything else. I know no other way. She needs discipline. Not discipline from a place of anger, but of love. I am not angry with her. Right now, all I want is to help her.

I am pissed. But not at her. At the men who hurt her.

She stands and looks at me with wide eyes.

"Lay over my lap."

She lays over my lap.

"I am going to spank your ass. If you think it is too much and need to stop or have a break, just say red. It's a safe word. Not a get out of jail free card. Otherwise, just be quiet. Do you understand?"

"Yes."

"Ok. This is going to hurt. I am going to spank your ass until I decide it's enough. Do you understand?"

I don't really want to do this. She almost killed herself for a second time. But I need to do this. As much for me as I do for her. She needs to be absolved and if this is what it takes. Then so be it.

"Yes."

"Good."

I lift the my hand and bring it down on her bare ass.

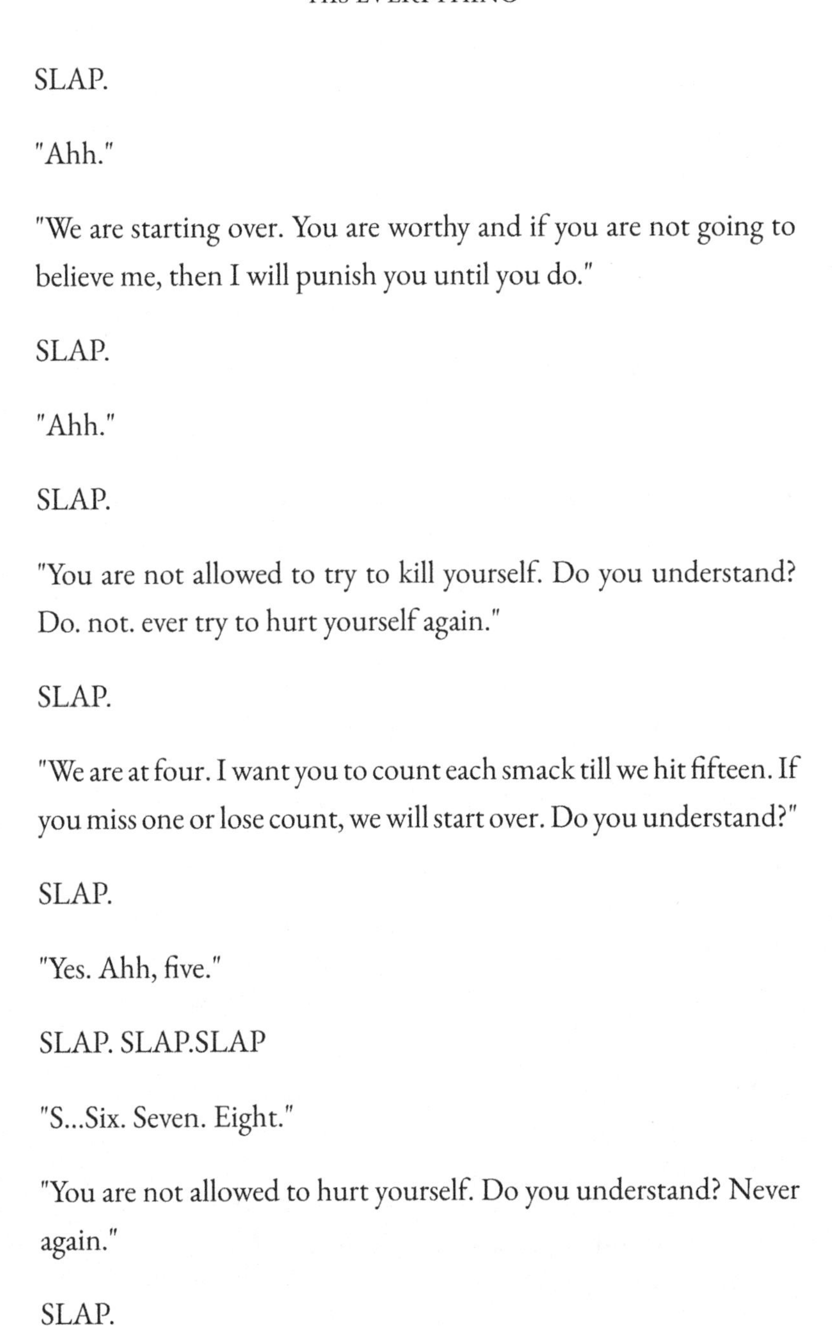

SLAP.

"Ahh."

"We are starting over. You are worthy and if you are not going to believe me, then I will punish you until you do."

SLAP.

"Ahh."

SLAP.

"You are not allowed to try to kill yourself. Do you understand? Do. not. ever try to hurt yourself again."

SLAP.

"We are at four. I want you to count each smack till we hit fifteen. If you miss one or lose count, we will start over. Do you understand?"

SLAP.

"Yes. Ahh, five."

SLAP. SLAP.SLAP

"S...Six. Seven. Eight."

"You are not allowed to hurt yourself. Do you understand? Never again."

SLAP.

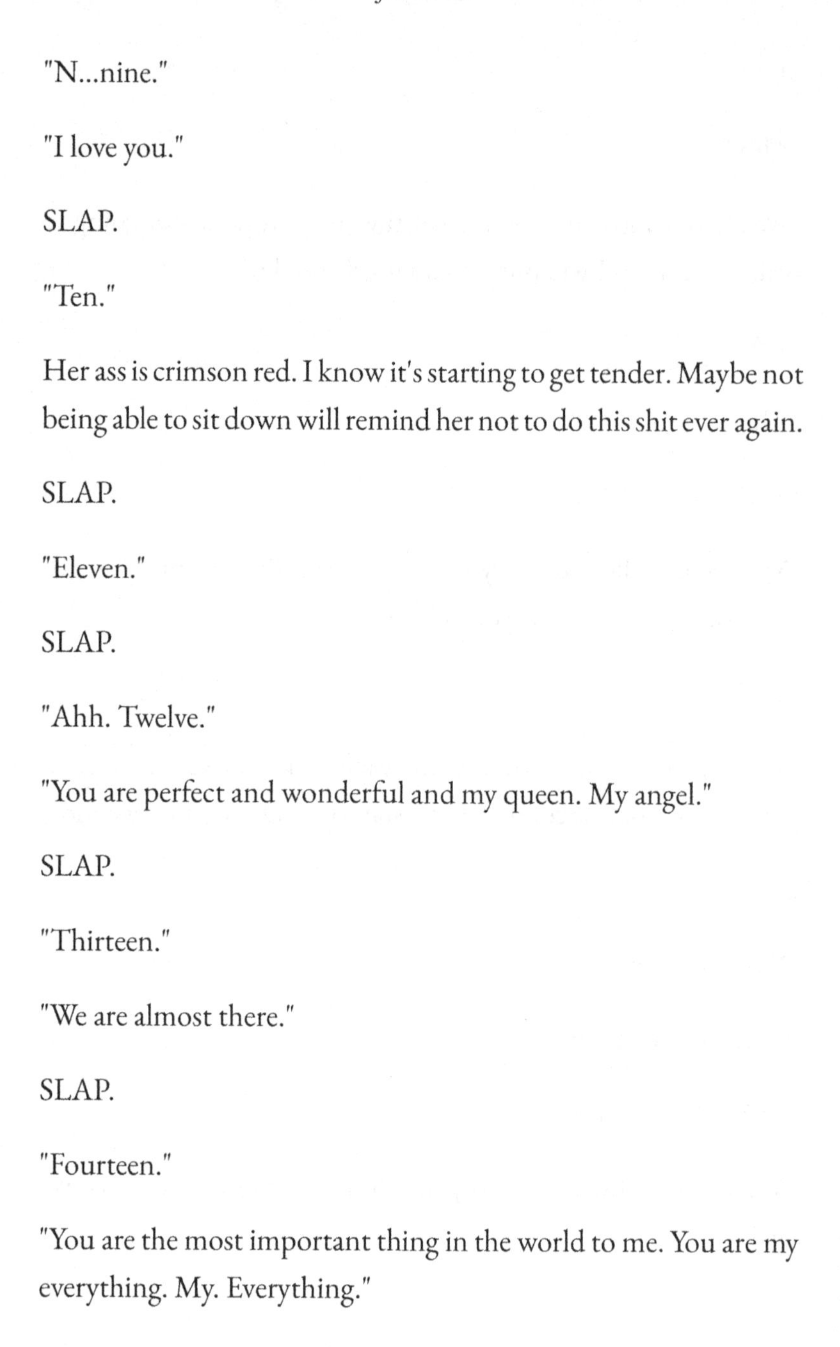

"N...nine."

"I love you."

SLAP.

"Ten."

Her ass is crimson red. I know it's starting to get tender. Maybe not being able to sit down will remind her not to do this shit ever again.

SLAP.

"Eleven."

SLAP.

"Ahh. Twelve."

"You are perfect and wonderful and my queen. My angel."

SLAP.

"Thirteen."

"We are almost there."

SLAP.

"Fourteen."

"You are the most important thing in the world to me. You are my everything. My. Everything."

SLAP.

"Fifteen."

"Good girl." I pull her up into my lap when she starts sobbing.

"I'm so sorry Daddy. Please, I'm sorry."

"It's ok, angel. It's all forgiven."

"I love you too. I'm sorry. I'm so sorry."

"I know, angel. It's ok."

"I'm so sorry."

"It's ok. I forgive you. And it's all forgiven. Shh. You are perfect and wonderful and mine."

"I'm yours."

I pull her to me. I want to cry into her hair. The fear I felt when I got this call. It was worse than when she was taken. But it's all forgiven.

"It's all forgiven, angel. Don't ever do this again. I can't take it. Do you understand I don't want a life where you are not in it?"

She cries for a long time. I don't mind. I don't care. I just hold her. She is mine, and she needs me the same as I need her.

I can feel her relaxing in my arms.

"Are you ok angel?"

"Yes."

"Good. Do you want to go to our room now?"

Years ago, I had the doc tell me everything he needed in order to keep me alive if something were to happen. This room is equipt to handle almost anything. Thank god it was here and Doc has been staying nearby because of how unstable Luna has been.

"Yes."

"Ok, up you go."

I wrap her in a sheet and lift her into my arms. I don't want to put her down. I would carry her everywhere if she would allow me to. I take us up to our room.

"Ok. Can we just sleep?"

"Yes, we can. Just sleep. I love you. Do you understand that? I love you."

"I love you too."

I lay her on the bed and strip us both before getting into the bed with her. I wrap her tightly in my arms and hold her.

"I'm sorry."

"Stop, no more apologies. It's done and over. We can move forward."

"Ok."

"Go to sleep. We will talk more after a nap."

"Ok. Please don't leave."

"I'm not leaving. Not now, not ever. I will never leave."

"Thank you. You are my world."

"And you are mine. My world. My angel. My everything."

She curls into my side and falls asleep. I really hope this has ended. I don't think I will be able to handle it if she tries to kill herself again. The gun was already a close call. I should have never left those pills here for her. What was I thinking? That decision almost caused me to lose her. She will need to be watched. She will not have access to any pills. She will have to get them from me. And I will give her as little as possible.

I hold her tighter and feel her soft breath on my chest. I can't lose her. I can't. She is my everything. I never knew what love was like before her. And I can't imagine living without her.

"Don't ever try to leave me again," I whisper to her sleeping form.

I don't want to live without her.

I fall asleep holding her tightly.

My Angel.

Mine.

"You will never hurt again. You are safe. And mine."

Mine!

Demetrius

I can’t help the feelings she brings out in me. Her pain is palpable. I can feel it in my bones. She needs me now. The only way I know how to be is to be myself. I have tried the more understanding way. The way of being soft and caring, but she is sinking further. It’s time to start showing her that she is mine. That she can and will survive this.

I can feel the bond we share. There is this ... connection. I can't explain it, but I know it exists. It is stronger than any other connection I've ever felt.

I don't know what to do with her, though. I want to take care of her and make sure she is safe. I need to protect her. I want to love her. I want to be the man that she deserves. It seems the spanking really did help. She has been doing better about some things.

I need to be the man that makes her happy. I want to give her everything she has ever dreamed of. I want to be the one that makes her smile and laugh, that makes her forget all the bad things in this world. But I know I am not a good man. I do many things that I am sure she would find despicable. I kill, maim, and destroy. But not her. She is my light. The only one that shines a light in my otherwise dark world.

It's time to make this connection grow and show her I am the man for her. The only person she can always depend on. I am going to be the daddy who takes care of her and loves her. I am going to be the man that shows her how beautiful she is and how amazing she is. I will be the man who makes her dreams come true. I will show her that what has happened doesn't define her. But first I have to make her trust me.

I pull the sheet that she has wrapped around her. She moves to hold it with a gasp.

"I said no clothes. Would you like me to spank my bad girl?"

She looks shocked and shakes her head.

"No."

I kiss her softly and then nuzzle her neck. "Good."

I stand up and lead her to the bathroom. I turn on the shower, remove my clothes, and step in behind her as I guide her into it. I reach around her and turn the water hotter. I lean forward and place my hands on her breasts and massage them.

"You are so soft," I whisper into her ear.

She whimpers and shivers.

I take her hand and guide it over her stomach. She gasps as her fingers glide across her wet skin. I cup one breast and rub my thumb against her nipple. It instantly hardens and goosebumps appear on her skin.

"Touch yourself," I growl in her ear

Her breath catches in her throat, and she slowly reaches between us. I watch as she glides her fingers across her clit, rubbing small circles. I love how responsive she is to me, even after what she just went through.

"I want you to touch me," I tell her.

I can see a small glint of fear in her eyes.

"I will never make you do anything. But I want you to touch me. Do you want that?" I take her other hand and I run her fingers through the hair on my chest and down my abdomen.

"Do you want to touch me?" I ask again.

She nods and I smile. I take her hand and guide it down my cock.

She gasps and closes her eyes as she strokes me.

"I want you to stroke me. Stroke me like you want me. Like you want me to be inside of you." She moans and starts to pump faster. "Can I touch you? I want you to feel as good as you make me feel."

She places her hands on my thighs and kneels down. I moan and my hips buck when she kisses the head of my cock. She looks up at me with desire in her eyes.

"Not now, my angel. This is about you. Maybe later."

She pouts when I pull her up to me. She looks so adorable. God, the things she does to me. I take her face in my hands and kiss her deeply. I slide my tongue into her mouth, tasting her. She tastes so sweet and I want more. I want to devour her. I want to lick every inch of her body and make her scream my name while she comes on my face.

“This is about showing you that life continues. What happened doesn’t define you. We will work on this together. I am here.”

I kiss her again, and she pushes her hands into my hair. I grab her ass and pull her closer to me. I grab her breast and pinch her nipple hard, causing her to yelp before I pull it into my mouth. I sucking and bite gently as she cries out. I love her sounds; they are music to my ears. I could listen to them all day long.

"Demetrius! Please!"

I bit a little harder, and she gasps “What should you call me?”

I savor her little moan before she says “Daddy.”

“That's right.”

I release her breast and kiss my way down her body. I can smell the arousal on her skin. I can feel it on my hands. I open her legs and stare at her beautiful pussy. I see that her clit is swollen and red. I lick it with a slow swipe of my tongue and she moans.

"You like that angel? I bet you want my cock right now, don't you?"

She nods frantically.

"Well, I'm not going to give it to you yet. I want you to wait. I want to make you feel good. We have time."

I spread out her legs more and I look up at her. She is panting and her eyes are wide.

"Tell me what you need, Luna. Tell me what you want."

"I want you. I want you inside of me. I want to feel you. I want to feel your cock. I want to feel you come in me. I want to feel you fill me up. I want to feel you everywhere. Please fuck me."

I chuckle. "Patience, my angel." I flick her clit with my tongue, and she gasps. I grab her hips and thrust my tongue deep into her pussy. I reach up and grab her tits and squeeze them. "I want to hear you scream my name. There will never be anyone else, just me. Only me."

"Yes, Daddy!"

I pull my tongue from her pussy and I look up at her.

"I am going to make you feel amazing. You're going to come so hard you're going to beg me to stop. Say it again."

"Please, Daddy! Please, I need it."

"That's right. Let Daddy make you all better."

I grab her ass and pull her towards me. I devour her with mine. I suck on her clit, and I run my fingers through her folds and push her little button with my thumb and stick two fingers into her.

"Oh, God! Yes! Oh yes!"

I pull my fingers out and I put them in my mouth. I suck on her juices, and then I shove my tongue back into her pussy. She grabs my hair and pulls me closer. I can feel her walls tighten around my fingers. I press harder and I can feel her orgasm coming.

"Daddy! Please. Please!"

I pull my fingers out and I lick them clean. She gasps and gives me a dirty look until I stand up and grab her by the waist. I'm happy to see that she still has some fire. Picking her up, I push her against the wall. Grab my cock and I position it at her entrance. I rub the tip of my cock against her lips and she gasps.

"Say it again. Tell me what you want."

"I want your cock, Daddy! Please, please!"

I pick her up and push her against the wall, and she instantly wraps her legs around me. I push the head of my cock inside her and she cries out. I keep pushing slowly until I am fully seated inside of her. My eyes roll back in my head at just how right she feels. Warm and like heaven. Like home. I don't care what they forced her to do. I only care that she is here with me.

"Don't worry, my angel. I will take care of you. Always."

I pull out and I slowly put my cock back into her. She screams out and her nails dig into my shoulders. I move in and out of her and I can feel her walls tightening around me.

"I'm gonna come. I'm gonna come in you, baby."

I can feel her clenching around my cock, and I feel my seed want to fill her. It's starting to try to force its way out of me and into her. I'm trying to be gentle. She doesn't need rough. She needs me to give her what she needs to get past all of this. She is mine. Now and forever. I pull out and I slap my cock against her clit and she screams.

"Fuck yes. Fuck yeah. That's it. You gonna come for Daddy? Come all over my cock."

She throws her head back and I can see the pleasure on her face. I grab her hips, notch my dick back up and I start to move into her again. She is screaming and begging. I can see her muscles moving under her skin, feel her pussy while it grips my cock, and I know she is close. I can feel her tightening around me, and I know she is going to come soon. I grab her hair and pull her head back.

"Come for Daddy angel. I want to feel that beautiful pussy come all over Daddy's hard cock. You have to have your pleasure, first angel. That's how this works. Come on, Daddy's cock."

I can feel her walls clamp down on me, and I explode inside of her. I can feel the warmth of my seed coating her insides.

"Ahh! Ahhh! Ahhhh! Yes, Daddy. YES!" she screams.

I hold on to her tight and I can feel her shaking. I kiss her cheek and I hold her to me.

"Did you enjoy that, my angel?"

She nods, and I take her mouth with mine in a searing kiss.

"Your mine! No one will ever touch you again. Say it, angel. Tell me you're mine and only mine."

"Yours. Only yours. I belong to you. You own me."

I smile and pull her up to me. "I do."

I take my time washing her hair and then her body. She needs to know that I will take care of all of her needs. She is safe with me. She is the center of my universe. I turn off the water and grab a towel. I dry her off and wrap her in a robe. She needs to eat. If she won't eat on her own. I'll feed her.

I walk into our room grab the plate beside the bed and sit at the small table.

"Come here, angel. Sit on Daddy's lap."

She walks over and sits next to me. I look at her for a moment to give her a chance to move. When she doesn't, I pick her up and place her on my lap.

"I said sit on my lap. Now eat, my angel."

"I don't want to sit on your lap and I'm not hungry." She says, turning her chin up.

"Eat or I will spank you. Don't test me when it comes to your health angel."

She narrows her eyes at me. Oh, this is what I want to see my girl getting feisty.

"I told you I'm not hungry."

I lift her chin, and I kiss her hard. She fights me, but I am stronger than she is. I stand her up and remove the robe from her and bend her over my knee. I smack her ass hard enough to leave a handprint.

"I said you need to eat."

I rub her beautiful ass. She gasps and whines.

"Only good girls get clothes and you just defied me."

I smack her ass, and she cries out. I rub her ass and she moans. Mmm, my bad girl likes this.

"Are you ready to eat? Tell me you're sorry and all is forgiven."

"I'm sorry, Daddy. I'm sorry." She begs me.

I lift her up and place her back on my lap. I pick up a piece of fruit and bring it to her lips. She opens her mouth and I slip the fruit inside. She closes her mouth and takes a bite. I pull it from her mouth and I lick the juice off her lips.

"Good girl. Eat."

I grab another piece of fruit and feed it to her. After eating half of the plate, she stops eating.

When I look at her she says, "Please Daddy, I'm full."

I stand her up, and I take the plate away. She instantly went for the robe that I discarded and told her she couldn't have. I grab it from her.

"HEY! I want that!"

"I said no clothes, you didn't earn it."

“Give it back!” She screams at me.

I swat her ass, and she looks at me in shock.

"I think you like being a bad girl. I want to play with my naughty little girl." I put my hand in between her legs and run my fingers between her lower lips. Ahhh, my angel is already wet for me.

She looks up at me with anger and desire in her eyes.

"What did I say about fighting me?"

She shakes her head. "I didn't fight you."

I smirk at her, and I pull her to the bed. I lay her on her belly and I spread her legs.

"Spread those legs. I want to see your pussy."

She spreads her legs and I look at her wet slit.

"Are you ready to be punished?"

She nods.

I grab a pillow and I place it under her hips. I grab her hair and I pull her head back. I take her lips in a searing kiss. My obsession. My Luna. I can't get enough of her. I pull her legs apart and give a stinging slap to her pussy. She lets out a loud gasp. But I can tell she also enjoyed it. I can feel her pussy throbbing.

"You have to earn clothes, my angel. You can't just take things. I want you to work for them. Do you understand me?"

"Why?" she moans out

“Because I’m your daddy and you have been a bad girl. Bad girls don’t get clothes. You have to eat and do what Daddy says to get those.”

I smirk. I think my angel likes to be spanked. I grab her ass and palm it. I lift my hand and smack her ass again. She moans when I rub it after. I take my fingers and run them down her ass crack. She tenses when I get to her tight little hole.

"One day, my angel. One day I will take this ass. But not today." I smack her ass again with my other hand. I can see her pussy pulsing and juices starting to drip. I grab my cock and I rub the head against her clit. "Tell me what you want, baby. What do you want me to do with you?"

I move my cock against her wet folds while she coats my cock in her juices. I can feel her pussy clench.

"I want you to fuck me. I want you to fill me up and make me come. I want to feel you everywhere. Please, Daddy. Please!"

I love that she is as needy for me as I feel for her. I've never had a weakness and fuck if she isn't mine. I grab her hips. I push myself inside of her. We both moan at the feeling of us connected.

"Say it again." I groan as her heat envelops me.

She gasps, and she tries to push herself away. I hold her tight and I thrust my cock inside of her. She screams out and I can feel her walls tighten around me. Her pussy is so warm and tight. I can feel her squeezing me. I can't help but rut into her this time hard and fast.

"Yes! Yes! I'm going to come. Give me more Daddy! Harder!"

I grab her hips and I pound into her. I can feel my seed moving up my cock while she screams. I pull out and I slap her ass. I push my cock back into her. I can feel her walls gripping me. I slap her ass again and again. I can feel her body trembling. She is so close to coming. God, she is perfect.

"Say it again."

She pants out, "I'm yours! Take me, Daddy, make me come."

I slap her ass again and reach around and pinch her clit. I can feel her pussy clamp down on my cock. She is crying out and I can feel her pussy contracting around me. It's a flood of small, intense orgasms. I pull out and I slap her ass. I can feel her body shaking from the intensity of her orgasm.

"Give me one more angel. Come for me." I groan.

I slap her ass again, and I can feel her pussy contract. I pound into her, making her moan so loud I'm sure the guards outside can hear her. That's right, she is mine.

"Mine, mine, mine," I whisper to her.

I can feel her pussy clamp down on me. I flip her over and put one of her legs on my shoulder and start pounding into her again. I can feel her walls tightening around me again. She screams out.

"I'm going to come. I'm coming. FUCK!" she yells.

I rut into her, chasing my own pleasure. I growl and I shoot my seed deep inside of her. I lay off to the side of her, pulling her with me. I brush the hair from her face. The feelings of protection that I already had for her have tripled. While I lay here with her wrapped in a warm cocoon of my arms, I know I'm going to torture and kill everyone who hurt her. Starting with that fucker that was sitting beside Salvatore at the auction. He thought he was being cute. I'm going to show him just how fucking cute he is.

Don't worry, my angel. I will protect you. I will always take care of her. Even if she doesn't know what I'm going to do in order to make that happen. She will feel safe and these men will pay for what they did to her.

Vinny

Demetrius

It's been a week, and my angel is doing so much better than she was. I still don't think she believes me when I call her mine. But she will eventually. I haven't had sex with her since that night when I had a moment of weakness. I should have never done that. She wasn't ready even if she did enjoy it. Soon she will be getting her clothes back and then I can show her around the house and the grounds. I know she is going to love it here.

But right now I'm watching that piece of shit that was with Salvatore turns out his name is Vinny. He has no idea how close to death he is right now. I'm like a shark hunting my prey. When the moment is right, we are going to grab him and bring him to my safe house.

I watch as a guard walks over to him. Grabs his arm and pulls him towards the door. They seem to be having a conversation before he walks in. I can't believe he actually raped my angel and thought he would get away with it. Just the anger of what he did is enough, but to hear him talk about it like he went to the store and picked up dinner? That pissed me the fuck off. Luna is so sweet and kind.

I've had enough of this bullshit. The next time he is alone, he is mine. I'm going to show him what happens to people who touch my angel. I watch as the guard opens the door and Vinny walks out. He looks around and he sees me standing there, leaning on my car. He smirks, and he starts walking towards me. Wrong move, mother fucker.

When he gets closer to me, he asks, "You here for something, Demetrius?"

"Yes, I am. You hurt someone special to me."

He laughs and says, "Oh, you mean that whore? Man, you're wasting your time on that delicious piece of ass. We broke her."

I stepped closer to him, my hand grabbing him before I even realized I was reaching for him. I grab him by the front of his shirt and I lift him off the ground. "What did you do to her? What did you do to my angel?"

"Fuck you, man. I'll fuck anything I want."

"Wrong answer." I pull my gun and smack him hard enough with it to knock him out. "This is going to be so much fun. You have no idea."

Anton steps out of the alley and helps me get him to the car.

"You sure about this, boss?" He asks in Russian.

"You know I am Anton. He touched what is mine and now he is going to pay. How can my angel ever find any peace with these scum bags walking free?"

"She wouldn't. You know I support this decision. I just want to make sure you are aware of what could happen if the Pakhan finds out."

I laugh and I throw him the keys. "Let me worry about Viktor."

He nods, and we toss Vinny in the trunk. This fucker is going to pay, and I'm going to enjoy it. I have so many little surprises in store for him. He is going to find out just how it feels. No one will ever make my angel feel unsafe again.

An Unexpected Visitor

Demetrius

Now that I have one of them, I need to go and make sure my angel is eating. She is doing so well that it makes my heart soar. I'm going to make him pay for what he did to her. However, right now I have a surprise for my baby girl. I know she is going to be so excited I can't wait.

When I walk into the room, my angel is lying on the bed watching TV.

"Hey baby," I say as I walk over to her.

"Hi," she whispers.

I bend down and kiss her lips softly.

"Did you eat today?" I look at her plate and thankfully, most of it is gone.

I spent a few days feeding her and making her sit on my lap to reinforce that she was safe with me. That she needed to eat and that there would be consequences if she didn't. It's my job to make sure she is doing the things she should. I'm not going to let anyone else take care of her. I'm going to keep her safe and I'm going to keep her happy. Her health is a big part of that.

She smiles and kisses me. "Yes, Daddy. I ate earlier. I was hungry and not sure if I should wait for you to feed me." She chews on her lower lip nervously.

I chuckle and I kiss her again. "You were right to eat, baby girl. You're such a good girl." I kiss her on the lips. "As a matter of fact, you're such a good girl that I have a surprise for you."

"You do?"

Seeing her face light up is the best thing this life has to offer, if you ask me. I will burn the whole world down to make sure it stays there.

"Yes, I do."

I take her hand and help her from the bed. I put a robe on her. No one is allowed to see my angel but me.

"I get to wear something? Oh, thank you Daddy!" she says, jumping up and down and clapping her hands.

I smile at her and lead her to the door. Her eyes get as round as saucers.

"I get to leave the room?" she all but whispers

"You do, angel, but that's not the only surprise." I take her hand and lead her down the hall to another room.

When we walk in, she squeals. "Pick anything you want angel and while we are away from the room, I will have the clothes put away for you."

"You bought me all of this?" I nod and smile. She leaps at me so suddenly I stumble, but catch my balance with her in my arms.

She grabs my face and kisses me hard as she wraps her legs around me. "Thank you, Daddy."

"You're welcome, angel. Now go pick out something pretty. I have some things planned for you today." I set her on her feet and swat her ass as she walks away.

The smile she gives me over her shoulder has my cock turning into a steel bar in my pants, and I have to adjust myself. I want to fuck her right now, but I have plans for her and I don't want to rush it.

It can wait. First, I need to take care of my angel.

I watch her while she picks out several dresses and skirts. She tries them all on and I have to admit; she looks stunning in every single one of them. Watching her happiness at something as simple as clothes tells me I have been doing right by her. She is learning quickly that I only do things to make sure she is ok and her health is the most important thing.

I know not everyone would agree. But I have watched her come so far just over the last week. I have seen the fear in her eyes fade away and replaced with confidence. I think it makes it easier for her to know she doesn't have to worry about anything because I will take care of it all.

"Which one do you like, baby?"

She looks at me and blushes. "All of them."

"Well, then why don't you try them all on? Give me a fashion show."

She giggles and runs to the bathroom. She comes out wearing a red dress that stops just above the knees and black heels. Her hair is down. God, she is so beautiful. I have to stop myself from taking her right here. I have to remind myself that I have a plan and I can't just take what is mine. She needs this. This is just for her.

She walks towards me and stops. "Do I look ok?"

"You look beautiful."

"I don't look like a whore?"

I immediately stand and walk over to her. "Never speak about yourself like that again. You are my angel. If anyone ever says that to you, I will kill them. Never disrespect yourself. You are gorgeous. If I ever hear you say that again, I'll spank that beautiful ass red."

Her eyes grow wide and she takes a step back. "You really mean that?"

"Yes, I do. And I will never allow anyone to treat you that way again. Never."

"Promise?"

"I promise, angel. No one will ever mistreat you again. Not as long as I live."

"Thank you, Daddy." She hugs me tight and I hold her.

"No need to thank me, baby girl. You are my everything." I kiss her head and walk her out the door, pulling her behind me.

I show her around the house and the grounds. She was so excited over the pool, I just had to smile at her.

"Now, angel, I am going to give you a few rules. You are not to be out of the room without me or Anton. It's for your safety, ok? This is important."

She nods her head enthusiastically. "I need words, baby girl.

Promise me you won't go anywhere alone and never ever without one of us. I don't trust anyone but Anton. He will be the only one other than me that can be alone with you. Do you understand?"

"I do Daddy. I won't go anywhere alone. I promise."

"Good girl. Now I have something else to show you. Come on." I take her hand and lead her to the extensive flower garden, where I have a table set for two.

It's time to show my angel just a touch of her life to come. I smile as I hold her chair for her and then push it in. I can see the confusion on her face.

"What?"

"I don't know what to say. You're too kind. I've never had anyone do that for me."

I chuckle and shake my head. "Don't say anything. Just enjoy." I take her hand and place it on the table. "Let's eat angel. You've been doing so well that I wanted to reward you. You can go anywhere on the grounds that you would like as long as...?" I wait for her answer. She smiles and answers quickly.

"As long as I have you or Anton with me."

"And why do you need one of us?"

"To keep me safe. He is the only other person you trust with my safety."

"That's right, baby girl. That's exactly it. So let's eat. I had Anya make you something special."

Anya brings out our food. I cut the steak in front of me and served her. She eats it slowly, and I watch as she enjoys each bite.

"I love this. Thank you."

I smile and nod my head. "You're welcome, angel." I love feeding her. It soothes something primal in me. To take care of her on this level is immensely satisfying.

After we finished eating, I took her hand and led her around the property. I show her the pond and she seems to really be enjoying herself. Today is about her. Making her happy. She has been such a good girl; she deserves the world.

Right now, I am working on getting her justice. I will make sure she has peace. We walk the path that leads around the gardens. I just want her to enjoy her day. My phone rings and I look at it. It's Anton. I know he wouldn't call me right now unless it was important. He knows how important this is to my girl.

"Sorry angel, I have to answer this."

"Of course, go ahead. I'm just going to look at the flowers."

I step away and answer. "Anton?"

"Boss, it's Viktor. He's coming."

My blood runs cold. I turn and look at Luna. I can't let him near my angel.

"Where is he?"

"He's on his way. The men at the front gates informed me."

"I'm bringing Luna back in now. Meet us at the back. I want her taken directly to the room."

"Yes, sir."

I hang up and approach Luna. "I'm sorry, baby girl, but we have to cut this short. But you can come out here whenever you want."

I can see the disappointment on her face and it breaks my heart. This fucker showed up at my house without calling.

"I'm sorry, baby girl, but Anton will be taking you to our room so that you are safe. As soon as it is safe again, I will come and get you. I promise."

"Ok, Daddy I understand."

"Ok come on, let's get you safe." I pull her into my arms and kiss her forehead. We head toward the house and Anton appears at the back door.

"Take her up the back way. Keep her safe, Anton."

"I will."

I give her a kiss. "Go angel, stay with Anton."

Anton takes her elbow and gently leads her away. I watch as they disappear through the doors. I hope he gets her into the safety of the room before my brother see's her. She is my everything and I will kill for her. I hope he doesn't make the mistake of thinking he can come to my home and demand things from me. Pakhan or not. No one will hurt my angel ever again. I love her with every fiber of my being. I haven't felt she is ready for that yet but I plan on telling her soon.

I walk to the front door and open it just in time to see Viktor's driver open his door. He steps out and I walk out to greet him.

"Bother to what do I owe this visit?"

"I have been hearing things, Demetrius. We will talk in your office."

You can't Have Her

Demetrius

I know what this is about. He's going to ask about my angel and then the disappearance of Vinny. I was expecting a call. But he must really think it's me if he is here at my house. I lead him to my office and he sits at my desk and puts his feet up on it.

"Must you be so disrespectful to others, brother?" I ask, narrowing my eyes at him.

"Do you realize that I am the Pakhan?" I nod. "But I keep hearing about my second in command going off the rails and doing his own thing. What's going on? Sit."

He waves his hand at my chair. I give nothing away. I sit down in a relaxed manner."So tell me what you heard."

"You were seen watching a club where it just so happens one of Salvatore's men was and then ... poof, he was just gone. I wonder where he might have gone ...."

He looks at me expectantly, but I just shrug. "I am unsure Pakhan, perhaps you can tell me. It wasn't my turn to watch Salvatore's men."

He looks at me sharply and I can see the anger on his face. "I will find out who is responsible for this and when I do, they will be punished."

"You will have to forgive me if I don't care what happened to that Italian, or any Italian for that matter."

"Oh, you will care. If I find out that you had anything to do with it, Demetrius... I will personally kill you."

I laugh and shake my head. "Viktor threatening me is never a good idea. You stay in that spot because I keep it that way."

"I am the head of this family. You will do as I say. Where is this girl you bought? None of this trouble with you started until she came around. I want to see her."

"I told you before, she is mine and I am keeping her safe."

"You better tell me where she is. If I have to find her ... it will be worse for you... and her. She will pay for your mistakes, brother."

He stands up and comes around the desk. "If his disappearance is because of you. I will take her from you. It's within my power as Pakhan. I will use her how I please and then kill her." He tells me as he looks at his fingernails.

I can feel the rage building when I stand up to my full height. My older brother may be the Pakhan, but he is stepping out of line. No one will ever touch my angel again.

"Be warned ... Brother. If you come looking for trouble, you will find it. I will protect her. And I will kill any man that touches her. It's best if you forget about touching what belongs to me."

"I will figure this all out."

"You do that brother, but you won't be touching what's mine. I don't care if you think it's within your rights to do so."

His face turns red, and he stalks out of my office. I close the door behind him. I can hear him stomping down the hallway as I walk back to my desk and grab my phone. I dial the number and wait.

"Da." I hear the deep Russian voice of one of my loyal supporters.

"I think it's time. Start finding out who is loyal to me." I say to him in Russian.

"Of course, boss. I will take care of it."

"Good. I will be in contact."

Luna

When Demetrius came back up to get me, I could tell something was wrong. He looks so stressed out and pissed.

"Are you ok? What's going on?" I ask as I try to get up.

"Stay still." His hands grip my shoulders and he pushes me back down.

"Demetrius, what's wrong?"

"I have to go away for a little while. There's some business I need to take care of. Anton will be here with you."

"But.. how long will you be gone?" I ask as I look at the floor.

"Not long. I'll come back as soon as I can. I promise."

"Why do you have to go away?"

"I have to take care of something. I can't tell you exactly what I am doing, baby girl."

I can feel the frown on my face. I don't want him to go. What if something happens to him? What would happen to me then? Right now I am under his direct protection and I can't imagine it would stay that way if he were to be killed.

"Please don't go."

"I'm sorry, baby girl, but I have to. I promise I will be back as soon as I can. I miss you already. Remember, you leave with no one but Anton."

I hug him tight and kiss him. "I understand."

"Everything I am doing is to keep you safe. Don't forget that."

"I won't."

He kisses me softly, and I watch as he walks out the door. I hate that he has to go. My heart is thumping loudly in my chest. I can hear him speaking with Anton in Russian. I know I am safe here. But I feel like he is abandoning me. I know it's strange. Maybe I have what they call Stockholm syndrome. You know where you think you love your captor. Love. Do I love him?

I lay on the bed and stare at the ceiling. I know he will be back. I just have to believe that. I'm not sure I want to leave the room when he isn't home. Whatever happened upset him enough that he has to leave to take care of something. I'm scared. I know he says it's nothing, but I can't help the fear that is running through my veins. I don't want him to go. I hear the door open. I look and see it's Anton.

"Letting you know. The boss says you can walk around."

"Thank you."

He smiles and nods his head. "You need anything?"

"No, thank you," I mumble as I look at the ceiling.

"Don't worry. I'm here to protect you. I won't let anything happen while Demetrius is gone. If you need something. You let me know. I get."

"I will thank you, Anton. I think I will just stay in here till he returns." He nods and closes the door.

I hear the locks click into place. The sound that used to frighten me now reminds me that I am safe. I sigh and rest my head against the pillow. I close my eyes and try to sleep, but all I can think about is Demetrius leaving me alone and if I really do love him. The way my heart aches, I'm going to have to say I do.

It should surprise me or maybe make me panic a little. But I can't bring myself to be worried about how I feel. If what has happened to me has shown me anything. It's that life is short and can change at any moment.

TIME TO DEAL WITH THIS

Demetrius

I'm heading to my safe house. It's time to take care of Vinny. I was going to drag this out over time. But with Viktor sniffing around, I need to get rid of him. It just means I will have to do the maximum amount of damage to him over a smaller amount of time. I hate that I had to leave Luna, especially so soon after Viktor left. I know this isn't a good time for me to leave her. But I need to take care of this prick.

If the Pakhan finds out, I know he will come for me. I am disobeying him, but I can't bring myself to care. Over the years, I have gained a lot of support from the men. They follow my orders and have for years. There are still many who are loyal to Viktor, but if it comes down to a fight, I know I will win. I don't want to kill my brother. But if he tries to touch my angel, I will chop him up into little pieces and feed him to dogs without even thinking about it.

I drive to the safe house and park in the garage. I step out of the car and head to the door. As I enter, I pull off my tie and roll up my sleeves. I go to the basement, determined to make him suffer for what he did to her. She was already mine when he raped her. I don't care if he knew it or not. That's not the point. I will show him how it feels to be violated. I will make sure he never does this to another woman.

I hear the sound of footsteps approaching me. I look up to see one of my men, Serge.

"Boss, the items you ordered have arrived."

"Thank you, Serge."

As I'm about to go downstairs, my phone rings. It's my brother Vladimir, who's at the Kremlin. He's calling because he must have heard something. I see his name on the screen and answer the phone.

"Vladimir."

"Demetrius is everything okay? I am getting reports that you have gone rogue. Want to tell me about it?"

We have always been close. I am not sure he will completely understand, and I will need my other two brothers to support me if this goes the way I think it will. I know he would never hurt my angel or tell Viktor about her.

"Hmm. Yes, that might be a good idea."

I step out the back door of my safe house and tell him everything. From the moment I saw her to what I am about to do.

"I understand, brother. You don't think Viktor will approve?"

I growl. "He has made bad choices about how he has spoken about her a few times already. I will not allow him to lay a hand on my angel."

"Ok. I will send word to the others. I understand. I would probably be the same way. But Demetrius, realize if you kill Vinny and continue to hunt down the men who touched her?"

"Yes, I know Vlad. I don't want it to come to that. But he has changed. I won't allow it and now he wants to work with the Italians."

I can almost hear him nod on the other end of the phone.

"I will tell Aleksandr to expect mayhem. We cannot come back right now. But if you need me. I will be there with as many men as I can gather. Do not worry, Demetrius, she will be safe."

I hang up the phone and head back inside. I need to get ready. I have to move fast. I grab my gun and holster it on my hip as I head down the stairs. I look at the body bag Serge has prepared. Time for this bastard to pay.

Justice

Demetrius

I walk straight into the back room that I had designed just for matters like these. It's the perfect torture room. There is a drain in the middle of the floor for easy cleanup. I installed restraints on a bed that looks like the one in an OBGYN's office. I had this ordered and brought just for him and the rest of the bastards that dared to touch what's mine. There is a bar hanging from the ceiling that has restraints on it and all the fun tools I could ever want, plus a few ordered just for this occasion.

I move around the room, gathering items I need for this mission. I will not stop until I have gotten justice for my angel. He will feel every ounce of pain that she felt and more.

I don't care how long it takes, but he will confess to his sins and then I can send him off to hell where he belongs.

But before that, he will learn what it feels like to be raped. I have quite a collection of toys here just for him. I take a deep breath and square my shoulders. I can do this. I won't let anyone hurt my angel ever again. He watches me while I walk around the room gathering tools on a steel table. They currently have Vinny restrained in a chair, but I will transfer him to the table shortly. He will scream for mercy. The same way I am sure he made my angel scream.

I will make him tell me what he did to her. And I will make sure he pays for it. When I grab one of the huge dildos and sit it in the area by the OBGYN bed, I smirk when his eyes get big. I got one of the largest ones I could find just for this.

The dildo is big, really big, like a truck tire big, or a python big, or anaconda big. The base is rounded and smooth as glass, and the tip is flared. It comes to a sharp point, quite unlike any penis I have ever seen. It will definitely work for this.

Now that I am all set up, I walk to the steel door and motion for two of my men to come in and move Vinny to the bed. He tries to fight them and scream, but it just makes my grin become an even bigger smile.

"You can scream all you want, Vinny. As a matter of fact, I encourage you to scream. This room is soundproof. They can't even hear you right outside of the door. So scream, yell, cry, whatever you need to do to let out your fear. But in the end, you will confess to what you did to my angel."

My men finish tying him down and making sure they secure his feet in the stirrups. I walk over to the bed. He's shaking now and I can see the fear in his eyes.

"Vinny, this is what you did to her. So this is what you will go through now. And you will tell me the truth. You will tell me everything and you will pay for it."

"I did what was well within my right to do." He tries to be brave, but all he manages is to make me even more pissed.

"Oh really? Well, let's see how you feel about that after this." I sneer at him. How dare he!

I cut his clothes off of his body. I grin as I grab the giant dildo and slowly insert it into his ass hole without lube. He screams in pain, but I don't stop. I relish in his screams of agony the way I'm sure he made my angel scream and cry. The way I am sure he enjoyed her agony. I have heard the fear and anguish in her cries at night, just the agony of that is enough for me to be even more brutal. I move it back and forth, faster and faster, until he is screaming for mercy. Tears of pain streaming down his face. I keep going until he is a trembling, sobbing mess.

"Still think what you did was within your rights?"

"I'm sorry. I'm sorry ok? I didn't know she was yours. She was just some whore laying on a bed."

"Wrong answer," I growl.

I narrow my eyes at him and line the dildo up to his ass again. I push it in with force and he screams as his ass rips.

"None of those women were whores. They were abducted and forced to be there. But you know that already, don't you, Vinny?"

He nods, barely able to breathe from the pain. I keep going for a few more minutes before finally stopping and pulling out the dildo. I left him shaking and sobbing in pain.

"You will answer for what you did, Vinny. You will pay for the suffering you caused. Now tell me what you did to my Angel."

He describes how when he entered the area she was not conscious. How he touched her, what he said to her, and the way she begged for him to stop in her drugged state while he took his pleasure from her. How he dragged a knife down her beautiful skin and then licked the blood from her skin. Enjoying every moment of it and then moving on to the other girls that were being held there. Of course, I had to coax it out of him by shoving my dagger into his legs. But in the end, he did tell me. I guess you could say he spilled the beans... and some blood.

"You will never do this again. You will never go near my angel or any other woman."

I am filled with rage and sorrow. I will take my revenge on him, but

I know it will not undo the damage that has been done. However, it might help her to know she will never see this piece of shit again. My Angel will never be the same again and neither will I. But I have found a way to find justice for her. I will hunt down those responsible for her suffering and ensure that they pay for what they have done.

Justice will be served, and my angel will find peace.

I smile at him as I grab the sharpest knife I have off of the steel table. I think I will do something that will strike fear into any man who touched her. I have been thinking of doing this for some time. It's a very brutal act, and he deserves it. They all do. I am an evil man, but I would never harm women and children. They are off limits.

Nothing will be a better punishment for this than a blood eagle. I can feel the evil smile on my face as my bloodlust rises. I have my men help me move him to the hanging bar. After my men re-handcuff him, I tell them to leave the room.

I toss my knife up and catch it by the blade, holding the handle in my right hand. I lean in and whisper in his ear.

"This is for my Luna. My precious angel."

He struggles, but it does him no good. I smile. The knife still held out. I raise the knife up above my head with both hands and plunge it into him hard. I hear the crack of his ribs, like tree limbs on a stormy night.

The scent of blood fills my nostrils as I run my knife down the skin of his back. The musky odor of sweat and urine joins the coppery smell of blood. I feel his fear deep in my soul. The fear of death is palpable. The longer I spend cutting him up, the more calm I feel. The more righteous I feel with my choice to make sure my angel gets justice.

I take joy in completing this masterpiece. I cut down his back, exposing his backbone and ribs. I make slow, purposeful cuts and pull all the skin away from his ribs. His screams turning into the most beautiful song I have ever heard. This is for my angel and I will bask in his pain and suffering. Every time he passes out from the pain, I wake him with smelling salts and then continue on with my work. I pull his ribs up and to the side, one by one. Loving the sound of each scream and the sound of each rib breaking as I spread them out.

I bask in his pain until finally it is done. I have created my masterpiece; justice for my Angel, who suffers in silence. I stand up and clean off my knife. He is now the symbol of Luna's justice. I turn to my work of art and take a moment to admire what I have done. My act will serve as a reminder of the pain and suffering she endured, and people will remember it. But it also will serve as a warning to those who might think of hurting her again.

I watch as the light leaves his eyes. Letting him feel the pain of every moment until he finally dies. No painless death for him. Justice has been served. Now I need to get back to my angel. I grab a towel to wipe the blood from my face and arms as much as possible. I open the door and tell my men to place Vinny somewhere they will find him. The look on their faces when they see what I have done makes me smile. Time for a shower. I can't go to my angel looking like this.

I Missed You

Luna

It's almost morning, and Demetrius still hasn't come back. I can't help but be worried about him. I think I might be crazy. I haven't even known him that long, but somehow I still trust him. I take a deep breath and tell myself to remain calm. I can't help but feel something for him. I think I love him. It's baffling. I head for the shower. Maybe the water will help me clear my thoughts.

As I stand there, the water washing away all the worries and doubts, I finally allow myself to think about Demetrius. I can't get the mental pictures of his face out of my head. This man is so enigmatic and alluring, I feel like I can't stay away from him. I step out of the shower and put on a fresh set of clothes. I'm so relieved I can wear them again. I smile at myself. I guess that's just something I took for granted. I take one last look in the mirror and tell myself that I am strong and capable. No matter what happens, I will be okay.

I knock on the door, and Anton opens it from the outside.

"Good Morning Anton."

"Good Morning Luna."

"I just wanted to go get some coffee. I'm still allowed?"

"Yes, you are."

I smile at him as I step past him and head downstairs. I make my way to the kitchen with his help because this house is huge. When I walk in, I smell the scent of coffee and moan to myself.

Ahh, the elixir of the life. I pour myself a cup and take a sip, enjoying the warmth it brings me. I sit down at the table and my thoughts return to Demetrius. What is he doing? Is he thinking of me, too? I lie my head down on the table and take a deep breath. I miss him and I can't help it.

I hear the front door opening. I jump up from the table. I rush out of the kitchen. I want to see him.

Demetrius is standing in the entryway, appearing exhausted and worried with heavy eyes. It's clear that he had a long night. As I approach him, he takes a step forward to meet me. We both stand there looking into each other's eyes for what feels like an eternity. I want to reach out and hug him, but I don't know if I should.

He closes the space and pulls me into his body. He wraps his arms around me and hugs me tight to him. I can feel his relief at being here with me again. Almost as if he couldn't relax unless he was with me. Which is exactly how I feel. Does he feel the same way I do? I know he says I am his. But talk is cheap. Even though his actions have spoken volumes.

"I'm sorry, my angel. I didn't mean to be gone so long. But I had important business to see to."

I breathe in his scent and close my eyes. "It's okay," I whisper.

He looks down into my eyes, and I can see the love and gentleness in his gaze. With one more embrace, he steps back and looks at me.

"Come, let's go for a walk. I want to hear all about your morning."

We walk around the grounds, talking and laughing. He doesn't tell me the business he had to see to and I don't ask. But he does ask about my night and I tell him about my morning. We spend the whole day together, just enjoying each other's company. When the sun sets, we find ourselves back at the rear door of the house.

He takes my hand and we stand there for a moment, looking into each other's eyes. I know that no matter what happens, I will always have Demetrius by my side. I know I can trust him. I am aware that my emotions have progressed beyond what I could categorize as Stockholm Syndrome. This is especially true because he had previously rescued me.

I think I am falling in love with him. I guess it isn't a think. I am. I know I am. He squeezes my hand and gazes down at me.

"I will always take care of you," he whispers.

My heart swells with emotion. I look up into his eyes, and for the first time, I feel like this is home. He is my home. Does that mean he has feelings for me, too? Is this what love feels like? I am confused about the things I am feeling.

I smile up at him as I say, "I know. I trust you."

He leans down and kisses me. I close my eyes and kiss him back. His soft lips against mine, his hands in my hair. I never want this moment to end. I want it to be like this forever.

He pulls me closer to him. Every inch of my body wanted to be against him to feel his warmth. It feels like we are one. I love the feeling of his body against mine. The pressure of his lips against mine. But I know it can't be this way forever. I know the world is out there, ready to tear us apart. I pull away from him and look into his eyes.

I break the silence. "I missed you last night. It was ... lonely."

He rubbed my cheek with his thumb. "I missed you too, my angel. But I had to go in order to make sure you are safe. Everything I do from now on is for you. Always for you."

I nod my head. "I know you will make sure I am safe," I say with such sincerity that I almost believe it myself. Maybe I really do feel that way.

He leans down to kiss me again. I curl my arms around his neck, pulling him closer. I feel his arms wrap around my waist and he pulls me close to him. He kisses me again and again. I know it should feel wrong to feel like this about him. But it doesn't it feels right. My captor, my owner, but I don't care. I want him, and I know he wants me. I wrap my arms around his neck while he trails kisses down my throat. I breathe in his scent, feeling his every touch. He lifts me up and I wrap my legs around him.

I cling on tightly, never wanting to release my grip. He carries me to the bedroom and gently lays me down on the bed. As he lies next to me, I can feel his gaze upon me. Our eyes meet, and I see the flames of desire within his. I smile back at him, knowing that somehow, some way, I am bound to him forever. Despite not knowing exactly what he does. I am aware that he is part of some type of mafia, a dangerous world. However, I am confident that he will never harm me. I know it now more than ever. He will always be my big, protective Russian.

The Bratva

Luna

I stare at his beautiful face and his strong muscular body. The way he holds me so securely and protectively. How he looks into my eyes with such adoration and deep emotion that I feel like he could never replace me. How he makes me feel safe and loved like no one else ever could.

He is everything I ever wanted and more. He is my protector, my knight in shining armor, my one and only love. I know I can trust him with my life and I will never have to worry about being hurt or betrayed by him. He kisses me one last time before gently pulling away. He takes my hands in his and looks deep into my eyes.

He smiles at me and says, "I promise to always protect you,

no matter what."

I smile back at him, feeling the love radiating from his body. I know that I can trust him and that I will stay by his side for however long he wants me here. Every day with him shows me that this hard, violent man treats me with care and maybe even love. I want to tell him I love him so much, but I don't know how he will react. I know he says all kinds of wonderful things about never letting me go. That I'm his and only his. Is that the same?

As I lay lost in thought, he gently began to stroke my hair. I close my eyes and let out a soft sigh as his touch sends shivers down my spine.

He leans in and whispers in my ear, "Luna, you mean everything to me."

My heart swells with happiness, and I can feel tears prickling at the corners of my eyes. I open my eyes to look at him and see the same emotion mirrored in his own.

"You mean everything to me too," I whisper back, feeling more vulnerable than ever before.

He pulls me into a tight embrace, holding me close to his chest. I feel safe, warm, and protected by this gruff man. We lay there in silence for a few moments, basking in each other's presence.

His phone rings, interrupting our moment of bliss. Cussing under his breath. He pulls away from me reluctantly and answers it. I hear a deep voice on the other end, speaking in Russian. I can't understand, but I know his face has changed and now he looks serious. When he hangs up, he sighs and runs his hand over his face.

"Is everything ok?"

"It will be. I need to tell you something, angel. I hope that you don't think any less of me for this."

I shake my head and reach for him. "No, I could never. I know you are a violent man with a violent job. But I trust you. I know you would never hurt me."

He looks at me, and I can see the surprise on his face.

"I found one of your attackers and made him suffer. You will never have to worry about him again. I know it's not the most romantic thing to say, but I needed you to know that I will always protect you. I will get you justice, no matter what."

I feel a mix of emotions - fear, relief, love, and gratitude. Fear for the man I love who is capable of such violence. Relief that he took care of my attacker. Love for him and his protectiveness, and gratitude for having him in my life. I throw my arms around his neck and hold him tight, burying my face in his chest.

"Thank you, thank you so much," I whisper, tears streaming down my face.

He holds me tightly, kissing the top of my head gently. "I will always protect you, my angel. You are mine, and no one will ever hurt you again."

I feel the possessiveness in his words and actions, but I know it comes from a place of love and protection. Not one of control and evil. I trust him with my life, and with my heart. As we stand there, wrapped up in each other.

"I need you to understand there is danger all around us right now. I am second in command of the Russian mob in this area. The Bratva. The man I killed and put on display for everyone else to see was in the Italian Mafia. They won't take that lightly. If they find out who did it, they'll come after me."

I gasp in disbelief. The reality of the situation is starting to hit me.

"What are we going to do?" I ask, my voice trembling.

"We have to be careful. I can't let anything happen to you," he says sternly. "But that scum had to pay for what he did to you. To what is mine. He is only the first of many."

I nod, knowing there's no point in arguing with him. He's a man who takes charge and gets things done. I trust him to protect me, even if it means getting his hands dirty. As the night wears on, he tells me everything about his world, the Bratva, and his role in it.

How his brother is the Pakhan and keeps asking questions about me. We talk until dawn, holding each other close. The surrounding danger only brings us closer together. As we lay there, I know that I'm in love with this violent man, and I'll do whatever it takes to keep him safe.

He explains to me that when he had me go to the room; it was because Viktor was here.

I look at him with wide eyes. "Viktor? Does he own the Whispering Russian?" He nods, his eyes never breaking contact with my own. "That's not good." I frown.

"Why isn't it good Luna?" A frown formed on his handsome face.

"I worked there before ... well, before."

"Yes, I know."

"He, well, he said some things to me."

I tell him all about my first day and the things he said to me. About the way he acted when I was clocking out and how he took me into the closet and tried to rape me. He definitely doesn't look happy, but there is no way I could keep that from him. If he already felt there was a threat to me, he needed to know. He wraps me in his arms, pulling me close. I can feel his anger and frustration radiating off of him.

"Anton called me before he intervened. I know about that one. But not the others. Don't worry, I will protect you," he says, his voice gruff and determined. "Even from him."

I nod, knowing he means it. I feel safe in his embrace, and I can't help but wonder how I ever got so lucky to have someone like him.

Even if he did technically buy me from that horrible place. I know he was already looking out for me. He searched for me and found me there.

"There is something I have been wondering, Demetrius."

"Ask. I will tell you all I can."

"How long was I missing? It's ... It's all blur."

He pulls me ever closer to him and runs his hands through my hair. I can tell it's not something he really wants to discuss. His jaw gets tense.

"I was looking for a week before I found you. Then I had to wait three days for the auction to take place."

"Ten days? I was gone for ten days?" I whisper.

He nods, his lips pressed together in a tight line. He's clearly unhappy about it.

"I wanted to burn the building down, but I was afraid you might not make it out." He murmurs into my hair.

I can't believe I was missing for ten days. I can only imagine what could have happened to me had Demetrius not found me. I was so drugged it didn't feel like I was gone that long. I take a deep breath and look up at him, smiling softly.

"Thank you. For finding me."

He cups my face in his hands and gives me a gentle kiss on the forehead.

"Luna, you are incredibly brave. I vow to protect you from any harm that may come your way. I will not hesitate to take down anyone who dares to even glance at you the wrong way. You are my precious angel."

I believe him. He has shown me that this is his plan, and I am thankful for all he has done for me. Without him, who knows where I would be? I nuzzle into his chest and take comfort in knowing that he is here to protect me.

My Angel

Demetrius

My brave Luna always holding her chin up. I worry though. That call was from Serge, letting me know they had found the body. I know the Pakhan will be calling me soon. But for now, Luna is all that matters. I never thought a monster like me could love. She is the light in my darkness. My guiding light. I have her here in my arms where she belongs. I never thought it would happen this fast, but she is so much stronger than I thought. My angel. My perfect love.

I can't help but smile as she snuggles into my chest, her breathing slow and steady. Luna is everything to me, and I would do anything to protect her. Even if it meant killing the Pakhan himself.

But for now, I just needed to hold her and forget about the underworld I am a part of. Forget about the violence and the power struggles. All that matters is Luna.

I press a gentle kiss to the top of her head, inhaling the sweet scent of her hair. She looked up at me, her eyes filled with love and trust.

"Demetrius, can I ask you something?"

"Anything, my angel."

"What's going to happen now? With the Pakhan and everything."

I sigh, running a hand through my hair. "I don't know, Luna. The Pakhan has been wanting to bring me closer for a while now. And with this... situation. I'm sure he'll be even more insistent. Don't worry, I will handle it all."

I press my lips to hers and taste her. She tastes so sweet. My cock is so hard it's starting to hurt. I want her. I need her. I pull her body flush against my body as I roll on top of her. I swallow her moan when I rub myself against her.

"There are too many clothes between us, baby girl," I say as I lift her dress over her head.

Her hands go straight to the buttons on my shirt as we quickly undress each other.

I kiss down her neck while unsnapping her bra and removing it. I pull her nipple into my mouth and pinch it with my teeth. I hear her gasp. My hand travels down her body, coming to a rest on her wet pussy. A grin spreads across my face as I feel how wet she is. She's always so ready for me. I smile evilly as I rub my fingers along her slit. She whimpers, looking up at me through hooded lashes.

She knows what I want, and she isn't going to stop me. Her hand reaches for my cock, wrapping her slender fingers around it. I can't stop myself from groaning. She strokes her hand up and down my shaft, squeezing it as she does so. I run my hand down her body until I reach her center. Her wetness coats my fingers as I slide one into her tight hole. She groans, bucking her hips against my hand. I rub her clit with my thumb and slowly pump my finger into her pussy.

"Yes, Daddy, just like that. Please don't stop."

I smirk

Bending down, I capture her lips with my own. She moans against my lips when I add another finger. Her walls tighten around my fingers as I pump them in and out of her. Her juices coat my hand as she grinds against it. I remove my fingers, only to replace them with my cock. I thrust hard into her, sliding all the way in. I go as deep as I can. She lets out a moan. I pull out and then slam back into her. She arches her back off the bed.

"Harder Daddy, please."

I grab a hold of her ass and pound into her as hard as I can. Her moans encouraging me to go faster and harder. I watch as her eyes roll back into her head. She's so close, it won't take much to get her to come. I slam into her over and over until she's screaming my name in ecstasy. I let go of her ass and grab the headboard of the bed, thrusting into her even harder as pleasure radiates through my body. I love her and she is all mine.

"Mine. Mine. Mine." Is all I can say as I pump into her.

Her tight pussy grips my cock like a vise as she screams.

"Oh, my god yes Daddy!!"

I come hard, my whole body shakes with the force of it. My warm seed filling her tight pussy. I pull out and collapse beside her on the bed. My breathing is ragged as I try to slow it down. I lay there and listen to her breathing calm. I pull her into my arms and she sighs in contentment. I know I don't deserve her, but I will never let her go.

"Thank you, Daddy. That was ...wow."

I smile against her head. I like it when she calls me daddy, like I told her to. I like it a lot. Maybe too much. The feelings of love that I have for her should scare me. But they don't I love her more than life itself. God help anyone who gets in the way of that. I don't care who it is. I will burn this city to the ground and then stand there to watch it burn.

I pull her tighter to my chest and kiss her forehead.

"I'm not sure what you are thanking me for, but you have nothing to thank me for. I know we haven't exactly had a normal relationship, but I will do anything for you. I feel lucky that you have accepted me."

She looks at me, and I can see the love in her eyes. "I will always be here, Daddy."

I kiss her on her lips. How did I get so lucky?

"Rest, my angel, I have you. Always."

As I lay there, listening to the sound of her breathing, my angel falls asleep in my arms - where she rightfully belongs. However, I am unable to rest because I know my brother will be calling me soon. Salvatore's henchman has already annoyed me. I made it clear that I can't tolerate him. I can't help but smirk as I recall the way I bounced Salvatore's head off the bar top - he definitely deserved it. After all, no one talks about my angel in that manner. He had the audacity to brag about raping her, and to me, of all people.

His day is coming. He will pay just like Vinny. But first I need to find some way of getting my baby girl to tell me what the others looked like. Or at least a man from the first few days. They will know the rest of the men who thought they could touch what's mine and live. They will all suffer the same fate as Vinny.

It may not be today or tomorrow, but I will find them all and they will pay for hurting my angel.

VIKTOR

Demetrius

Three days later

I thought for sure Viktor would have called me in before this. There is something up. I can feel it in my bones. A few of my trusted men have told me that Viktor appears more unstable every day. When he called today, I could hear the strain in his voice. I placed more men on my property just to ensure Luna is safe. He will be sorry if he ever pushes the issue about her. He will never get his hands on her. She is mine and I will protect her from everything and anyone. I don't give a fuck who it is.

If they thought I was a monster before, they haven't seen anything yet.

Once I know what is going on with Viktor, I will get to the bottom of it all. Until then, I have to be prepared for anything. My priority is to protect and take care of my Luna, and I will do whatever it takes. No one will ever harm her while I'm alive. My obsession keeps her on my mind always. She lives in my head rent free. Forever.

The man at my brother's gate is Serge, which is good for me. It means I have eyes on outside of this place since most of my loyal men are guarding my angel. I park my car outside Viktor's mansion and walk in. Upon walking in, I see at least six enforcers. They are all men who I have worked with for years.

A few I know for a fact are loyal to me. I nod to them and they nod back. It's odd there are so many here. Whatever this is, Viktor is expecting me to cause trouble. I was already tense but now I am expecting the worse. I'm not sure what he wants. I swear when it comes to Viktor, I'm never sure what's going on anymore. I think the power went to his head. I can't trust him or his ways. There was a time that we would have trusted each other with our lives. Now I don't think I would trust him to spell his name correctly.

I see him in his office having a conversation with someone with the door open. What the fuck is he doing? He knows I'm coming in. Who is he talking to?

"Viktor. What do you want?" I say in a low voice.

I look at the man sitting in the chair and see Salvatore. That fucker has the audacity to smile at me. I narrow my eyes at him. But smirk when I see his face is bruised.

What the fuck is going on here? Why is Viktor talking to him? Viktor looks tired. He appears as if he hasn't slept in days. He looks like shit. I don't trust him and I have no idea what to expect from him. I watch him closely. I'm waiting for him to make a move. What in the hell is going on with him? Fuck if I know.

"There are some things happening. I want you to come to a meeting with me tomorrow evening. Salvatore has come to speak with me about the murder of his right-hand man Vinny." he stops and looks at me and I can't help but smirk. I gave him one hell of a brutal death. He narrows his eyes at me. "You wouldn't know anything about that, would you?"

"Not a thing, Pakhan."

"Keep in mind what happens when you lie to me, Demetrius. Brother or not."

I tilt my head to the side a little as I study him. "Why would I know?"

"You were spotted speaking with him right before he disappeared, and we both know he was at the auction."

I hate this man. If I could kill Salvatore right now, I would. He is nothing without his muscle.

"I don't know anything about that. I was there to buy a woman, not murder a man."

"Yes, well, if you did have anything to do with it, you seem to have forgotten about it."

I look at him and raise a brow.

"I've not forgotten about anything. I don't sleepwalk that I know of. But if I did, I'm sure you would be number one on that list of people I would visit." I look straight at Salvatore and smile.

He squints at me and declares firmly, "I have said all I need to say. You must attend the meeting tomorrow. It is imperative that you are present, so you will be. You are responsible for going to Salvatore's property and dealing with this situation. However, let me caution you, Demetrius. If I discover that you are behind any wrongdoing, I will not hesitate to end your life, regardless of the fact that you are my brother."

I raise a brow. "Why would we meet at Salvatore's estate? So they can spy us on?"

"I don't trust you," Salvatore says.

I smirk with one side of my mouth. "You don't trust me because they saw me in the same place as your second in command or because you know I can kill you."

He stands and gets in my face and I can't help but smirk. Please, please do it. I need a reason to let out my anger at what he did, my angel. I will get you, Salvatore.

"What do you think you are going to do, Salvatore? You beat and abuse women. Only your guards can handle men." I growl at him, stepping into his space. "I will beat you until you aren't recognizable. Go ahead, try me."

"Demetrius!" my brother barks at me.

"Yes, Pakhan?" I say, never taking my eyes off Salvatore.

"Don't test me. Do as I say. Back off now."

"We were done anyway. I will see you tomorrow, Demetrius." He nods at Viktor and strolls out.

"I'm done here. I have better things to do," I say to Viktor.

"What would those things be? Get back to your precious Luna?" He says with a sneer. I look him in the eyes and say nothing. Shit, he knows it's Luna that I saved. "What? You thought I didn't know that the whore you bought was that perfect little piece from my club? Brother. You are losing your touch. It looks like pussy is clouding your judgment."

"Viktor," I growl in warning.

"You will do as I say. You WILL go to Salvatore's tomorrow and you will behave."

He has something planned. I feel like this is a setup to get me out of the way. But I don't have a choice. I will have to go.

"Why is there a meeting?"

"Oh, because we are going to make peace with the Italians and then we are all going to make a lot of money."

"How?"

"Human trafficking, of course."

I narrow my eyes at him. "Dad stopped that shit long ago. We don't deal in women."

"We do now. You will be there at nine for that meeting or I will take your little pet," he smiles at me, "and show her what a real man is like."

I ball my fists at my side as I look at him. Does he really think he could? I ignore him and make my way to the door. I don't say a word to him. I'm pissed and I need to get out of here before I lash out.

"Demetrius."

I don't turn around. I know without looking, Viktor has followed me. My voice is low, and it has a hint of anger in it.

"What."

"I know what you are thinking. You want to kill Salvatore, don't you?" He says with a smirk.

"You would be a fool if you didn't think that," I say and walk out. "I've made it no secret how I feel about him."

"You won't touch him, Demetrius. If you do, there will be consequences."

Fuck him! I will kill you, Salvatore, and I will enjoy every fucking minute of it.

NOT WITHOUT A FIGHT

Luna

When I woke this morning, Demetrius was already gone. He must have left a long time ago, since his side of the bed is cold. I know he has been worried about Viktor, and I know nothing good is coming. He thinks I haven't noticed that more men are around the house and that he beefed the security up, but I have noticed.

It's just another thing to worry about in this world we live in. I just want to relax and enjoy my time with him, but that seems impossible now. I don't want him heading into danger, and I certainly don't want him heading into danger with Viktor. His older brother is not trustworthy. I am too scared that he would betray his younger brother if the situation demanded it. I can only pray that he comes back home safe and sound.

I can only hope that Viktor hasn't found out that I am the one he bought from that horrible place. Just from the little amount of time that I spent around Viktor, I can tell he is an evil man. One who is used to getting his own way.

I take a deep breath as I look around our room. Demetrius is out there in danger. But yet here I sit like a princess in a castle. Being guarded while my man is out there risking it all for me. I can't even think about something happening to him. Just the thought fills me with dread.

I know that he can handle himself, but the thought of anything happening to him terrifies me. What would I do if his brother crossed him? Or worse, killed him. My goal is to ease fears and think optimistically about Demetrius returning home unharmed, so we can reunite happily. But I know I can't relax until we take care of Viktor once and for all.

There's a loud knock at the door, which startles me out of my thoughts. My heart skips a beat as I stand up quickly and make my way towards it. Who could it be? Where is Anton? I can't open the door, he knows that. A million thoughts run through my head as I slowly reach for the handle, scared of what might be waiting for me on the other side.

"Yes?"

There is no answer, and the door doesn't open when I try the handle.

"Who is there?"

Only Demetrius and Anton can open the door. Even now, I cannot leave this room without one of them as a safety precaution. When no one answers, I just stand there frozen in place. The fear of being taken again has immobilized me. The flashes of the things that those men did to me keep me frozen in place.

Unable to move. What if Viktor is on the other side? What if he has come to take me? I can feel my heart pounding in my chest, the fear making it almost unbearable to stay where I am. I want to move, but I can't. I want to scream, but nothing comes out. I can only stand there hoping that Anton or Demetrius will come soon and save me from whatever is waiting for me on the other side.

What if something happened to Demetrius and Anton? Why isn't Anton outside of my door? He has never left his post before. Suddenly there is a loud bang and the whole wall shudders with the impact. I scream I run to the window and try to open it. I don't care. I would rather jump to my death than face whatever is trying to get through that door. It won't open. Fuck! I glance at the grounds again and I don't see any of the guards patrolling. What the fuck is going on?

There is a loud noise and the wall shutters again. I scream as I turn around to face the door, only to see it blow open. My heart is racing as I try to calm myself down. But as soon as I see who is standing in front of me, my heart drops. I'm on the verge of a panic attack.

It's Viktor.

My worst fears have come true. Is he here to take me back to that place? To do unspeakable things to me all over again. Tears stream down my face as I back away slowly, trying to find something - anything - to defend myself with. But Viktor doesn't move. He just stands there, watching me with a strange expression on his face. For a moment, I'm confused. Then I realize what he is doing.

He's watching me.

Initially, it seems inexplicable. How can this man, who I'm aware desires to harm me, simply remain still? However, as I glance at my hands, I observe blood. I can't recall grabbing a shard of the shattered vase on the table.

"Don't come any closer." I can hear the tremble in my voice and feel the fear that's gripping my body.

I'm trying to not show how scared I am. I can feel myself trembling. I know he thinks that it's a threat to him, but really, I would rather die than be taken. I don't know what his plans are for me. I won't go through that again. I look past him and I see Anton bleeding out on the floor.

Fuck.

Viktor takes a step forward, and I flinch, ready to cut myself with the broken vase. I bring it to my arm quickly. But he is faster. He grabs my hand and stops in front of me. He looks down at the blood on my hands and the slight cut on my wrist that I didn't get a chance to finish.

Fuck.

"What have you done?" he asks, his voice soft.

I don't answer. I can't. My mind is racing a mile a minute, trying to come up with a plan, an escape, anything. But all I see is Anton's lifeless body on the floor, and I know that there's no way out of this now.

There is only one thing that I am hoping for, and that is for Demetrius to locate me. Because I know he is going to take me from my home. Away from Demetrius.

"You're coming with me," Viktor says, his voice firm. "And if you try anything, I won't hesitate to hurt you."

I nod, not trusting myself to speak. I know that if I resist, he'll only hurt me more. But when he grabs my arm and starts to drag me towards the door, something inside me snaps.

With a scream, I grab a lamp and swing it at his head. I hear the sickening thud as it connects. He lets go of my wrist when he falls and I take off running through the house. But as soon as I burst out of the house, I run into two of his goons and they grab me.

"No, you can't do this. Demetrius will come for me. You can't please let me go." I scream as they drag me towards a black van parked in front of the house.

One goon laughs in my face. "Demetrius won't be able to save you now, sweetheart."

I struggle against their grip, kicking and screaming, but it's no use. They throw me into the back of the van and one of them climbs in after me, pinning me down to the floor.

As the van starts to move, I realize that this is it. I'm going to die here, alone and terrified. But then something inside me shifts. I think about Anton and all the other innocent people that these monsters have hurt or killed. And I know that I can't just give up without a fight.

With a surge of strength, I push the goon off of me and scramble to my feet. I slam my elbow into his face, feeling the satisfying crunch of bone beneath my skin. He stumbles backward, giving me just enough time to grab the door handle, but before I can open it, he is on me again.

"You stupid bitch."

That's the last thing I hear before blinding pain and darkness.

Falkner

Demetrius

When I left Viktor's house, I got a call that one of my men had tracked down another of the men that had hurt my angel. But when I got there, I noticed something was wrong right away. I stepped out of my car and my man Igor couldn't look me in the eye.

"The man is in there tied up waiting for you, boss."

I shifted my gaze between him and the rundown shack in the middle of nowhere. His trembling figure gave away his guilt as my cold eyes bore into him. It was clear that Igor had set me up, but I would deal with him later.

"Give me your gun."

"Sir?"

"Now."

He nods and hands it to me. I roll my shoulders and walk for the front door. If they want a fight, they will get one. But now I know I need to get back to Luna. What if this is all a ploy to keep me from her? Fuck. My brother set me up.

I need to deal with one betrayal at a time. I take a deep breath and steel my resolve. I will kill them all. It doesn't matter how many are in here. I will win because I need to get back to Luna. I need to make sure my angel is safe.

Right before I kick open the door, my phone pings with a text. I glance at it.

> Anton: Viktor has her. I am wounded. They have killed many men. You need to come home.

> Me: Call the in house doctor. I am on my way.

Mother fucker.

These are all dead men. I feel the red rage as it takes over. My muscles tense. I know I'm not invincible, but I feel like I am. Kick the door with enough force. It flies off of the hinges and I open fire as I enter. The room lights up with the sound of gunfire as I take down the first two men with precision that only comes with years of training.

They fall to the ground, lifeless, as I advance on the rest of them. They're no match for me. I've been in battles like this before, and I know how to come out on top. You don't give them a chance, you just fucking kill them. No mercy. They should know better. They have all seen how I work. The room is filled with the smell of gunpowder and death as I make my way toward the back, where I know the last of them are hiding.

I reload as I am walking down the hallway. I pull up the gun and shoot through the flimsy door. I rush it and push it open with my shoulder, shooting at the first man I see. He collapses in a pile and I move on to the next. I put a bullet in between his eyes. His brains fly all over the wall behind him. Seeing there is no one else, I turn and check the rest of the house.

When I walk out, I eye Igor. I put his own gun up to his forehead.

"You think I'm fucking playing with you? Tell me what you know." I scream in Russian.

He falls to his knees, begging for my forgiveness.

“Please, you need to help me. My daughter has been taken by someone who threatened to sell her to Gabriel if I didn’t comply with their demands. I can’t let that happen to my child. The Pakhan assured me that she would be mistreated. She’s only 16 years old. You've witnessed the atrocities they commit. Please, I beg of you, help me save my daughter. I had no choice."

I know my eyes softened at that. What else could he do? I've seen what they do firsthand. This is why I want no part in anything like that. They don't care if it's just a child. I hand him his gun.

"Come. Let's end this. I will deal with your treachery later."

I pull out my phone as we jump into my car and speed toward my house.

"Vlad."

"Demetrius?"

"I need your men and I need both you and Aleksandr to come back. Viktor has taken my angel. I will burn this entire city down, Vlad. You know this. She is my light. He can't have her." I growl. "He is a dead man."

"Alright brother. We will be there. I will do what I can from here to get you the manpower."

As soon as he hung up, I punched the steering wheel in frustration. Viktor better hope he hasn't harmed her in any way, or he'll be six feet under. I've never allowed my emotions to consume me like this, but I know there will be consequences. I feel like a ticking time bomb, ready to detonate at any moment.

When we finally get back, I see Anton and Serge, both bleeding from wounds I know aren't life threatening, but still, it's not something I like to see. I run to our room because I have to see it with my own eyes. She can't be gone. As I approach, I see they blew the door off of its hinges. I can see a few of my men on the floor dead.

But it means nothing to me. Only Luna matters. I step over the broken pieces on the floor, searching for my angel. And then I see it - a shattered vase and drops of blood. My heart sinks. It seems like my girl didn't go down without a fight. I feel a sense of pride knowing that she could give her a run for her money. But now, I'm not sure if she'll recover from this. I call Viktor, and he picks up while driving. I can hear the smile in his voice, and it irritates me. I growl in response.

My chest tightens with anger and frustration. I can feel my heart racing, my adrenaline pumping. My hands shake as I grip my phone tightly. The emotions inside me are so strong that it's almost like a physical pain. I can't believe Luna is gone, and I can't believe I wasn't there to protect her. My mind races with thoughts of revenge and justice. I want to find whoever did this to her and make them pay. The anger and desire for revenge are so intense that I feel like I could explode. I take a deep breath, trying to calm myself down, but it's no use. The rage inside me is too strong. I need to find Luna, and I need to make sure she's safe.

"Viktor. Brother or not. Pakhan or not, you are a dead man. Touch her and die. I will find you and when I do, it will not be a painless death. Remember how Vinny looked? I will do worse."

He laughs. "Oh, brother, you've always been so melodramatic. I am just going to get myself a taste of your beautiful whore. She will scream. I will make sure of it. It's within my right. I warned you. Then she will die. She will die because you dared to defy me. So remember, this is your doing."

"You so much as lay a finger on her, Viktor, and I swear on my life that I'll make you suffer in the most excruciating ways I can imagine," I growl.

My chest heaves with anger, and my hands shake with the intensity of my emotions. The mere thought of anyone hurting her fills me with a burning rage that I struggle to contain. I can feel my muscles tensing and my jaw clenching as listen to Viktor. The adrenaline coursing through my veins makes me feel both invincible and vulnerable at the same time. I am ready to defend her at all costs, no matter what it takes.

He chuckles once more before speaking. "Do you truly believe that you can locate me, my dear brother? You are merely a pawn in this game. You will never find us, mark my words. As I have already conveyed, I intend to revel in her company, and I shall do so. It is I who holds the title of Pakhan, not you. You would be wise to keep that in mind."

"I will stop at nothing until I find you, Viktor. All will perish in my wake, so make no mistake. Brother, I will locate you and hold you accountable if any harm befalls her. Remember that gruesome Blood Eagle I performed on Vinny? You may well beg for such a fate if you cross me."

"That was you?" I can almost hear the fear in his voice, and it brings a wicked smile to my face.

"This will not end well for you, Viktor. She is mine. No one touches what is mine."

"This will end exactly how I want it to, Demetrius. And what I want, I already have. You can not win. I am the Pakhan."

The line goes dead and I roar in frustration. I pace around my room. I know I need to do something. But what? Fuck Viktor. What is he going to do to her? If he touches her, I will make him feel the worse pain imaginable. He has no idea what he has done. He thinks he can hide behind being the Pakhan. What he doesn't realize is I don't give two fucks about that I. Will. Murder. Everyone. My fury explodes in a fit of rage and I destroy everything in my path..

Anton walks in after a while and looks at me. I've destroyed the rest of the room. The only things left untouched are the things that belong to my angel. I can't bear to think of destroying her things. I look at him. He is all patched up and ready to go.

But I can see the concern in his eyes as he takes in the scene of destruction. My hands are shaking, my heart pounding in my chest. My breathing is ragged and I can feel the sweat on my forehead. The anger has consumed me, taken over my body, and left me feeling drained and exhausted.

Anton approaches me cautiously, as if afraid I might lash out at him. But I know he's just worried about me. I take a deep breath, trying to calm myself down.

"Viktor," I say through gritted teeth. "He's got her. I don't know what he's going to do."

Anton nods, understanding the gravity of the situation.

"We'll get her back," he assures me. "But first, we need a plan." I nod, feeling a sense of purpose wash over me. Anger may consume me, but I know that I am going to do whatever it takes to save my angel.

"Call everyone that's loyal to me. I want them all. Everyone. Every single enforcer, every drug dealer, everyone. Vlad already has some of his men en route, but it might take a while for them to get to us."

Serge enters the room and apologizes, "Boss, I'm sorry I couldn't prevent them from arriving. At the gates, when we got there, I drew my gun."

I walk up to him. "You did what you could, Serge. None of this is your fault. But if they hurt Luna. I will burn this city down. I will kill anyone and everyone who gets in my way. You should call your families and tell them to go away. Tell everyone to send their families away." They nod.

I pick up my phone. Time to call in a few pros to find her. I have to find her. I have to. My head is reeling, and it's hard to think. I promised her I would keep her safe. He made me into a fucking liar. I knew. I knew it was a ploy. I should have turned right around and left. I should have come home and protected her. I have to find her. But how do I do that now? She is gone from me. Taken. I can't lose her. I will kill Viktor. No, I will kill them all. All of them.

Aleksandr just gave me a call to inform me that he's currently on the private jet, and he mentioned that Vlad is also on a separate private jet from the Kremlin. They both pulled some strings and managed to bring additional men with them. It won't be long before they arrive here.

I want to throw my phone. I feel my nerves fray. My patience is at an all time low. I look around the room. I have to keep it together. I have to save her. I will not lose her, not now, not ever. I look up when I hear a gun cock behind me.

I gradually pivot to face a senior gentleman garbed in black leather, sporting salt and pepper hair and a lengthy beard, his weapon trained on me. I raise my hands in surrender while Anton and Serge point their guns at the stranger, ready to react. I shake my head to signal them to stand down, then cautiously approach the old man.

"Who are you?"

He has a lot of nerve coming here right now. I know if looks could kill, the rage on my face would be enough to do it. He looks me in the eye passively and speaks in Russian.

"My name is Gospodin Falkner."

I know this name. He was a hitman for the Bratva in Russia until he disappeared a few years ago.

"How did you get in here?" Anton asks.

"I have some skills I use them sparingly, but they are good for times like this." He shrugs.

"Are you here to help me find her?"

"Yes."

"How did you know she was gone? I haven't called anyone yet."

"Because Viktor told me." He answers simply.

"What do you mean, Viktor told you? How do I know I can trust you?"

He shows me a photo of Luna when she was small. The picture is taken from a distance. I give him a quizzical look.

"She is my daughter."

"That's not possible. She is an orphan."

He agrees with a nod. "We simply can't afford to waste any more time. Her mother passed away during childbirth, and I used to work as a hitman. It's not a suitable environment for a child to grow up in. I arranged for her to live in Montana, hoping to keep her safe from all of this. However, she chose to move to Brooklyn. To make matters worse, she moved right into the heart of Bratva territory." He expresses his disappointment by shaking his head.

"How did you find her?" I ask.

"You can't keep anything from me. She is my baby. I knew the moment she left and moved here. I knew what could happen."

"Why didn't you intervene and stop he from being taken by Gabriel?" I growled out in anger. My poor angel. He could have stopped it all.

"I found out too late to save her. By the time I got here, you already had her."

"How can I trust you, Falkner? You said Viktor told you. I thought you were retired?"

"You can't trust me. But you need me. If you don't want to lose your angel, I suggest we start searching for her." I look at him and he pulls out his gun and points it right at my head. "She is my only child. If Viktor kills her, you are a dead man, Demetrius."

I maintain eye contact with him to convey my seriousness. "You still haven't answered the question. If anything were to happen to her, I wouldn't want to go on living. Life wouldn't be worth it."

That's the scary truth. I wouldn't want to live a life where she wasn't a part of it. She is my life now.

I feel a lump form in my throat and my chest tightens with a mix of fear and desperation. My eyes begin to water, but I refuse to break my gaze from his. I need him to understand the gravity of the situation and the depth of my feelings. My hands tremble slightly, and I clench them into fists to steady myself. This is not a conversation I ever imagined having, but it's one that I need to have.

We both stand there for a moment before he nods his head and walks away.

"He wanted me to take you out. Get me your men. Let's find that bastard Viktor and get Luna back. He can't have my daughter. I already have feelers out for her. I will be in touch."

I watch him walk out of my house like he owns it. Anton looks at me, eyebrows raised.

"Boss. Do we trust him?"

"No. But we have no choice and he knows this side of life better than me. He was known as the human hunter for a reason."

Only Demetrius, Ever

Luna

As I awaken, I'm greeted by the consistent hum of engines and a throbbing headache. Looking around, I realize that I'm strapped to a chair in some kind of aircraft. Trying to gather my bearings, I take a few deep breaths and assess my surroundings. The feeling of nausea overwhelms me as I realize that I must be on a private plane. Despite never having flown before, it seems as though I'm in a room of my own.

My hands are firmly secured to the chair using tape. I exert all my energy in an attempt to break free, even wriggling to loosen the hold, but to no avail. It's not like I have anywhere to run to, even if I was to break free. My only escape would be to take a leap out of the plane, hoping to meet a quick death upon impact with the ground. The thought of it causes my heart rate to skyrocket, and I start hyperventilating. I'm struggling to stay calm, but it's proving to be a difficult task.

The sound of the plane's engine is deafening and the smell of fuel fills my nostrils. Turbulence makes the plane shake violently, adding to my terror. I can feel the sweat on my palms and my breathing becomes shallower. My mind races with thoughts of what could happen next. Will I ever make it out alive? Will anyone come to rescue me? Will Demetrius be able to find me?

I try to push these thoughts away, but they keep coming back, haunting me. I close my eyes and take deep breaths, trying to calm myself down. But the fear is too overpowering, and I can feel my body trembling. I am trapped, helpless, and at the mercy of my captors. The only thing I can do is pray for a miracle and hope that he can find me before it's too late.

The door to the room I am in opens and Viktor walks in. I stare at him in fear and shock as it all comes back to me. He came into Demetrius' house and killed everyone. Then blew the door off of its hinges. I ended up hitting him with the vase and I tried to escape. The last thing I remember is one of his goons catching me and knocking me out. I look at Viktor and he stares at me with the cold eyes. I glare back at him.

"What are you going to do to me?" I ask with as much force as I can manage.

"Anything I want." He walks closer to me, smirking. "I heard the rumors about you and my brother." He glances at me with a look I can't decipher.

"He saved me," I answered defiantly. "What the fuck do you care? You just took me from my home."

"So you slept with him to get away from me," he growls

"He saved me!!" I scream at him. "I didn't know he was your brother."

"So you think you can fuck anyone you want?" he asks, stalking closer to me.

"I only fuck Demetrius," I whisper. "He is the only one. I am his and he is mine."

He glares at me. I knew my answer would not please him. He grabs my chin and forces me to look him in the eye. I struggle to get free, but he holds me tighter.

“You are mine! I saw you first!”

As soon as he leans in to kiss me, I shut my eyes. He slides his tongue over my lower lip, but I keep my lips pressed tightly together. I don't want him to kiss me; I only want Demetrius. What if something happened to him? What if he's... I can feel tears starting to stream down my cheeks. He licks my face, and I can't help but gag. His hands wander up my thighs towards my crotch. I clamp my knees together as tightly as possible. No, God, not again. Don't touch me! I scream in my head. Instead of being scared, I get angry. I'm not a toy to be played with.

"Don't fucking touch me," I yell as venomously as I can manage.

My heart is pounding in my chest, and I can feel my palms starting to sweat. I want him to get away from me. The memories of the last time someone touched me without my consent come flooding back, and I can't shake them. My body feels like it's on fire, and I can't escape the feeling of being trapped.

I take a deep breath and try to calm myself down. This isn't going to happen again. I won't let it. Not without a fight. I open my eyes and look at him, trying to convey all the anger and disgust I'm feeling. He seems to back off for a moment, but then he leans in again, his hands still creeping up my thighs.

"No! Don't touch me." My voice is shaking, but I'm determined to stand my ground.

Thinking about what happened is too overwhelming. All I can do is try to forget.

He moves away from me and I stare at him, my eyes revealing my fear. He grins at me and tears apart my shirt, exposing my breasts to him. With lustful eyes, he fondles my breasts through my bra and begins to stroke his manhood. I look away, hoping he won't force me to do this. Suddenly, he pulls out a knife and all I can think is, "Please, make it quick. End my life."

As he approaches, I can see the glint of the blade in the dim light. Suddenly, he cuts the tape, and I feel the tension release from my wrists. Before I can react, he yanks me from the chair and I am thrown onto the cold, hard floor. My head smacks against the metal, causing a sharp pain to shoot through my skull. The metallic scent of blood fills my nostrils, and I try to catch my breath.

I can feel the cold steel of the knife moving up my legs, and I shudder with fear. The sound of fabric tearing fills my ears as he cuts my jeans off of me. I try to move, to fight back, but my legs are still bound together. He rolls me onto my stomach, and I feel him moving my panties to the side. I scream and cry, my throat raw with the effort.

As he takes his pleasure, I feel a sense of violation and disgust wash over me. I try to fight him off, but his strength is too great. All I can do is lie there, helpless and vulnerable, as he continues to growl with pleasure.

He slams his dick into my pussy, hard. I scream from the pain. It hurts so much I can hardly breathe. He is so big I feel like it is tearing apart my insides. It hurts. I try to fight, but I can't do anything. Even with my hands free, I can't reach him. I can't even lash out.

“You’ll take it, you whore,” he moans in my ear. “Yes, that’s right, take my cock.” He slaps me across the face, and a groan of pleasure escapes his lips as I scream.

“Please, don’t do this,” I sob.

I can feel his dick begin to grow and throb inside of me. I don't want this no. Oh, my god no. He is thrusting into me and I can feel the warmth of the blood running down my thighs. It hurts. I can't take this anymore. I know I will die like this. I just know it. He keeps thrusting and I just give up. I turn my head and look at the wall. I let my mind take me to all the wonderful moments I had with Demetrius. All the kisses and sweet words. The love he showed me. How tender he has been with me.

"Fuck! I am going to come." Viktor yells in my ear.

As Viktor reaches his climax, I feel a wave of nausea wash over me. I can feel my body shaking with sobs as tears stream down my face. My mind is a jumbled mess of pain and confusion. I feel violated and dirty, like I will never be clean again. The physical pain is excruciating, but the emotional pain is even worse.

He bites down on my shoulder. I can feel his teeth pierce my flesh. His cock pulses. I shudder in revulsion and puke on the floor. He doesn’t care. He is still thrusting into me with wild abandon. When he is done, he stands up and smiles down at me. Viktor collapses onto me, his body still shaking with the aftermath of his orgasm. He doesn't seem to care about the damage he has done to me, the pain he has caused. All he cares about is his own pleasure.

I just stare at the wall. I don't move my eyes away from the words in front of me. I just stare. Hollow once more. Alone. Hopeless. I feel the warmth of my tears on my cheeks.

"You are mine to do with what I want."

He lifts me up by my arms and throws me back into the chair. He tapes my hands to the chair while I side there in my bra and panties. Blood making my legs crimson. He yanks my face up to look at him.

I clench my jaw as he tells me to clean him off, blaming me for the mess he made. He forces my mouth open with his thumbs and shoves his penis inside. When I try to bite down, he threatens me with violence, holding my jaw tightly. He thrusts in and out of my mouth, causing me to gag and taste the unpleasant mixture of his semen and my blood. Finally, he ejaculates down my throat and compliments me for being a good whore. I attempt to pull away, but he grips my face even harder.

He scowls. "You had better get used to this, you whore. I will take you anytime I want. That is some good pussy. I can see why my brother was keeping you for himself. But I am not going to be greedy. I'm going to share you."

"He will come after me and when he does, you're a dead man, Viktor. You know he won't stop."

He laughs at me. "You don't know my brother."

"I do. I know Demetrius will never stop until he finds you. And I know he will kill you. I think it is you who don't know your brother." I spit in his face.

He wipes the spit off his face and strikes me. "You're mistaken about one thing." The blow is so intense that I can sense the metallic taste of blood in my mouth and feel a sharp pain on my face. "Demetrius is no more. He won't be coming after you." He grins and winks at me before exiting the chamber.

My heart shatters. I sob hysterically. I can't catch my breath. I feel like my chest just caved in. I want to die. I have no reason to go on. No. Please no. No, no, no, he can't be dead. It can't be true. I sob and scream. I yank on the tape and the ropes. I can't breathe. My chest hurts so much. Viktor is lying to me. Demetrius can't be dead.

Oh god what am I going to do? What will happen to me? I look down at my arms. My wrists are bloody and raw from pulling at the tape. I scream in anguish. I can't do this anymore. I just give up. I have nothing left. All I feel is pain. I hear the door open again and Viktor comes back with his phone. I can see a man sprawled on the floor that might be Demetrius. It's a very bad picture. I can't see his face.

"Do you see that? It's your fucking Demetrius."

"He is not dead. You're lying he isn't dead. He isn't," I sob "That's not him."

I have nothing to live for. Viktor already raped me. I sit here, bared for all to see my shirt in tatters, my pants cut off. My blood coating my legs in some macabre type of covering. I don't care what Viktor does to me anymore. I want to die.

"I will never willingly give myself to you. You aren't half the man Demetrius was."

"You will regret what you just said."

"No, I won't. Demetrius loved me." I sneer at him. "and I still love him. I will forever until my last breath."

"I don't care. I will use you until I am done and then toss you to my men. Then they will do what they want to you. When you are all used up, I will just sell you"

I stare at him with cold eyes. "Do your worst Viktor."

He laughs at me. "Oh, I will. I promise you." He licks my face, causing a shiver of revulsion to go through my body.

"I am going to kill you. I swear it. I will be the last thing you ever see." I look him straight in his eyes.

He gets right in my face. "You couldn't even if you tried." He laughs as he leaves the room again.

I stare at the door full of hate. I don't care how long it takes. He will get sloppy and I will kill him. He killed the only man who ever meant anything to me. My reason to live is now to see him suffer as I watch him die. I want to see the look of surprise on his face as I stand over him.

I am left alone, bruised and bleeding, wondering how I will ever be able to move on from this. Thoughts of Demetrius consume my mind, and I know he would have never treated me like this. All I can do is cry and hope that someday, somehow, I will escape from this nightmare.

Fuck Him

Luna

We've been on this plane for what seems like an eternity, although I'm certain it's only been a few hours. My body aches and my head is spinning. My sorrow for Demetrius's loss has imprisoned me. I feel suffocated and nauseous.

My eyes are heavy, and my vision is blurred from the constant tears. My throat is dry and scratchy from the sobs that have wracked my body. Every breath feels like a struggle as if I'm trying to pull air through a thick fog. My stomach churns with a sickening mix of grief and anxiety. I can't bring myself to eat or drink anything, even though my body is screaming for sustenance. The thought of being trapped on this plane for even a moment longer fills me with dread. I just want to be home, alone with my thoughts and my memories of Demetrius.

Viktor has yet to return to the place where he's holding me captive. The dried blood on my legs reminds me of the pain he caused. I want revenge, but I refuse to let him break me. He wants me to feel like a slave, but I won't give him that satisfaction. His angry phone call revealed that I was raised in foster care and he referred to me as a slut to his men. I will not let his words define me.

"I wish that were true," I say with a heavy heart. If only it were, maybe this pain wouldn't be weighing so heavily on my soul. I've always tried to be a good girl, but now I see that it was all a facade. Demetrius saw me as a good girl too, but he didn't know the truth about me. He didn't know about everything that happened to me. And now that I've lost him, I can never tell him. The mere thought of him brings tears to my eyes and I break down in sobs. I wish I could just die and make this pain go away. He was my safe haven, my shelter in the storm, my protector in this cruel world. I yearn for him, but I know I'll never see him again.

As the plane begins to descend, I sense its rough landing. Soon after, the door opens and Viktor strides towards me. Without warning, he clasps a metal collar around my neck and releases the tape from my arms and rope from my legs. With a sneer, he pulls me up and tightens his grip on the leash. I am yanked off the plane and when I reach the stairs; I stumble and fall, tumbling down a few steps before regaining my balance.

I can see a man waiting for us. When I get a good look at him,

I freak out. My body freezes. One of the men from the auction where I was raped over and over is waiting for us at the edge of what looks like a jungle. I feel desperation seep into my very soul. Why is this happening to me? What did I do to deserve this?

Viktor laughs when I tense up. I try to pull away, but he yanks the leash and pulls me back. He drags me to the man and shoves me forward. I fall on my knees in the dirt. I hear someone approaching me, but I'm too scared to look up. The man screams in pain.

The man is holding his stomach with a shocked look. His intestines are in his hands. He falls to the ground, writhing in pain. I feel sick watching him. But truthfully, I don't care that he's dying. He deserved it, as far as I am concerned.

Viktor looks down at me. "Get up. Now." He kicks me in the ribs.

I gasp in pain, and he pulls me to my feet and pushes me forward. I stumble forward, trying to gain some balance. He yanks me back to him by the collar and grabs me by my hair.

"Walk bitch or I will kill you."

I can't bear the thought of dying this way. I need to take revenge and kill him first. Struggling to regain my composure, he finally releases me and starts trailing behind. I'm clueless about our whereabouts, just blindly following the path, my bare feet sore and constantly tripping on sharp objects.

He pushes me toward an old compound. I don't care why it's here,

I just want this to be over. We enter and he speaks to the men in Russian. I can't understand. But I know they're talking about me. I don't want to know his plans for me. He's said enough. Their eyes are all over me and I tremble. They look at me like a meal they all want a piece of. I'm shaking with fear.

He forces me down a corridor and into a room.

"I have a job for you," Viktor says looking at another man. "Get in here."

The man enters the room behind him and closes the door.

He holds up his arm. "Take your knife out and cut my arm," the man obeys and brings his knife up. The man slices his arm and then pulls the knife away. He presses his hand into the cut. Blood seeps down his arm. Viktor grabs my head and forces me to look up at him.

"Now kiss it. Kiss my wound and suck my blood." He hisses.

"No." I shake my head.

"What did you say?" He asks.

"I said no. I will never do that. You can beat me, but I will never do that."

"Oh, my precious." He grabs my throat and starts to squeeze. "You act as though you have a choice."

I can't breathe and I try to kick him in the balls, but he blocks it.

"You are mine. You will do as I say. Now fucking kiss and lick the blood off of my arm."

He tightens his grip above my collar, causing my vision to blur. In that moment, I almost wish he would just kill me and be done with it. However, he eventually releases his grasp, and I gasp for air. The knife is within reach, and I consider taking it to end my misery. He notices my gaze and smirks before letting go of me entirely. Without hesitation, I grab the knife and make a run for it, clutching my leash as I flee. As I rush through the halls, I can hear him barking orders to his accomplices.

"Get her! Bring her back. Bring her back now! I'm going to beat the shit out of you when we get you back, precious. You're going to wish you were dead." I hear his voice echoing off of the walls.

I hear them yelling and chasing me. I am running as fast as I can. The men are gaining on me and I can't keep up the pace up. My body is weak and broken. They catch up with me and shove me to the floor.

"No," I scream when they grab my leash and pull me across the floor.

"Fuck you, bitch." The man kicks me in the face.

I can see the edges of my vision as I fight the fog, trying to take over. I take the knife and stab it into his leg as hard as I can. I pull it out and do it again. I hear him scream and I feel his fresh blood spraying down my arm.

"You fucking whore. I am going to kill you!" He screams and yanks the knife from his leg.

I am writhing in agony as the blade pierces through my shoulder. The excruciating pain blinds me and I cry out in desperation. Death seems like a welcome relief, as I hope this man will kill me soon. His brutal kicks to my ribs and face leave me prepared to embrace my fate. Viktor has already murdered Demetrius and now, I have no reason to live. Just as another blow is about to land on my battered body, he is pulled away from me.

"Stop fucking kicking her."

The man's face is contorted with anger and hatred.

I am dazed, listlessly lying on the floor in a puddle of our shared blood. My own spreading out further around me. I may not have won the battle, but he knew I was there. Fuck him.

"Get out of my fucking way." I hear Viktor below through the hall. "If you kick her one more time, I will fucking kill you. She is mine. When she dies, it will be because I am finished with her."

The man gazes down at me and murmurs, “You better wait, bitch. I’ll make sure he stays away from you for a while.” He grins as he steps back. “I have all the time in the world to make you pay.”

My heart is pounding in my chest, and my head is throbbing from the blows I received. I try to move, but my limbs feel heavy and unresponsive. The pain is overwhelming, and tears stream down my face as I struggle to catch my breath. I can feel the warmth of the blood spreading across the floor and pooling around me. The room spins, and I feel like I'm going to pass out. But I can't let myself give up. I have to keep fighting, keep pushing forward, no matter how impossible it may seem. As I lie there, battered and broken, I vow to myself that I will never let him win. I will never give up, no matter what he throws my way. I will keep fighting until my last breath, and I will never let him break me.

I MISS YOU

Luna

They bandaged me and left me alone in the room. I stayed awake as long as I could. I'm scared to sleep too, afraid someone could come in. But no one ever came and eventually, I drifted into a restless sleep. I had dreams of Demetrius.

Our first days together and a flash of little ones running around. Looking into his smiling face. The smile I know he only reserved for me. I wake up with tears streaming down my face and an ache in my chest. I can't believe he is dead. I feel like I am hollowed out. A walking zombie. Completely gutted.

I dream of his smile. His laugh. The way he said my name. I can't stop the tears streaming down my face. I don't know how long I sat here thinking about him. The life we could have had together. My head is pounding and my throat feels tight from the constant sobbing. The tears have left my eyes puffy and red. I try to take a deep breath, but it feels like there's a weight on my chest that won't go away. My stomach is in knots and I feel like I might be sick.

I look around the room, trying to distract myself from the pain. The walls are bare and there's only a small window high up near the ceiling. The room is dimly lit and the only sound is my own ragged breathing.

I feel so alone. The only person who truly understood me is gone. The thought of never hearing his voice or feeling his touch again is too much to bear. I try to focus on the good memories, but they only make the pain worse. I feel like I'll never be happy again. How can I move on when a part of me is missing?

I know I need to be strong. Demetrius wouldn't want me to give up. But right now, in this moment, all I can do is grieve.

Everything hurts and I don't need a mirror to know how bruised I am. I can hardly move the shoulder I was stabbed in. They put a makeshift bandage on it. But they tended to nothing else. Hopefully, I get an infection and die.

I am able to hear Viktor conversing with another person about what to do with me. Viktor instructs the other individual to "Do what you want with her." The other person laughs. My only hope is that they plan to kill me like they did Demetrius and not what I fear they are discussing. Unfortunately, I know that I won't be that fortunate. I remain seated, sweating and trembling, when the door opens.

"It's time." Says Viktor.

"Time for what?"

"Time for you to get up and be of use to me."

I'm not moving. I can hardly move at all. Whatever. I look up at him with a hateful glare. He steps closer and yanks me up by my hair.

"I said get up, you fucking bitch!"

I attempt to pull away from his grip, but my strength is lacking, and the agony is too much to bear. He hoists me up to my feet, and pushes me against the wall, I stumble, tumbling to the floor. He seizes a fistful of my hair, tugging me upright, and I wail in agony as he strikes me across the face. My head jerks to the side, and I plummet to the ground once again. As everything fades to black, his words echo in my ears:

"Breaking you will be a pleasure."

When I come to again, the sun is high in the sky and I am fastened to the wall with a short chain that connects to my collar. They have stripped the rest of my clothes off of me, leaving me completely bare. My whole body hurts from the beating I took. Besides removing my bra and my panties, it seems he didn't do anything else. Although one of my eyes is almost swollen shut from the hit I took.

The collar is too tight and restricts my throat. I can barely move more that a few steps. I have just enough room to lie down without choking. My hands are burning from the cuts caused by the tape. The wound where I was stabbed is throbbing and looks angry with purple and red colors. The hole is large, and it seems like he twisted it when he pulled it out.

I can see my shoulder through the thick blood clotting around the wound. It's hot and pulsating, radiating my body heat. The surrounding skin is stiff and scaly, like that of a reptile. The pain is so intense that my hand recoils when I touch it. I smell of blood and death, and I can tell that it's quickly becoming infected. If he was going to take care of it, I think he would have done it by now.

I don't know how long I've been here for. For all I know, this may be the last day of my life. I would like to stay alive and not die before I get my revenge. I will try to survive until I have a chance to kill this bastard for what he did to Demetrius. He has taken the only man I have ever loved and I never even got the chance to tell him just how much he meant to me.

My heart is heavy with grief and anger. The pain of losing Demetrius is always there, like a dull ache in my chest that never goes away. But I know that I must stay strong and focused if I am going to avenge him and bring justice to his memory.

As I sit in the corner, I have no idea how much time has passed before I hear the sound of the door opening. Viktor walks in, accompanied by a large, well-built man who is dressed only in a pair of jeans. Without hesitation, Viktor points directly at me.

“Get over here,” he hisses. “Kiss him,” Viktor adds. I remain still, standing naked with a collar attached to the wall. I can’t go far. The man looks at Viktor, then at me. Suddenly, Viktor pulls out his knife.

"No." I shake my head.

I can see the smirk on Viktor's face.

"Are you going to keep saying that?"

"Yes. I told you. I will never willingly give myself to you. That also means anyone else you want to watch me with."

"I am the boss here. You will do well to remember that. I can do what I want and right now I want to see you with this man."

"You want me to watch a man rape me? You killed the only man I ever loved. You can go to hell. If you want to see me with a man, you have that ability. I can't fight you. I don't care. The only man I will ever willingly kiss is dead."

Tears streamed down my face as I spoke, my voice shaking with anger and grief. My body trembled with the intensity of my emotions, and I felt my heart pounding in my chest. The thought of being forced to take part in this horrific act made my stomach churn and my skin crawl. I feel sick to my core, and the mere suggestion of it filled me with a deep sense of revulsion and disgust. Despite my fear and sadness, I refused to give in to the demands of my captors. I would not let them break my spirit or force me to betray my love. I was determined to stay strong, even in the face of unimaginable cruelty and suffering.

The man he brought into the room is standing there, growling and breathing heavily while staring at my naked body. I can sense that he doesn't care whether I'm willing or not. They can use my body, but my soul will always be mine. However, I doubt it matters to him. They won't care that it's not consensual. I'm just a plaything to them. They can have their way with me, but that's all that's going to happen. I learned how to check out in the awful place I was at before.

I can perceive the fury, and animosity reflected in his gaze. Viktor is gripping the knife in his hand, and the man is staring intently at both Viktor and the weapon. Viktor nods in acknowledgement and the man advances towards me.

"I don't have any use for you if you won't do as I say." Viktor smirks.

I shrug my good shoulder and close my eyes in anticipation. I'm aware of what's about to happen and I don't want to witness the pain he's about to inflict on me. However, avoiding the reality won't change anything. I hear his footsteps getting closer and feel his touch. Despite trying not to react, it's difficult to control my response. Surviving this ordeal requires me to divert my thoughts elsewhere. So, I escape to a different place and focus on Demetrius, reminiscing about all the ways he showed me how much he cared. I remember the tender touches and the smiles that were only meant for me.

"Don't think of it as rape. Think of it as lovemaking." The man whispers.

My body shakes with each sob and tears stream down my face uncontrollably. I feel a lump in my throat, making it hard to breathe. My chest tightens as my heart races, and I can feel the weight of my emotions crushing me.

"I am going to enjoy this. Play nice and you might just survive." He whispers in my ear.

"I don't care if I survive."

"You will care when I am done with you."

"You can do what you want. I am going to die either way. I will never willingly give myself to you or anyone else."

I feel his cock rub against me.

"Oh, but you will." He grins.

I sense his hands moving across my body, but it causes my stomach to churn. The touch of anyone other than Demetrius is disgusting to me. It gives me goosebumps. If I had eaten, I would have likely vomited on him. However, they haven't provided me with food or water yet. As this man touches me, I can feel Viktor's gaze on us.

"Move," he says in a husky voice. I open my eyes at the sound of his voice and I see him palming himself through his jeans. He is hard as a rock. He is stroking himself right here in front of us. "On the floor."

I start to panic, trying to lower myself down.

He laughs. "Oh no. I have other plans for you."

He seizes my injured shoulder and pushes me down onto my knees. Agony courses through my body as he grips it, causing fresh blood to trickle down my skin. Though I attempt to keep my mouth shut, the pressure he applies to my jaw with his thumbs becomes unbearable, and I'm forced to part my lips.

"Open your fucking mouth or I will break your jaw and use you, anyway."

He forces my mouth open and shoves his cock into my mouth. My eyes water as I struggle to breathe, my hands clawing at his thighs in a desperate attempt to push him away. The taste of him is bitter and overpowering, and I feel a wave of nausea rise in my stomach. But he doesn't let up, his hips thrusting forward with each gagging gasp I make. I feel violated, humiliated, and utterly powerless, trapped in this degrading act with no escape.

"Fuck yeah."

I gag and almost throw up around his length. I try to push him away with my hands. The pain makes me try to scream. But he's so much bigger than me that he just pushes in further, blocking my airway. He can do what he wants with me, and it's beyond terrifying..

"That's it. Take it." he moans

Tears are flowing down my cheeks. Out of the corner of my eye. I can see Viktor stroking himself as he watches the man fuck my face. The man is holding my head so that I can't move away.

"Fuck." Viktor hisses. "Her mouth looks so perfect. I can see why my brother wanted to keep her for himself." he groans, "Take your clothes off." He orders the man.

I gasp for air the moment he moved away from me.

The man grins at me before hastily removing his pants. He stands before me fully naked, eagerly awaiting instructions. His erect cock protrudes from his body as he licks his lips while staring at me. Viktor remains in place, stroking his own cock while observing us. He slowly approaches me, grabs me by my hair, and passionately kisses me. When he pulls away, I retaliate by spitting in his face. He takes a step back, wiping the spit from his face.

"Use her anyway you want. You will pay for that, you whore."

The man grins at me. "Open your mouth."

"No."

He grabs my hair and yanks my head back, digging his fingers into my jaw, forcing it open. He slams his dick into my mouth, causing my teeth to grind against his cock. He moans loudly.

"Yes." He hisses.

He's thrusting in and out of my mouth vigorously, making it difficult for me to stop him. He's moving too quickly, and his penis is being pushed down my throat. I'm struggling to breathe, and the panic is starting to set in.

"Yes, yes, yes." He grunts. "Gag on my enormous cock. Let me feel it."

I repeatedly gag as the pressure builds behind my eyes, and he shows no signs of stopping. My vision starts to darken as I struggle to breathe. He grips my head tightly, and a deep moan escapes his lips as he climaxes in my mouth. His hot release sprays inside of my mouth, and he withdraws, gazing down at me. I let it fall from my mouth onto the floor as I gasp for breath.

"Swallow the rest." He hisses.

I shake my head no as I continue to try to spit it all out. He slaps me.

"Swallow it or I will cut your throat."

Viktor grins at me. My face twists in disgust as I force down the unpleasant taste. I can feel my stomach churning in protest. Viktor's grin only grows wider at my discomfort. Despite my revulsion, I can feel a sense of satisfaction radiating from him. It's as if he's pleased with himself for making me do something I find so unpleasant. His eyes gleam with a twisted sense of pleasure, and I can't help but feel a shiver run down my spine.

“Good girl,” he says as he pulls out his knife and holds it up for me to see.

He steps forward and places the icy blade against my neck.

“Now, lay down. We're not done with you yet.”

Trembling and shaking, I obey and lay on the floor. The man and Viktor stand over me, stroking themselves.

“You're so beautiful,” he says.

He strokes my body with his fingers. I start to cry. Not again. I just want to die. It's not like this will be my first experience, but at least before they had the decency to drug me. I do remember bits and pieces, but not with the clarity I will have now.

My body shakes with sobs as his fingers continue to roam over my skin. I feel violated, helpless, and alone. The memories of experiences flood my mind, making me feel like I'm drowning in a sea of pain and shame. My heart pounds in my chest, and my breath comes in quick gasps. I want to scream, to fight back, but I'm frozen in fear.

As his fingers move to my face, I close my eyes and try to escape into my mind. I imagine myself in a different place, a place where I'm safe and loved. But the images are blurry, and I can't hold on to them for long. The reality of the situation snaps me back to the present, and I feel a surge of anger.

Why me? Why does this keep happening? Am I just a victim, a pawn in someone else's sick game? I want to fight back, to take control of my life, but I don't know how. All I can do is endure the pain and hope that someday it will end.

"That's right, bitch cry. Fight me. Make it hurt. I love a challenge." He grins.

He kneels between my legs, spreading them wide. The cold air hits me as he pushes his finger against my pussy, rubbing and stroking his dick while looking at me. He slides his finger inside as Viktor forces his cock into my mouth, starting to thrust. His cock slides down my throat, and suddenly I have a flashback to my time in the human trafficking ring. I remember those two men breaking me in. Panic sets in and I push Viktor away with my hands, hurting myself in the process.

I try to scream, but I can't. Instead, he forces himself in further and makes me gag.

"Yes, that's it fight. Fight it. God, that makes it so much better." The man says while rubbing my clit.

He pulls out his finger and lines himself up. I can't breathe. Viktor has me locked down and his cock is in my mouth.

"I want you to feel this. I want you to feel everything I am doing to you."

He rubs his dick up and down my pussy. It's wet and slippery. I hate my body. Why does it still react even when I don't want it to? I feel disgusted with myself. The shame hits me like a Mac truck. My heart races and my stomach churns with nausea. I feel trapped and helpless, my body betraying me even as my mind screams for it to stop. Tears stream down my face as I try to block out the sounds of his grunts and moans. I want to disappear, to escape this moment and never have to face it again. But I know that the shame will linger long after he's gone, haunting me with its heavy weight.

"Fuck you are so wet." He grins.

I feel the head of his cock slide along my slit, and then he thrusts forward. He is so big; I scream around Viktor's dick. Viktor takes that moment and thrusts in further.

"Mmmhmm."

I feel Viktor pulling out of my mouth. He steps back. I take a deep breath.

"That's right. Fuck her, be brutal. I want to see you use her like the whore she is." He says, stroking his cock while he watches.

The man slaps me and pinches me everywhere he can, causing pain as he rapes me. I try not to cry out, but the pain becomes too much and I can't help but scream.

"Yes. You feel so good."

"So tight."

"So warm."

He slams his cock into me as hard as he can. I can feel him throbbing inside of me. He pulls out and thrusts back in.

"Fuck. You are so fucking tight."

He starts to thrust harder. He grabs my legs and holds them up and then slaps me so hard blood flies from my mouth. I am trying to focus on anything other than what is happening. He slaps me again on the other cheek.

"That's it. Don't fucking close your legs. I want to see all of this."

He slaps me again. I am starting to feel dizzy from the force of his slaps. I can't focus. Hopefully, I pass out.

"So tight." He grunts "I love your pussy. So soft and wet. So fucking warm. You are a good little fuck. Fuck, fuck, fuck, that's right bitch." I feel his hands on my breasts. He pinches my nipples and twists them. I scream out in pain. "Yes. That's it. Give it to me."

I feel him spasm. Viktor has walked back over, and he is stroking his cock.

"I'm going to fill you with my come. You are going to have to drink all of it." I shake my head no. I don't want that. Viktor grabs my head and forces me to look up at him. "You will drink it." He hisses.

He thrusts his cock in my mouth and I can feel him spurting in my throat.

"Now I will take your pussy again. I have been waiting to have you anytime I want. Ever since I first saw you in my club." He says as he lines his cock up.

"You are going to be begging for more. Just wait Luna. You'll see, you will want me. I'm so much better than Demetrius could ever have been. I'll make you want me"

I feel his entry and let out a gasp before breaking down into sobs. Suddenly, a sharp slap across my face sends me reeling, and the edges of my vision start to darken rapidly.

"I didn't tell you to cry."

I try to focus on anything other than him. My mind keeps going back to when Demetrius first made love to me. He was so gentle. He was so patient. He took his time. I have flashbacks of how he would kiss me. How he would touch me and fold me into his arms protectively.

"Yes. So good. So warm. Fuck yeah." He moans as he pumps in and out of me. The other man is watching with a smile on his face. "You are such a good fuck. So fucking tight. You feel so good. I'm going to come again. This is so fucking good." I feel his semen pouring out of me. "Oh yes. Oh, fuck."

He pulls out and steps away.

"Get up and clean yourself off." He hisses. He throws a towel at me. I struggle to move. I look at Viktor. He is sneering in my face. "You are mine now Luna. You will do as I say or else."

"Or else what, Viktor? Are you going to kill me? I am already dead."

"I have much worse planned for you. I look forward to watching you give up. No one is coming for you. You will be my little fuck doll until I grow bored with you. It might take a few years. Who knows, you might survive the first year." He grins down at me. "Until then, enjoy."

He and the other man exit the room, shutting the door behind them. I'll take his life before I shatter. It's my only option now. If I could only find a means of escape, if I could simply endure. I'm at a loss. He can use my body, but my soul is untouchable.

That's Demetrius's alone. He's taken my heart and soul with him wherever he may be. I yearn to join him there. I already miss him terribly. I curl up on my side, cradling my shoulder and my used body, and sob myself to sleep.

You're a Monster

Luna

I'm not sure how long I have actually been here. It feels like forever, but I think it's only been a few days. Last night was freezing. I curled up in a ball as tightly as I could, trying to stay as warm as possible. My dreams were of Viktor killing Demetrius and there was nothing I could do about it but scream.

When I woke up, my throat was sore from screaming and my eyes were swollen from crying in my sleep. The reality of my situation hit me hard, and I felt a heavy weight on my chest. I tried to shake off the feeling of despair and hopelessness, but it lingered like a dark cloud over my head. The hunger pangs in my stomach reminded me that I hadn't eaten in a while, and I wondered how much longer I could survive in this place without food or water. The thought of being trapped here, alone with my fears and nightmares, made me shiver with dread. I knew I had to find a way out, but the prospect seemed daunting and impossible.

I'm pretty sure I am running a fever now. I'm shivering from the cold. The scream from my dream is what woke me up. I am covered in sweat and freezing cold.

Great fever dreams.

It's still dark outside. I sit up and pull my legs in front of me trying to cover as much of my naked body as I can. My shoulder hurts so much that all I can do is cradle it.

I can hear the doorknob jiggling. Whispers and laughter fill the air, but fear has taken over me. I curl up into a ball, trying to cover my face with my hands. Suddenly, the door swings open and two hands yank my ankles, dragging me toward them as I kick and scream in terror.

"I told you I would come for you, bitch."

The fear that ripples through me is almost overwhelming.

"No. No, no, no. Not you. Not now. Please." I scream and cry.

I hear a click and feel the weight of the chain fall from the wall.

"Please."

"Oh, you will be saying please. Very soon. You stabbed me and now you're going to pay."

He is pulling me through the door. I can't see what is going on. I am being dragged along the floor.

"Help. Help me! Please!"

I scream, and he laughs. "No one can hear you, princess."

He laughs and drags me to a room with a bed. He tosses me onto it. I look down at what he has in his hands.

"You stabbed me. I should have killed you when I had the chance. Now I'm going to make you pay for that little over site."

As I look closer, I can see that he is tightly gripping a sharp and shiny knife, glinting in the dim light. The sound of his heavy breathing fills the air as his eyes dart around the room, searching for his next victim. The metallic scent of the weapon lingers in my nostrils, making me feel uneasy and on edge. I can't help but feel a chilling sensation down my spine as I realize the danger of the situation. He continues to hold the weapon with a menacing grip, ready to strike at any moment.

"Please."

He laughs at me. He holds up the knife while striding toward me.

"Not like this."

'I can't die like this,' I thought frantically as panic consumed me.

"Like what? This is what you get. You stabbed me." He is leaning forward. "You will die, but not before I have fun with you."

"No, no, no. Don't."

As he chuckles, he suddenly seizes my hair and forcefully pulls my head backwards. The sharp blade of a knife is pressed against my neck, and I can distinctly sense it breaking through my flesh.

"Open your eyes."

I close them tighter.

"Now."

I open my eyes and look up at him.

"Don't move. Any movement and this will go deeper."

Tears are streaming down my face. He laughs and I feel the knife move. I scream. I can feel him climbing on top of me and settling between my thighs.

"Oh, I love your screams. They are so pretty. Scream more, baby. I'm so hard for you."

He takes the knife and moves it across my chest. I cry out at the burning pain.

"Don't move."

He cuts me again, and I scream out in pain and terror. He laughs. "This is just the beginning. We have a long night ahead of us."

"Please. Don't hurt me."

I feel him inside me. "It's too late for that. You hurt me."

"Please."

"Please what? What do you want me to do? You stabbed me. Now I'm going to fuck you and you are going to love it."

I sob, and he laughs. I feel him slam into me, and he pulls the knife away. He moves around a bit and then he laughs.

“Wow, that blood looks beautiful,” he exclaims as he runs the knife down my chest, causing me to scream in agony. He then proceeds to lick the blood off my skin. “You taste so delicious. All of this blood belongs to me, and no one can take you away from me, ever,” he boasts while laughing. “You’re mine now, and nobody can change that. After the Pakhan is done with you, I’ll request to have you all to myself.”

I am screaming and sobbing loudly.

"Stop crying." He slaps me.

I cry harder. My chest heaves with each sob, and tears stream down my face, blurring my vision. I can feel my whole body shaking with the intensity of my emotions, and I struggle to catch my breath between sobs. It feels like my heart is breaking into a million pieces, and I can't seem to stop the flood of tears.

"Don't make me hurt you more than I already am. This is all your fault."

I can't help it. This is all so much. I can't stop sobbing. It's as if the dam broke and this is all that's left.

"I told you to stop crying." He slaps me. He is laughing at my pain. "You will heal. And then I will get to do it all over again. You will never leave this place. You will never leave my side. Stop crying or else you will really see my anger."

I can't stop sobbing no matter how hard I try. He slaps me harder and I taste the copper of blood in my mouth.

"Your man is dead and now I get to use you all I want. He was so greedy trying to keep you for himself." he grunts pumping in and out of me "I can understand why though. Your pain is so delicious. The feeling of your pussy wrapped around my hard cock. You're so warm it feels like a furnace. The feel of your blood dripping down my face. I'm going to make you bleed and enjoy every second of it."

"You're a monster," I scream, and he hits me.

"Be quiet."

I feel the knife slide along my body. I can feel the pain as it cuts through me. He is grunting and thrusting faster.

"I love you." He moans as he moves inside me.

I am shaking and crying. "I don't want this."

"You are mine. Now and forever. And you will do as I say. If not.." he leans over and kisses me "I will kill you. When Viktor uses you. You had better remember that. You belong to me." He groans and I feel him come inside of me.

He pulled me back down the hallway to my holding place and reattached the collar's chain around my neck. He then forced his semen back inside me and said, "This belongs in you so you won't forget who you belong to."

He's crazy. How am I going to make it through this to seek my revenge? The sensation of my blood on my exposed flesh is akin to slick oil being drizzled over me. Every inch of my bare skin is drenched in my own blood, oozing from my wounds and splattering onto the concrete floor with a resounding thud, almost resembling the rhythm of a heartbeat. I tremble, not only from the physical trauma, but also from the fever that has taken hold. My head is throbbing relentlessly.

When the sun starts to rise, I just sit there and stare at the door. I only need to hold on long enough to kill Viktor. after that, I don't care what happens to me. I have already lost everything. In another world, Demetrius would be looking for me and I would have hope that he would come and save me. But that world is over and done with. Now I only have revenge to keep me going.

No Turning Back

Demetrius

My brothers arrived a couple of days ago and it's really taking a toll on me. I feel like more of a monster than a man at this point. It's been too long since I've seen her and I fear for her safety. I made a promise to keep her out of harm's way, but I'm failing miserably. I lost control and trashed my office; books were scattered everywhere with pages littering the floor. Unfortunately, nothing seems to be helping this unbearable pain in my chest. I'm filled with rage and I swear to take down that bastard.

My hands are shaking and my heart is pounding so hard that

I can feel it in my ears. My breathing is shallow and erratic, and my vision keeps blurring. I can't seem to calm down, no matter what I do. The anger and frustration are consuming me, and I don't know how much longer I can hold on. Every time I think of her in danger, my blood boils and I feel like I could tear down walls with my bare hands. It's a terrifying feeling, but I can't seem to shake it off. I need to find a way to channel this energy before it annihilates me.

They have been doing their best to track her down. Falkner called me an hour ago with news that he thinks he found the location where they took her. He's gone ahead to scout the area and confirm. Apparently, they've taken her to an old remote compound that's heavily guarded and doesn't even belong to the Bratva. But I won't let him get away with taking my angel. I'll do whatever it takes, even if I have to burn the jungle down. I'm pacing back and forth in my room when Vlad walks in and hands me a whiskey. I accept it without a word.

"What do you think Falkner will do?"

I shake my head and sip my drink. "I don't know. He's a man of many mysteries. But we need to be ready. I don't want to get in his way. He knows his way around a gun and has taken out more than one enemy with it. But this is my angel. I don't care if it's his sperm that created her. She is my woman and I love her. It's my responsibility."

Vlad nods and stands next to me. "We'll get her back. I know it. We just have to be prepared and be patient. We need to make sure that when Falkner goes in, he has our full support."

I take another sip of my whiskey and nod. "We will. I'm not leaving until she's safe. I'm going to make sure that Viktor pays for what he has done. He won't ever hurt her or anyone else ever again."

Vlad gives me a sad smile and nods. "I know, man, and I am here for you both when this is over. We will get her back and then we will make sure Viktor pays for what he has done."

I nod and finish the whiskey in one gulp. I stand up and grab my gun, sliding it into my holster. "Let's go get her. We know where he is by the time we land. Falkner will already have the details. I doubt if his intel is wrong."

He nods "Let's go. I have a cargo plane ready for us."

We make our way to the hangar and board the plane. I choose a seat beside Vlad and mentally prepare myself for the inevitable. Once we touch down, there will be no going back. I'm determined to do whatever it takes to retrieve her and ensure that Viktor pays for his actions.

If he laid a finger on her, he'll beg for death. I'll demonstrate to him the same fate I bestowed upon Vinny, only this time, I'll prolong his agony. The blood eagle will require days to complete, and he'll endure excruciating pain.

Falkner is waiting for us on the tarmac when we land. He knows for sure she is there. He heard guards speaking about it. It's time to go in and kill them all.

"Save Viktor for me," I growl

"Of course," Falkner says with a smile on his face.

"Let's go."

We're en route to the compound where Luna is being held by Viktor, and I'm eager to get there quickly. It's a few miles away from our current location, so we trek through the jungle towards it. The compound is concealed and heavily fortified, revealing that Viktor is more intelligent than I anticipated. We systematically eliminate the guards patrolling the perimeter of the compound, one by one. We move with urgency and stealth through the compound, executing anyone in our path. We will leave no one alive.

It takes us some time to reach the building that we believe is holding Luna. Since it's heavily guarded, we must exercise caution. Fortunately, they appear to be oblivious to our presence, which is exactly what we desire. As we turn the corner, the front doors abruptly swing open, and a man dashes out before coming to a sudden halt. When he sees me, I can't help but display a feral grin, and I watch as he pisses his pants. I raise my firearm and aim it at his head.

"One word and your brains will be all over that door." I walk towards him and he backs away. "Where is Viktor?" He swallows. "Fuck, I don't have time for your shit. Where is he?" He points to a building on the other side of the compound. "Where is my angel?" I growl.

I hear the door open and Falkner walks out. "I don't think she is in this building. There were a few sleeping guards. They won't be a problem anymore." He says, wiping the blood off of his face.

The man that just pissed himself goes even whiter. I see his hand go under his shirt. "No, you don't." I shoot him between the eyes. Thank god for silencers. I turn to look at Falkner.

"I say we try to one Viktor is in." He says.

I point towards the building the guard said Viktor was in.

He nods and we head that way. As we get closer to the door, it opens and a guard steps out. He is holding a gun. Falkner moves lightning quick much faster than a man his age should be able to. He shoots him in the head and then steps forward and kicks the door open. The place is eerily quiet. I look behind us and I see my men clearing the other buildings.

I hear my angels' screams echo through the halls. I can't tell where it came from. But fuck if that's going to stop me. I look at Falkner. "Let's go."

Nodding in agreement, we swiftly navigate through the building, clearing anything that obstructs our path as we approach the source of the commotion. The sound of Viktor's voice becomes increasingly audible as we draw nearer to the room from which the scream emanates. I hear him laughing cruelly.

"That one." Falkner growls.

I can hear the anger and rage in his voice. This is my angel, but he is her father. Her sperm donor. It doesn't matter. If Viktor has hurt her even one time, I will kill him. I am not leaving here without her. I will never leave her. We are moving fast and then we see the door open. I can hear my angel screaming even louder now. I see red.

"Luna!" I roar.

I rush into the room and see Viktor standing over my angel. He has a knife in his hand and she is covered in blood. There are cut marks covering her body. The very first thing I notice is he has his dick inside of her. I look over and see her eyes. They are empty and filled with despair. He looks at me and smiles. My eyes focus on him. My singular target.

My heart is pounding in my chest, and my hands are shaking with rage. I feel a surge of adrenaline rushing through my veins, and my vision becomes tunnel-like as my focus narrows on Viktor. I can feel the fiery anger bubbling up inside me, and my fists clench tightly as I step towards him.

My mind is racing with thoughts of revenge, and it filled my body with a primal urge to inflict pain upon him. I can feel the raw power coursing through my muscles as I prepare to attack. The sight of my angel's broken body fills me with sadness and regret. I know that I can never fully make up for what Viktor has done to her. I can only love her with everything I am.

"Ah, Demetrius. Good, you are here."

I pull my gun and shoot him. The bullet tears through his shoulder. He screams and falls backward. Leaving my angel laying there bloody and battered. This mother fucker was raping her. I'm going to rip him apart. I stalk forward and grab him. Pulling him to his feet and shoving him against the wall. He laughs and I lose it. My fist connects with his face.

"You fucking bastard! I will kill you!"

I kept hitting him repeatedly until he finally fell to the ground, and then I proceeded to kick him. My anger was getting out of control and blood was splattered everywhere. All I could see was red. Suddenly, I felt a hand on my shoulder, and when I turned around, I saw Falkner's face. This snapped me back to reality, reminding me that I needed to take care of Luna.

"She needs you." He says.

"I know. Take him and tie him up." I growl in anger.

He grins and nods. "I've got this. Go."

I hurry towards Luna, but she's struggling to reach me due to her battered condition. My heart shatters as I gaze at her.

"Oh, my beautiful angel."

She is sobbing. I gather her in my arms and she screams in pain.

"They said you were dead," she sobs, clinging to me. "They said you were dead. I thought you were dead. Am I dead? Did he kill me?"

"I'm not dead and neither are you, angel. I'm here. Shhh I have you."

Upon glimpsing the collar around her neck, I turn my gaze towards Viktor and snarl, "You're a bastard."

"Don't worry about that right now. Get her out of here," Falkner says.

"I can't. They attached her to the wall."The words make me sick. They chained her to the wall. "Fuck. Ok, angel. I will get this off."

I kiss her forehead and lay her back on the bed. She whimpers.

"It's ok, baby. I'm going to get it off. Shhh, my angel. I'm going to need the keys, Falkner. Viktor should have them on him."

Falkner walks over and starts looking through Viktor's pockets.

"Hurry, please."

Falkner hands me the keys and I take a deep breath. I walk over to the bed and try to unlock the chain from the collar. I try a couple of keys and finally the chain comes off. She gasps and starts crying.

"Shh, Luna. It's going to be ok."

"Demetrius."

"Don't worry, baby," I say as I pull her against my chest. "Shhh, you're safe now. I have you."

She is weeping and whimpering uncontrollably, and it's evident that she's been through a lot. Strangely, she seems worse off now than when I first rescued her from that dingy warehouse. Her body is covered in blood, and the scent of other men lingers on her. It breaks my heart to see my sweet angel in such a wretched state. How could this happen to her again? Oh, my poor angel.

I quickly remove my shirt and place it over her to keep her warm. I lift her up and hold her close, finding it difficult to let go. It feels like an impossible task.

My fists clench tightly as I feel my pulse quickening and my chest heaving with rage. My vision becomes blurred with a red haze as my anger takes over. The room feels smaller and my breaths become shallow and rapid. I can feel the adrenaline pumping through my veins, urging me to take action. The thought of sparing anyone crosses my mind briefly, but I quickly dismiss it. They all deserve to pay for their sins. The only thing that matters now is revenge.

"I want them all dead. Everyone here dies." I growl, "There will be no survivors."

She is still bleeding from the knife wounds he carved into her. Her shoulder looks like they shot her. It's red and puffy. I can see the infection and she is burning up. She needs a fucking doctor.

"Shh, baby. We are going home. You are safe."

"Home." She sobs. "Demetrius. He said you were dead." She sobs even more frantically. "He showed me a picture. If this is a dream, please don't let me wake up. Just let me die if this is a dream."

"I'm here angel. I'm here. I'm not dead."

She's shaking and sobbing. "I thought you had left me. I had nothing to live for," she says between sobs, her body trembling.

"I will never leave you. I love you, Luna. I'm never letting you go. You are mine and always will be."

As I carry her out of the room, I sense her body trembling due to the trauma and fever. Despite my anger and rage, she takes priority over everything else. I must get her on the plane, to a place where I can tend to her and nurse her back to health. A place where she can feel secure and protected.

"Demetrius."

She is whimpering my name. She is terrified and hurting. My heart is breaking for her.

"I have you, angel. You're safe. No one will ever hurt you again. I will never leave your side again. Ever."

She nods and curls into me. I look at my men.

"Burn it. Leave no stone unturned, no building not searched. Burn it all down. Kill them all."

They nod. They are all just as enraged as I am. I have to get her out of here. I have to get her somewhere safe. She is barely holding on and I'm afraid she is going to pass out.

"Demetrius," she says again.

"What, angel?"

“You were gone,” she sobs, her tears wrenching my heart.

“I’m not gone. I’m right here,” I reassure her, holding her tightly.

She clings to me, weakened by the fever and shock that must be coursing through her.

"Don't leave me again. Don't go. I was so scared and heartbroken. I thought he killed you."

I walk outside, and Falkner is dragging Viktor out. He is a bloody mess. I would love to kill him right now, but I have plans for him. I can see the rage on Falkner's face and it mirrors my own.

In Russian, he says as gets into Viktor’s face, "That is my only child. Look at what you have done to her. You will die a slow, painful death. It's the least you deserve for what you have done to her."

Viktor tries to say something, but Falkner punches him in the jaw.

"Do not talk to me." He spits on him and looks at me.

I'VE GOT YOU.

Demetrius

I turn to Falkner and instruct him, "Please escort him to the plane and secure him in one of the cells. I'll take care of her wounds."

He nods. Falkner leads the way through the jungle, kicking Viktor the entire way.

"Kill everyone! No one gets out of here alive." I yell to my men.

They all nod and rush off.

I carry Luna through the compound, and past the fire that is consuming the buildings. I can hear the sound of gunfire as my men kill everyone inside.

"Demetrius."

"Yes, my angel?"

"You left. He took me."

"Shh, angel. I will never leave you again."

She nods and closes her eyes. I hold her tighter. And I never will. I will follow her for the rest of her life. I will ensure that no one ever controls her again.

As I embrace her, I feel my heart pounding in my chest. The weight of my promise to protect her feels heavy on my shoulders, but I know it is a burden I am willing to bear. I can feel the warmth of her body against mine, and I know that at this moment, she feels safe and loved. I kiss the top of her head and whisper softly in her ear,

“I’ve got you, always. Don't fall asleep on me yet, angel. Stay with me. Talk to me."

"I tried to escape."

"What did he do to you?"

"He shot me and then he beat me. I couldn't run. I tried, but he caught me. Then he locked me in that room."

"Oh, Luna."

She is the epitome of bravery. My Luna, my guardian angel, the beacon of hope in the midst of my darkness. She is the only one who truly matters to me; the center of my universe. The sound of her voice, the touch of her hand, the scent of her hair - they are all I need to feel complete.

“He watched one of his men rape me and then joined in.” Her words cut through me like a knife, leaving me gasping for air. I etch the memory of her pain into my mind, a haunting image that I cannot shake off.

“Fuck. Oh, god. Luna, I’m so sorry.” I press my lips to her temple, hoping to convey the depth of my remorse.

I hold her tighter, wishing that I could take away all her pain. The warmth of her body against mine is a comforting balm, reminding me of what truly matters in this world.

"Then he chained me to the wall by the collar."

I nod. "I know, baby. I'm going to keep you safe. I won't let anyone hurt you ever again."

She whimpers and shakes her head.

"He wouldn't stop. I begged him. He just laughed and did it, anyway. He said you would never come for me because he killed you." sobs wrack her body

"He will pay for what he did to you. Shhh I'm here. I'm here."

I can feel her body trembling in my arms as she continues to cry.

Her fists clench and unclench, and her breathing comes in short gasps. I stroke her hair and murmur comforting words, but I know that the memory of what happened to her will not fade easily. Her skin is cold and clammy, and I can feel her heart beating wildly against my chest. It breaks my heart to see her like this, but I am determined to be strong for her. I hold her close, hoping to provide some measure of comfort and security in the midst of her pain.

Once I kill Viktor, I will become the head of the Bratva and take my brother's place. It's not something I ever wanted to do. But it is something I need to do. There is no one else strong enough to run the Bratva. My other brothers are still working on other parts of their lives. Vlad will become my second in command as soon as he is done in Russia.

As I feel my angel's body relaxing against mine, I glance down and realize that she has fallen asleep. It's not hard to imagine how exhausted she must be, especially with the fever that has resulted from her infection. My only hope is that it hasn't turned septic yet. As we step onto the plane, I know that I'm going to hold her close all the way home.

I can't imagine being separated from her anytime soon, if ever. I've made sure that she's in the cabin with me, and she's sleeping soundly. She's been through so much that I decide to grab the first aid kit to see if I can help in any way. Vlad and Aleksandr follow us, and Vlad watches me struggle for a moment before offering to take the kit from me. However, I growl at him, unwilling to let anyone else take care of my angel.

"Demetrius, let me help. You just hold her. I swear I won't harm her." I know Vlad would never do anything to hurt her, but my instincts are still on high alert. He steps back and nods. "Sorry, man. Just trying to help."

"I know. Thank you. But ... I can't let you touch her. Before we leave, I need water so I can clean her."

Aleksandr nods. "I will get it for you, brother."

“Thanks. I’ll do my best to clean her up, but these wounds need stitches,” I say, gesturing to her shoulder and other deep cuts. As I examine her battered body, I notice an infection in her shoulder. “I have to check if the bullet is still in there.”

“Please, let me assist you,” Vlad offers.

I shake my head.

"Ok. At least let me get the stuff you need to fix her up."

I nod. "Thank you."

I know he is right, but I can't let him touch her. Not yet anyway. He walks away to get the things needed.

Luna starts to thrash around and cry out. "No!" she sobs. "No more. Please."

I hold her and whisper to her.

"Shh angel, you're safe. I have you. I'm here." I brush the hair from her face. "Shhh it's ok. Wake up, for me."

"Please."

"Shh Luna."

Her eyes open. She is crying and shaking. "Demetrius?"

"Yes, my angel. It's me. I have you. You're safe. He can't hurt you anymore."

"Oh god. I'm dreaming. Please tell me I'm not dreaming."

"You're not dreaming, angel."

As she gazes into my eyes with her stunning gaze, tears trickle down her face, shattering my heart.

"How is this real? Am I really here? Are you really here?"

"I'm here, angel."

"You were gone. He wouldn't let me go."

"Shh. You're safe."

She whimpers and looks around the plane.

"You're on my plane. I have to patch you up, my love. Your wounds are bad."

She nods and her eyes close once more.

"Can I help her?" Vlad asks.

I growl and shake my head. "I will do it. I have to do it."

I hold her in my arms and as I finish cleaning her wounds; I look at the places she needs stitches.

He shakes his head. "I will never hurt her brother. She will be my sister. I swear I will do everything in my power to help her. Always."

I nod in agreement, allowing him to tend to the wounds that I couldn't handle. The gashes were deep, and I could see where he had to remove a significant portion of the flesh to ensure that the stitching would be clean and damage-free. I observe his every move, every gentle touch, as he takes his time and works with caution. After completing the stitches as best he could, he carefully wraps the wounds.

"We should take her back home for her recovery. I'll get in touch with Doc and ask him to meet us there with all the necessary items. In case she wakes up, please give her this to keep her calm." He hands me a sedative and expresses his concern.

"I want her to be okay, and I know she'll need rest. How can I assist her after this?" I turn to my younger brother with a heavy heart. "I rescued her from a human trafficking ring, only for Viktor to do this to her. What can I do now?" A tear rolls down my cheek, and I can sense the weight of the situation.

He wipes my tear away with his thumb and places his hand on

my shoulder. "I know, brother. We will all do what we can for her. Time and someone to speak to will be the best."

Aleksandr comes back with the water in a large bucket. He takes hold of his shirt and rips the bottom hem off of it.

"To clean her with," Aleksandr says, handing me the water and soap.

I nod "Thank you, brother."

Luna is currently experiencing bouts of sleep, but her fever has left her feeling disoriented and groggy.

"This might sting."

"Ok." she whispers.

I slowly and carefully wipe the blood from her skin. The blood clings to her flesh like a veil, the maroon dried blood turning bright red as it streams down her skin. There is so much red. It is all over her and all over me. I don't care if it's on my clothes, but I need to remove it from her. I clean the cloth often as I remove the blood in soft strokes. I finish cleaning her face and rinse the rag.

I squeeze the water out of it and slowly wipe the blood off of her body. Taking my time and being as gentle as possible. She is trembling as I gently clean her. Her skin is hot to the touch. When I am done cleaning her body. I make sure to clean in between her legs the best I can. I lay her down on the seat so that I can dry her off. Aleksandr takes the rag from me and sits down across from me.

"I'm sorry this happened to her brother." I look at him. I see the sadness in his eyes.

I am handed a blanket to cover her with as the men begin to return to the cargo plane. Upon spotting me, they nod and hush, leaving ample room for me.

"I am too," I whisper. "But not as much as I am for not being there when she needed me. If I had known, I would have never left her side."

He shakes his head. "Don't think that way. There is no way you could have known. You were trying to get justice for her. You went after a person who hurt her. But we are all here now and we will make sure she is ok. She has a family to support her."

I nod.

"At least let me help with her shoulder. You will need to lean her up a bit so I can see if the bullet came out the back."

"Alright."

I carefully move her so he can look at her back. "The bullet didn't come out. There is no exit wound."

I nod. "We will have to dig it out. Fuck."

"I'm not the best at that, but I can try."

"No, it has to be a doctor. I can't take a chance with her""

"We can have him come to the house. That way, she doesn't have to go anywhere. I know she will be safer there."

After a few minutes of silence, he looks at me and I see the question in his eyes.

"Are you going to kill him and take over as head of the family?" He asks me as he carefully cleans her shoulder. Re-bandages it due to puss.

"Yes. It's not something I wanted. It's not even something I'm proud of. But it needs to be done and the only one capable of doing it is me. I am next in line. He will pay for what he has done and I will use it as a warning to anyone else who thinks they are man enough to touch what's mine."

He nods. "I will help you in any way that I can. It is our responsibility."

I look at him and smile. "Thank you, brother." He pats me on the shoulder.

"Anytime. Thats all I can do for now." He nods and walks away to help Vlad get everything sorted for take off.

He knows I won't be leaving her. I wrap her in the blanket and hold her to my chest while I stare down at her beautiful face.

"I have you, my angel. I'm never letting you out of my sight ever again. That's a promise." I say to her, stroking her hair.

She opens her eyes and looks at me.

"My beautiful angel. I love you so much."

"I love you too."

I smile. "You should try to sleep. It will help you heal."

"I can't sleep. Not yet."

I kiss her forehead. "Vlad. My other brother gave me this for you to take. It's a sedative to help you stay calm and here is something for the fever. You need rest."

She nods and takes the pills. She cuddles closer to me and rests her head on my chest.

"I was so scared you were dead. He kept telling me over and over that he had killed you. It crushed me."

"I'm alive. I'm here and I will always be here. If something ever happens and I die. I will still be here. Haunting you. I love you, my beautiful angel. You are mine, and I will never leave you again. You aren't ever leaving my side again. You will be my wife. You are my everything. Nothing else matters."

She smiles and her eyes close. "I will never leave you either. I'm so happy to know you are here."

"Careful how you move. We had to stitch the deeper wounds. I cleaned you off with water and a rag. But your shoulder is bad."

She nods.

"Lay back. Relax and sleep. You need it. I will be right here holding you. I'm not leaving you."

I can sense the tears burning my eyes as I think about my beloved angel, my gorgeous girl. I plan to convene a meeting and make an example of Viktor as I inflict pain on him for his actions. I will use him to send a message to anyone who even considers causing harm to my angel. He will suffer a slow and agonizing death.

"What did you do with Viktor?"

"He is chained in a cell. I will make an example out of him. You won't have to watch, my love. But it will happen and it will be painful."

She nods. "I want to see it. I don't think I can move on until I do. What of... the others that were there?"

"I had them all killed. No one walked out of there alive but Viktor. Sleep now. We can discuss this later."

Her eyes flutter shut. I sit here looking out the window as the plane takes off.

I WANT TO WATCH HIM SUFFER

Luna

Upon waking up, I am immediately alert, but the softness of my surroundings quickly calms me. Slowly opening my eyes, I realize that I am back home - it wasn't just a dream. As I take a look around, I notice Demetrius sitting beside me, holding my hand while his attention is fixed on the TV.

"Demetrius," I whisper in a raspy voice.

He turns and looks at me. "Yes, my angel."

I can't help the tears that spring to my eyes. It wasn't a dream. He is alive. He is here. He is next to me.

"It wasn't a dream."

He smiles and brushes the hair from my face.

"No, it's not a dream. You are safe. He will never touch you again."

"I thought you were dead. You were gone. They told me you were dead."

He pulls me into his arms and I cling to him. "Shhh, baby. I know. But I'm here. You are safe now. They won't be coming for you again. You are safe." I can't stop the sobs. He climbs into the bed with me and carefully holds me against his chest.

"I thought you were dead. I had nothing to live for." I say, sobs wracking my body.

"Shhh. I'm not dead. I am here. You have nothing to fear. I won't leave you again."

"What happened? When I woke that morning, you were gone."

He sighs and tightens his hold on me. I can see the regret in his eyes.

"Viktor called me to come into his office. After I left, I got a call from one of my men saying they had found another one of the men who hurt you. When I got there, I knew instantly that it was a setup. I should have left, then I knew what it was. Instead, I killed them all and drove home as fast as I could get here. But I was too late. Viktor already had you."

"What about Anton? I saw him on the floor."

"He is alive. But there are a few things we need to speak about. One of them being that your biological father helped us find you."

The sudden jolt caused me to move faster than my stitches could handle, and I let out a cry of agony. He responded with a growl.

"Don't do that."

"I don't have any parents. I'm an orphan."

"You have one. He is still here if you would like to meet him."

"Can you please let me see him? I need to know."

He kisses the top of my head. "Of course."

"I have a father? Where the hell has he been?" I muttered to myself. My life had been spent in the foster care system, and it was nothing short of a living hell. The other children were cruel and malicious, and it was difficult for me to believe that my father had simply allowed me to suffer. Suddenly, he reached for his phone and pressed the call button.

"She is awake. Do you want to come here?" He listens for a second. "Alright, we will be waiting."

"Where is he?"

"In the library. He will be here in a moment."

"Ok. Why is he here?"

"He came to me."

"When?"

"Right after we found out you were gone. I was in my office and he walked in."

"Why would he abandon me and put me into foster care?"

"That's for him to share, angel. But keep in mind, he helped me find you."

As I hear the sound of the locks clicking on the new door, I nod in acknowledgement. Suddenly, a tall, older man enters the room and catches my attention. Despite his age, he's quite handsome with his salt and pepper hair. I can't help but wonder if he's Russian. Looking over at Demetrius, I realize that I bear a striking resemblance to the man.

"Luna. This is Falkner, your biological father."

He gazes at Demetrius and then shifts his focus to me.

"May I sit?" He says in a thick accent.

"Yes."

"Luna, I am so happy to see you. I know you must have a lot of questions. And I promise to answer them. I would like to get to know you if that is ok."

"Where the fuck have you been?"

My face twisted in anger as the words spilled out of my mouth. My fists clenched and my jaw tightened as I glared at the person in front of me. Despite my initial joy at seeing them, the sudden outburst had left me feeling frustrated and betrayed. I took a deep breath, trying to calm myself down before speaking again.

"I am sorry for what happened to you. I didn't know until after he already had taken you."

"That's not what I mean," I whisper

"I'm sorry Luna. Your mother died in childbirth. I am.. was a hitman for the Bratva and there was no way I could keep you safe. So I left you at the hospital. I kept tabs on you and came here immediately when I found out you had moved to the heart of Bratva's territory."

"So why did you never come to find me?"

"I was a coward. I didn't know what kind of life you had and didn't want to mess anything up. But when you got taken, I came immediately. I came to find Demetrius and offer my assistance. I called in every favor I had left to find you."

"But why are you here?"

"Because you are my daughter. I will not walk out of your life again. You can have the time you need. But I will be close by. I have a room in the house. If it is ok with you."

My heart feels heavy with a mixture of emotions - grief, anger, confusion, and relief. My hands are shaking, and tears are rolling down my cheeks. I can't believe that the man in front of me is my father, and a hitman for the Bratva at that. My mind is racing with questions, but my body feels numb. My father reaches out to me, but I flinch away from his touch. I need time to process everything he has just told me. I nod slowly, indicating that he can stay in the house, but I don't say anything. I need to be alone, to let everything sink in. I look at Demetrius.

"I would never keep you from a parent, angel."

"I have a father?" I ask looking at Falkner.

"Yes," he answers in a voice that now sounds thick with emotion

"I would like that. But I ... I need some time."

"Anything you need. I am going to get out of here and leave you two to talk. I will be right downstairs. You need to rest, daughter."

"Thank you, I will ... Dad." He stops and smiles at me and I smile back. "Demetrius, are you going to stay?"

"Of course, my angel. I'm never leaving your side ever again."

My father. It hits me like a ton of bricks - I actually have a dad.

As he walks out of the room and closes the door behind him, I hear the distinct sound of the lock clicking into place. It's funny how that noise now brings me a sense of comfort. I glance over at Demetrius, trying not to let my worries consume me, but I can't help the nagging feeling in the back of my mind.

"What's going to happen to Viktor?"

Demetrius clears his throat. "I am going to make an example of him for everyone to see."

"I want to be there. I have to watch."

He sighs and nods. "I wasn't sure you would want to."

"I have to. He watched while his men brutalized my body and got off on it. While telling me you were dead. I have to see him suffer and die for what he has done to me. No one will ever hurt me like that again. I want to watch him die. It's the only way I will ever feel safe."

"Of course, my love. But I will warn you it will be very brutal. Everyone needs to know you don't touch what is mine and get away with it. But it can wait until you are well enough to stand strong."

"Thank you."

"You need to rest now, my sweet angel. I won't leave you. I will be here when you wake."

"I will. I need to ask something else of you."

"Anything, name it."

"I can't sleep alone. Will you lay in the bed with me? I know it's stupid but..."

"Shh, not stupid. Never."

"But?"

"Not another word. Of course, I will lay in the bed with you. I am never letting you out of my sight again if I can help it."

He pulls me carefully into his arms, wrapping his massive body around my smaller one protectively. I snuggle against his chest and close my eyes.

As I lay there with Demetrius holding me, I can feel my heart rate slowing down and my muscles relaxing. The tension that had been building up in my body for days starts to melt away. My breathing becomes deeper and more even, and I can feel myself drifting off into a peaceful sleep.

It's amazing how much our emotions can affect us physically. When we feel safe and secure, our bodies respond by relaxing and releasing tension. On the other hand, when we're stressed or anxious, our bodies can become tense and tight, making it difficult to relax and sleep.

But with Demetrius by my side, I feel like I can face anything. His powerful arms around me make me feel protected and cared for, and I know that I can trust him to keep me safe. As I drift off to sleep, I know that I will be ok, as long as he is beside me.

My Beautiful Angel. My Precious Gift.

Demetrius

A week later

I've got her back and she's safe now. However, I keep having

nightmares about my brother raping her, and no matter what I do, I can't seem to save her. Every time I sleep, I witness it all over again. Sometimes, I dream of her lifeless body lying in a pool of her own blood. But once I wake up, she's right there in my arms, unharmed. It's been a week since the incident, and she's almost fully recovered from the physical injuries. Although her ribs are still tender, most of the bruises and lacerations have disappeared. But what concerns me the most is the emotional trauma she's experiencing. Every night, she has nightmares that leave her crying out for my help. All I can do is wake her up and hold her until she feels better.

However, I have noticed that the emotional trauma is taking a toll on her physically as well. She has lost her appetite and has trouble sleeping through the night. Her eyes are constantly puffy and red from crying, and her normally vibrant personality has become subdued and withdrawn. I worry about her mental and emotional well-being and wonder how long it will take for her to fully recover from this traumatic experience. I know that it will take time, patience, and a lot of love and support to help her heal, but I am determined to be there for her every step of the way.

I am still holding Viktor in the basement of my safe house. I have been working out a plan for his punishment. Arranging a place to torture him publicly. I will put him up on an X with his arms and legs strapped to it. I will do the Blood Eagle the same way the Vikings did it. For all to see. Then once he is dead, I will place what is left of him so everyone in the city can see what happens when you touch my angel. Let it serve as a warning to them all.

Luna is lying against my chest. I can't stop the rage I feel from when I saw her covered in blood and cuts. My brothers and I have been trying to keep her busy with whatever we can think of. Vlad and Aleksandr will both have to leave soon. To wrap up everything they were doing so that they can return home.

Now that my angel is recovering well, it's time to finalize the plans and proceed with his punishment. This will establish my position as the Pakhan and serve as a warning to everyone not to mess with what's mine. Once this is done, I can ask her to be my wife. I've given her ample time to recuperate, but I can't seem to get enough of her. My body instinctively knows that she belongs to me and I'll protect her at all costs. We haven't been intimate since she was taken, and although she sleeps next to me in the nude, I can't touch her. She needs more time, and it's driving me crazy. My body is constantly on edge, and I feel like I need to prove to myself and her that she's still mine. The urge to claim her is overwhelming. But her well being means more than anything else and I will never push her into anything she isn't ready for.

We are lying in our bed, and I am wrapped around her and she is cuddled into my chest. My cock is hard as a rock and it has been. She has been sleeping peacefully but I can't take it. I slowly slide out of bed. I walk into the bathroom and grab the lube. I walk back into the bedroom. Luna is still sleeping peacefully. Her hair is a mess. Her beautiful dark eyes are closed. Her long lashes resting against her cheeks. Her full breasts are rising and falling with each breath she takes. Her body is healing. It is just smooth skin.

I walk around the bed and stand over her. I can see the outline of her pussy. It's beautiful, and it is mine. I open the lube and pour a little on my finger. I put it on my cock and wrap my hand around it as I watch her sleep. I slide my hand up and down the length of my cock as I watch her.

She is perfect. This woman is mine. The one woman who will give me children. She has a beautiful body and an even more beautiful heart. Her soft skin is smooth. Her long, luscious hair flows over the pillow. I watch the rise and fall of her breasts as I stroke myself. She is so beautiful and I need her so badly. But she needs space to heal. I have to take care of her first. Always. I stroke myself faster as I imagine her mouth wrapped around my cock. Her beautiful eyes staring up at me with want. I can feel the pressure building. I am so close to coming. I pump faster, imagining pulling her nipple into my mouth.

I'm yearning for her so much that I can feel my testicles retracting. My semen is slowly moving up my shaft, and I can sense its warmth as it spreads over my hand and onto her chest. She lets out a soft whimper while sleeping. I adore how she looks with my seed on her. I massage it into her skin to make her smell like me. She's still asleep, so I lie back down next to her and embrace her tightly against my chest. Mine.

I have a responsibility to care for her; it's the only thing I can do. The anger inside me is overwhelming for what he did to her. He has violated my angel and will pay the price for it, slowly and painfully.

When she wakes up, we can talk and I will explain everything to her. She is mine, my angel, my woman. She has been through so much, and I know she needs time to heal, but I can't wait. I need her desperately; it's like a beast inside me that always craves more. When I hold her in my arms and feel her soft skin on mine, I want her. I need her.

My heart races as I hold her close, the adrenaline pumping through my veins. My hands shake with the intensity of my emotions, and I struggle to keep them steady as I stroke her hair. My breathing is shallow and rapid, and I can feel the heat rising in my body, a physical manifestation of my desire for her.

But I must control myself. I cannot let my emotions get the best of me, not when she is still recovering. I take a deep breath and try to calm myself, focusing on the rise and fall of her chest against mine. She is my priority now, and I will do anything to protect her, even if it means suppressing my own desires.

I gently kiss her forehead, feeling the softness of her skin against my lips. She stirs slightly, and I pull back, not wanting to wake her. I watch her sleep for a few moments, marveling at her strength and resilience. She has been through so much, but she still manages to shine like a beacon of hope in the darkness.

I know I cannot fix everything for her, but I will be there for her every step of the way. I will hold her hand and guide her through the darkness, and together, we will emerge into the light.

She is safe, and she is here with me. I won't let anyone else hurt her. No one will ever touch her again. No one will ever hurt her again. No one will ever take her from me again if they try. It will be worse. I will burn them alive. I will kill anyone and everything that ever meant anything to them. I am not a good man. But I am the man who will do anything for her. Anything to keep her safe. To keep her in my life.

My beautiful angel. My precious gift.

Touch Me

Luna

A week and a half later

Demetrius is driving me insane. He won't leave my side. I can't take much more of this. He is constantly watching me. He won't touch me and it's driving me crazy. Is it because his brother raped me? I wouldn't think so but it's been close to a week and a half and he hasn't so much as kissed me. Sure we sleep in the same bed and he always holds me. But he doesn't kiss me or touch me. I know he wants to. He has a hard on all the time. But he won't let it happen. He won't let his body have what it wants.

"Luna. You need to eat."

I look up at him on the other side of the kitchen as he takes a plate out of the refrigerator. I shake my head at him. I am not interested in food. What I really want is him.

"Do I need to hand feed you again my angel?"

I scoff. What I want to say is 'Oh you'll touch me now?' But I don't. I don't want to be snippy with him even if I feel rejected.

"Why won't you touch me? Is it because of what happened? Don't you want me anymore?"

I can feel the tears trying to fall. I'm not going to let them. I've done enough crying to last a lifetime.

He turns and looks at me. "Of course I do. Why would you think that?"

I can see the surprised look on his face. It kinda makes me feel crazy. Like I'm missing something.

"I don't know. You are always watching me. You haven't touched me or kissed me since you rescued me. You are always in bed with me but you never touch me more than to hold me. Even then you hold me like I am fragile. Why? You aren't that kind of man."

He walks over to the table and places the plate down in front of me.

"You need to eat and you are not fragile."

"Why won't you touch me? Did what happened with your brother bother you that much? Am I not your type of woman? Should I leave?"

I can't help the tears that fall down my cheeks. I need him so much my chest hurts. Just him always him. His touch, his voice. It is him who I think about every single day. The smell of his skin. The way his voice sends shivers through my body. It's him. Only him. This rejection hurts.

"No, my angel. You are the only type of woman for me. You are the only woman for me. My love for you is not something that is based on your body. I always want you I always need you. But I don't want to push you. I know you need to heal."

"It's been a week and a half. It's been too long." I wipe the tears from my eyes.

"What do you mean?"

"I need you. I need you more than you realize. I need to feel you in my body. Please make love to me Demetrius."

He walks toward me and gathers me in his arms.

"Luna."

He leans down and kisses my lips softly. My heart is racing. It's like I can feel him everywhere. His hands are on my face.

"Are you sure this is what you want? The last thing I want is for you to feel you have to do this."

I nod.

"I have needed you so much. My body needs you so badly. I have been dreaming of your hands touching my skin. Of you kissing me. Please. Demetrius, I need you to make love to me. I thought I had lost you. You don't understand the way that broke me."

He kisses me again. His lips are so soft and tender. He pulls back and looks into my eyes.

"My angel. I never meant to make you feel like I didn't want you. I wanted to give you time to heal."

"Demetrius please touch me."

He stands up and lifts me up into his arms. He walks into the master bedroom and lays me on the bed. He slowly undresses himself. My eyes are glued to his body. He is gorgeous. I watch as he climbs up on the bed and lays over me. I look up into his eyes.

"I love you, Demetrius. Please."

He kisses me and slides his tongue into my mouth. The kiss is slow and sensual. He kisses me for a long time. His lips are soft and full. He tastes like coffee and something sweet. He pulls back and looks at me.

"I love you too." He kisses me again.

He slowly and softly kisses my jaw and down my neck. He slowly kisses his way down to my nipples. He sucks one into his mouth and then the other. My nipples are already hard and sensitive.

"Oh, Demetrius."

His teeth gently tug at my nipple. He kisses his way down my stomach and spreads my thighs. I can feel myself getting wetter and wetter. He kisses my hip bone. Then down over my mound. His hands are holding my thighs apart.

"Look at me."

I do. I am watching him. His eyes are staring into mine.

"I love you. Nothing will ever change that. Do you understand me?"

I nod.

"You are the only woman I have ever wanted. The only one I will ever want."

I nod again.

"Words angel I need words."

"Yes. I understand."

"No one will ever take you from me. Not even in death will you be taken from me."

"I never want to leave you."

He kisses my mound and the inside of my thighs. He uses his tongue and laps at the wetness pooled between my legs.

"Demetrius." I gasp

I can't help but to move my hips. I lift them up and let out a moan as his tongue touches me. More I need more.

"Fuck. Yes. Please."

His tongue strokes me up and down. His lips are sucking and pulling at my clit.

"Oh fuck. Oh fuck. I'm gonna come." I moan as I lift my hips.

"That's it, my angel. Let it go. Come for me."

He sucks my clit into his mouth. It's too much. Way too much. I feel it. My whole body is shaking. It's like a volcano inside me. His tongue is circling my clit.

"Demetrius. Oh God yes."

He sucks me hard. My orgasm hits me. Hard. My body is shaking and he doesn't stop. He is sucking on my clit. Oh my God. He keeps going.

"I'm coming. Oh god, I'm coming."

I can't stop the orgasm. It just keeps going. My pussy is spasming around his tongue. My juices gush out of me onto his face coating us both in my orgasm. His fingers are pushing inside me. My juices running out of me.

"Yes. Oh Fuck."

I am panting. He is still sucking my clit. He isn't stopping. The pressure buildings again. It's so quick that it shocks me. My head is thrown back. My body is on fire. My back is lifted from the bed as I arch up.

"Oh. Oh. Oh."

I can feel the heat building inside of me. It feels so good. Then he does it. His tongue slides up and presses against my asshole.

"What are you doing? Oh god. That feels so good. I can feel it. It's so good. So fucking good."

He pushes his tongue into my ass. My body is moving against his.

"Oh, Demetrius. I'm coming again."

He slides his fingers from my pussy. He puts them in his mouth.

"Mmmm."

"You taste so sweet, my angel."

He sucks his fingers.

It's Time

Demetrius

My body is on fire. Her pussy is so wet. She tastes like heaven. It's all I can do not to slide my cock into her right now. I want her so bad. I'm so hard it hurts.

"Are you ready for me my angel?"

"Yes. Yes. Oh god yes. I need you, Demetrius. I need you."

I kiss up her body. I slide into her warm pussy. She is so fucking wet. I push in slowly and easily.

"Fuck. You feel so good, baby. So fucking good."

She moans. Her pussy is squeezing me. "Demetrius. You feel so good. Please fuck me."

I take her mouth with mine. I need her. I have to have her. I pull out and thrust back into her. She moans into my mouth. I start to move in and out of her. I can feel the heat inside me growing.

"Demetrius."

"Oh, god baby. Your pussy feels so fucking good. I am so fucking close."

"Yes. Fuck me, Demetrius. I want to feel you come."

I pull back and look at her. "I need you to come first, my love."

Her pussy feels like my dick is wrapped in heaven. It's warm and wet. Her hands are wrapped around my neck. Her eyes are staring into mine. I pull out and push back in.

"Yes. Demetrius. That's it. Keep fucking me. Don't stop. Please."

"Your pussy is so fucking tight. I love the way you feel around my cock. Come for me, baby. Let me feel your sweet pussy come."

I am staring into her eyes. I can feel the pressure building. The tingling sensation starts at my tailbone and works its way to my balls. Fuck she is home. Where ever she is, is home. Fuck. She is moaning he mouth open in a small O. So beautiful. I need to see her come. I love the look on her face. It's so beautiful. Like the most beautiful piece of art in the world.

"Fuck. Oh fuck."

I can feel my balls tighten as he walls start to ripple.

"I'm coming. Oh god, Demetrius."

I can't stop it. I push all the way inside of her and explode.

"Fuuuuucckkk."

She is squeezing my dick. I continue to pump in and out of her prolonging both of our orgasms.

"Demetrius. I love you."

She says as I kiss her. "I love you too my angel. I love you too. You are mine, my love."

"Always yours. You own me. I belong to you."

I kiss her. "You do. You are mine. Forever."

"Forever." She whispers.

We lay there and hold each other. This is the best feeling. I feel her body relax as she starts to drift off to sleep. I kiss her forehead.

"I will protect you. I will never let anyone touch you ever again."

"I love you, Demetrius. You are my everything."

"As you are mine."

Luna

It's been two weeks now and Viktor is being held captive. But today is the day he will make an example out of him. I want to be there. It is not something that will be easy for me to see. But I know it is what is needed. The underworld of this city will see him die and see what happens when they touch what belongs to Demetrius and I will get my justice for what he did to me.

"Are you ready to go?"

I nod and sit up. It has been a few days since he last made love to me. I have healed and I feel whole. I just need him. My heart had a missing piece that clicked back into place when we made love. He held me for a long time. It was nice. I felt safe and warm. I have been in love with him since I met him. And now that I am in his arms again and back where I belong I never want to let him go.

"Are you ready for this?" He asks me.

"I am. But I am also nervous."

"I will be there to keep you safe."

"I know. But this will be the first time I will be facing him since ...."

He sighs. "I know. But you will never be in any danger. Not while I am here."

He kisses me.

"Demetrius. Please. Make love to me before we go."

He lifts me up into his arms. "That is something that will never be a problem. You are mine and you know it."

I kiss him and wrap my arms around his neck. "I love you so much."

I need this distraction. I'm not sure how I will handle this but I know that I need it in order to fully move on.

"I love you too my angel. You are my everything."

He lays me down on the bed and kisses me. His hands are stroking my body. He is being so gentle. So loving.

"I will never hurt you. Never."

"I know."

He kisses my neck. His soft lips are soft against my skin.

"You are the most beautiful woman in the world. You are everything I want and need in this world."

I wrap my arms around his neck. "I love you. Make love to me."

"Anything for you. Your wish is my command."

He walks toward me and removes his clothes. He crawls onto the bed where I have already perched myself.

"Open your legs for me, angel."

I do as he tells me. He stares at me. His eyes are dark. His hair is mussed. His lips are plump and swollen from our kissing. He looks so sexy.

"Spread your legs more. I want to see all of you."

I let my knees fall to the bed.

"Fuck you are the most beautiful sight I have ever seen."

He strokes his cock. He is already hard and he isn't even inside me yet.

"Touch yourself. I want to see you play with yourself."

My hand drifts slowly down my body to my clit. I slide two fingers into my wet center.

"Oh."

He moans. "Play with your clit." he says in a husky voice

I rub it and slide my fingers back and forth. I love it when he watches me.

"Oh. It feels good." I moan

He pushes into me. I look up at him.

"Let's make sure it feels really good."

He strokes into me.

"Oh, Daddy. Oh my god."

"I love it when you call me that."

He slams into me.

"Oh."

He pulls out and thrusts back in.

"Oh, Daddy. It's so good."

"You like that baby?"

"Oh yeah."

"You like it when daddy fucks you like a whore."

"Yes. Fuck me, Daddy. Oh god, that's good."

I am moaning and squirming. I can feel the orgasm building.

"You're going to make me come."

"I want to see it, baby. I want to watch you come on my cock."

"Oh. Oh. Oh."

I am pushing my hips up against him.

"That's it, baby. Come for Daddy."

I can't hold it back. The orgasm hits me like a freight train.

"Oh, Daddy. Oh yes. Oh yes."

My body is spasming around his dick. I can feel every inch of his cock as he thrusts in and out of me.

"Fuck. Yes. Take my come baby."

He starts to thrust faster.

"I'm going to fill your pussy with my come baby. I'm going to fill you so full. You are mine."

"Oh. Yes. Give it to me. Oh god. Oh."

He stills. I can feel his cock pulse as his come shoots into me. The feeling is divine.

"Fuck. You are so tight, baby. You feel so good taking Daddy's cock." I wrap my legs around his waist. He is still buried inside of me. He lays on top of me and kisses me. "I love you so much."

"I love you too."

He smiles at me "Now I guess we should get redressed we have somewhere to be. Today is the day you get justice."

D Day

Demetrius

Today is the day of Viktor's execution. I would love to say I have been looking forward to it. But the facts are he is still my brother, even after all the horrible things he has done. I will take pleasure in his pain only because of what he did to my angel. But that doesn't make it any easier. It will also be when I officially step into the role of Pakhan. The underworld will know I am the leader.

I have another announcement to make, one that is of greater significance. Today, I will be proposing to Luna, asking her to be my wife. However, I won't be doing it immediately after I have dealt with Viktor. I have a meticulously planned schedule for later tonight. Luna will have to accompany me to several meetings throughout the day, which may raise a few eyebrows. Regardless, I won't allow her to leave my sight again.

I need her by my side. I want her by my side always. They will have to get over it. She will be involved in everything I do. There will be no secrets between us. It will be the one thing that everyone in this city will know. Luna is the woman who I love and want to be by my side. We will rule the Bratva together.

At this moment, my focus needs to be on the task at hand. Anton pulls up the car and opens my door. I step out first, then offer my hand to assist my beloved from the vehicle. I sense her unease, and I don't blame her. She is about to confront the man who snatched her from our residence.

"Are you sure you want to see this?"

She nods and takes my hand. "Yes. I need to see him suffer for what he did."

"You know I will be here by your side every step of the way."

She nods.

"If you see anyone who took part in the ring, you were in. I want you to point them out to Anton, and we will take care of it. Understand?"

"Yes. But."

"No buts. They need to pay for what they did. So that you can rest easier. Trust me."

"I know. I trust you. I love you."

"I love you too."

Hand in hand, we enter the building and I instantly notice the newly built stage, covered in plastic. I can't help but smirk, knowing that cleanup will be a breeze. In the center of the stage stands a giant wooden X, with my tools resting on a small table nearby. My heart races with anticipation, but Luna remains silent, taking it all in.

"Where is he?"

"He's in the back room."

Anton takes us to a long hallway. I open the door and see Viktor on the floor, chained and on his knees. His arms are tied behind his back and his mouth is gagged. He looks scared, and rightfully so. He's in for a lot of embarrassment and pain soon.

"What the fuck?" He tries to scream, but the gag muffles it.

"Shut the fuck up," Anton says as he removes the gag.

"You fucking bastard. Let me the fuck go."

"Oh, fuck no. You're about to pay for what you did to my angel."

"I am still your Pakhan. You will obey me."

"You are nothing to me. Don't fool yourself Viktor."

I can feel the slight tremble in Luna's hand. I pull her tighter against my side.

"I'm sorry. This is what it has come to. But I will avenge you in the most brutal way possible. And that is a promise." I squeeze her for reassurance, lending her my strength.

Viktor stares at her.

"You still want her even after so many men besides you have had her? She is nothing but a whore." Viktor sneers.

"Shut the fuck up." I kick him in his face. "You are about to meet your fate. I will make it worse if you keep it up." I growl at him.

"I will never bow to a weak man such as you. You are no man. You are a child. A weak child. You let a woman make your decisions for you."

I turn and look at Luna. I grab her face and kiss her on the mouth hard.

"Anton, take her out and get her situated, please."

He agrees with a nod and leads Luna by her elbow. Three additional men trail behind them as they exit the room. I stride towards Viktor, confronting him directly.

"That will be the last thing you say about her. She is mine. You knew that when you took her. You also knew the repercussions that would happen to you if you touched her. I warned you. I tried, but you wouldn't listen. You saw what happened to Vinny. Did you admire my work of art so much that you wanted to join him?"

He spits at me. "Fuck you."

I smile. "I am the one who will be fucking her. I am the one she cries out for. I am the one who is Pakhan. Face it, brother, I warned you. You should have known better."

I acknowledge two of the men who remained in the room by nodding my head. They approach and lift Victor from his kneeling stance. We exit the room and are joined by four additional men who assist in fastening him to the X, with his back turned to the audience. I turn to face the group.

"Thank you for coming to my show today. I am about to make an example out of the man who attacked one of ours. Pakhan or not, there are always consequences. I am sure that everyone knows that touching what belongs to another man is one of the biggest crimes you can commit. I am making an example out of Viktor to show everyone that no one is safe. That is the Bratva way. We take care of our own. So everyone knows you don't touch what belongs to us. Most of all, NEVER touch what belongs to me. This is everyone's only warning."

I look out and see Salvatore and some heads of the Italian Mafia. The Don nods at me I nod back. I scan the crowd and see that even Gabriel from the cartel has shown up. Good, they will all know firsthand. I know this will broadcast that I am the one who did the blood eagle on Vinny, but I couldn't care less. This will be my calling card for anyone who dares to think about crossing me. Especially if that means touching my angel.

"What the fuck is this? Are you seriously going to make a fucking example out of me? You fucking asshole. I am your brother."

"And you are the man who took what is mine and touched her. You knew that when you did it."

In a show of support, Vlad and Aleksandr sit on either side of Luna. I nod at them both and they nod back.

"You have brought this on yourself. You raped my angel after removing her from my home and killing your fellow Bratva brothers. But first. Part of your punishment is that I am going to show you how that feels." I walk up to him and whisper in his ear, "Ever been fucked in your ass, brother?"

His eyes widened, and he turned his head to look at me. "You wouldn't."

"Oh, I would." I pick up one of the knives from the steel tray.

I cut his clothes from his body, leaving him completely exposed to the crowd. They all go completely quiet when I pick up the dildo that is the size of my arm.

"This will hurt, brother. But don't bother screaming because I don't give a fuck. The same as you didn't when you violated my angel. For that, you will die a slow and painful death."

"Please don't. Please don't," he begs.

"Did you care when my angel said that to you? No, you didn't. You told her instead that you had killed me. Now let's see what kind of a man you really are."

I shove the dildo into his ass without lube. He screams like a girl. It takes all of my strength not to laugh. I start to move it back and forth slowly.

"Fuuuuccckkk. Pleeaaassssseee. Stop."

"You are begging me already? You aren't even going to last the first minute. Good."

I shove the dildo in, moving it harder and faster.

"Ow. Ow. Ow. Ow." he screams out in pain.

I push the dildo in as hard as I can, bottoming it out inside of him.

"Ahhhh. Oh, God."

"Do you think that is the worst I have to offer? Do you think I am going to be gentle with you? Nope. I am going to fuck you with this massive dildo until you are raw. I am going to make you scream until your throat is sore. Want to know the best part?"

"Please. I am begging you. Stop. Stop. It hurts so fucking bad."

"Your body will come even if you don't want it to. Does that mean you are enjoying it?"

I move the dildo smoothly in and out of his ass.

"Fuuuuuuckkkk. Fuck."

"Do you feel that? Your cock is starting to get hard. You are enjoying this. The pain is mixed with pleasure and that is what the brain will want more of. How do you feel, brother? Does it hurt so good? It can't be that awful. I mean, you are obviously enjoying it. Even your cock is hard. You want this, don't you?"

"No, no, no, I don't want this. Oh god. It hurts. So fucking bad."

"You think my angel enjoyed the pain? Do you think she wanted to be violated? No, she did not. Did you stop when she asked? How about when she cried and screamed? You wouldn't listen to her, no matter how much she begged. And I am going to make sure you never touch her again."

Some might think I am taking this too far. But I said I was going to make an example of him. The first way I am going to do that is by proving that even if you don't want something, the body will still respond. Smoothly fucking his ass with the dildo, I pull it out and hit his gspot over and over, causing him to moan out in pleasure even though it hurts.

"Fuuuuckk. Fuck. Oh fuck. Stop. Please." he moans.

I start to rub his prostate with the tip of the dildo. I push it up and hit his gspot hard.

"Oh god. Oh, God."

"Are you going to come?"

"No. No. It feels good. Oh, fuck, it feels good."

I keep going and when he is close to coming; I ram the enormous dildo into his ass, causing him to scream as he comes all over the stage.

"No. No. No. Please. Don't. No more."

"Look at you. Look at your body responding. I knew it would." I stop moving the dildo. "You must have enjoyed that, Viktor. Look at your come all over the stage. Tsk, tsk."

"No. No. Please no more."

I shove the dildo in as deep as it will go and he screams.

"What a weak man."

I remove the dildo. The crowd is utterly silent. I'm not sure if it's a stunned silence or an I am a crazy lunatic silence. Either way, I don't care as long as they learn this one valuable lesson. Don't fuck with what's mine and don't even fucking think about touching her.

"This is just the beginning. I have more planned for you."

I take the sharpest knife I have here and cut the skin on either side of his backbone. I carve the skin away from his ribs. Then peel the skin free as he screams.

"Still feeling good, Viktor. Bet you're wishing for that dildo in the ass right about now." I laugh.

When I move away to grab the small hatchet I had brought in just for this, I hear Luna gasp. My eyes find hers immediately. I can see the shock on her face. But I can also see the relief in her eyes. It makes me feel better that she is here. She will always know that I am the one who is going to make sure no one ever touches her again. She is my everything. No one will ever harm her again.

I turn and walk toward him. "What now, brother? Ready to beg for mercy. I will gladly give you some."

"Fuck you. I will never bow down to you."

"So be it."

I grab the hatchet and use it to disconnect his ribs from his backbone one at a time. His screams are like music to my ears. I use the knife to carve down his spine and then have the men flip him over to face everyone. The crowd goes quiet. They have seen much death in their lives, but none have ever seen the blood eagle. I have only done it once before. Vinny also deserved it. But this is Viktor, and he deserves a lot more than this. I am just starting with him. I will torture him for as long as I can. Everyone will think of this if they ever think about touching my angel again.

I have cut away the skin from his chest, revealing his exposed ribs, lungs, and beating heart. Despite being alive, his heart is on the brink of stopping. His agony is so intense that he is attempting to scream, yet he is unable to vocalize. The excruciating pain overwhelms him, taking his breath away and leaving him incapacitated. I am on the verge of lifting his ribs to expose his lungs one by one, while keeping him alive enough to feel every bit of the torment. However, in that moment, I hear a sound that interrupts my plan.

"You earned this Viktor. You must have known what would happen. But you touched me anyway." I hear Luna say from the crowd.

She walks up to the stage. The men who are supposed to protect her are right behind her.

"You took me and raped me. You tortured me and hurt me. You ruined me. But I am not done with you yet. Not until you are dead."

"Luna no. No. Don't. Stop. You don't want to do this." He gasps.

"No. This is what you deserve. This is what you get. This is the way that Demetrius deals with those who dare to touch his woman. And that is what I am to him." She pulls a knife out that I didn't even know she had and slowly walks toward Viktor. "You are a disgrace. You are an evil, pathetic man." She grabs the skin on his chest and slices it away. "You are weak. You are pathetic. You are nothing but a rapist. You aren't even a man." She cuts through the muscles in his chest and exposes his heart. "Just a small worthless piece of shit." She sneers at him.

My chest swells with pride for my angel.

I have to stop her even though what she just did made me so hard I am sure everyone can see my arousal. But I don't care, she is absolutely perfect. Made to rule the Bratva with me. Soft and loving. But will dish out vengeance. If I didn't already love her more than anything in this world, this would have cemented those feelings.

"Patience angel. I have big plans for him."

You Have a Heart After All

Luna

I never planned on walking up onto the stage to take part in this. But before I knew it, my feet were climbing the steps, and I was moving toward Viktor with a knife I had hidden. I cut the rest of the skin away from his chest. I fully intend to grab his heart and show it to him.

"You are weak. You are pathetic. You are nothing but a rapist. You aren't even a man." I cut through the muscles in his chest and exposed his heart beneath his breastbone. "Just a small worthless piece of shit."

His heart is beating. The blood is pumping. I can see the bottom of it as it thumps. It is still alive. He is still alive. He is suffering. But Demetrius stops me before I can reach into his chest cavity and pull it out. I have never felt so savage before.

I have seen and pointed out a few men here that I saw at that warehouse. I want to make sure they understand what's going to happen to them. I am no longer that small frightened girl they used. I will have my vengeance. We are coming for them. I see the blond and the dark haired man in the crowd and the color has drained from both of their faces. Good, they should be terrified.

Demetrius will make them suffer the same fate Viktor is going to endure. I know he will do it. I have no doubts. I nod and move to the side when he steps back in front of Viktor and yanks one of his ribs to the side. I can hear the cracking of the rib. The rib snaps with a sickening crunch. I watch the look of pain spread across Viktor's face as Demetrius grabs another rib and pulls it to the side. Every time he passes out, he has him woken with smelling salts and continues on with the blood eagle.

I can hear the groans and sounds of dismay coming from the crowd. The sound of breaking bones is sickening. Watching Viktor's skin and muscles pulled apart is something I never thought I would have to witness. But I needed to see it. He deserves everything he is getting. And when he is gone, the others who hurt me will get what they deserve, too. I stand beside Demetrius and watch him work. I have to admit, the giant dildo was a nice touch. If I had to guess, I would say he came up with that one after I tried to kill myself.

When he has pulled all the ribs away from Viktor's chest, making a macabre work of art. He wipes his hands and rinses them. He turns to me and kisses me full on the mouth.

"He is yours, angel."

"Thank you, my love." I place my hand on his chest. "I love you so much."

"I love you too."

I stand in front of Viktor. His eyes meet mine and I can see the pain. As much as I don't like the hate that is in my heart, it is there now. Because of men like him. The look he gives me is filled with hatred and anger. But it is also the look of a defeated man. I reach into his chest cavity and wrap my hand around his heart and squeeze. When he mouths a silent scream, I smile at him.

"Goodbye Viktor."

I pull his heart from his chest and the blood gushes all over me. I can feel it trying to pump in my hand as I remove it from his chest cavity. I hold it up to him and shove it into his open mouth.

"Here is your heart and here I thought you didn't have one. I suppose I was wrong after all." I sneer at him as I watch his life fade from his eyes.

I walk down the stage steps covered in blood. Looking like I was in a horror film. Demetrius follows me. We make our way over to Vlad and Aleksandr. I turn around to see what Viktor looks like from far away. He is hung, spread like he has the wings of an eagle, his arms outstretched like an X.

He is fully exposed. All of his organs are spilling onto the floor except for the heart that is now in his mouth. His head is tilted up toward the sky. His face is swollen and his eyes are closed. He looks like an angel. He looks like a saint. But he is nothing but a devil. He was the very embodiment of evil.

"Come, Luna, let's get you cleaned up. I am so proud of you. My avenging angel. No one will ever want to face you again. Don't think I didn't notice the ones in the crowd that went ashen when you walked up on the stage. Their day will come. Don't worry about that. I am going to make sure every last one of them will pay."

My legs are weak. I feel them wobble before he grabs my elbow. Now that it is over, I feel drained and peaceful. Like I can finally sleep.

"Are you alright?"

I nod. "I just don't know what happened. I felt so ...."

"Savage." he smiles at me.

I nod. "Yes. Savage. I knew what he had done. But seeing it. Doing it myself. It is different."

I look down at my hands and arms, still stained with blood. I think maybe I am in a bit of a shock that I did that. I know he deserved it, but I have never felt that kind of hatred for someone before. The relief is almost debilitating. The moment his beating heart was in my hand, I felt a peace I haven't felt since before the warehouse.

"He raped and tortured you. You have every right to be savage."

I looked at him. "What about you?"

"Me?"

"Did you feel savage?"

"I did. But I am different from you, my angel. I am not a good man. I could do this to anyone and everyone but you. I only care for you and eventually, the children that we will have. But anyone else I could kill and never think twice. Anyone who touches what belongs to me is going to pay. And believe me, they will pay."

"Children. We will have children?"

He nods. "I want to have a large family. Will you give me a large family, my angel?" He asks as he guides me from the building to our car.

"Yes. I want to have a house full of children with you. If that is what you want."

What a strange conversation to have when we are both mostly covered in another person's blood.

"It is. More than anything. It is something I had never considered until the day I saw you get out of that old beat up truck. But then the idea of having children with you became the most important thing in my life. Besides you, of course."

"What?" I look at him as helps me into the car and hands me a towel to wipe the blood off of my face. "You saw me the very first day I was here?"

I look in the mirror and what looks back at me reminds me of that Steven King movie Carrie. Jesus.

"Yes. You were looking up at the buildings before walking in and I couldn't look away. You were so beautiful."

"But I was all yucky from traveling?"

"You were perfect. You still are. I would have found you perfect even if you were yucky and covered in mud. I didn't know what it was about you. I was drawn to you. Then when I saw you again in the corner store, it took everything in me to not grab you and make you mine. I had to find out if you were single. I knew then that I had to have you. But my life isn't safe, and I knew I needed you to be protected. But you are safest with me. Always."

I smile at him and think about that day. "You looked so beautiful I almost reached out and touched you. I had to stop myself. Thank you for saving me. For protecting me. Thank you for loving me."

"I will always love you and protect you. You are my heart. You are my everything. You are the woman who completes me. I love you, angel."

We pull up to the house, and he guides me out of the car and straight to the shower.

My Good Girl

Demetrius

Watching my angel become an avenging angel is the hottest thing I have ever seen. When she shoved his heart into his mouth I almost came right there in front of everyone. Seeing his blood spurt out and cover her was ... I close my eyes in bliss just thinking about it. She is perfect.

We are now back home and the meeting has been called to an end. Only a few are left and I know that they will follow my rules. More will come when they hear that the new Pakhan is strong. This is an area for Russians and when they find out you take care of your own first they will join. I will run the

Bratva the way our father did. With fairness and mercy where it is deserved. I will make alliances where I can. But the Italians are on thin ice. The only thing that is stopping a full out war is the peace my father negotiated. But even that won't be enough to stop me in the end.

But for now, I need to concentrate on my beautiful angel. I guide her to the bathroom and start the shower making sure the water is perfect for her. I help her take off the blood soaked clothes and toss them straight in the trash.

"Bend over slowly."

She looks at me and raises her eyebrow.

"Do not argue with me. Daddy said to do it. I need to see your pussy. Now."

She places her hands on the shower wall and slowly pushes her ass back toward me. I run my hands over her back and down to her ass.

"Beautiful. So fucking beautiful. Do you know what you did to me on that stage? Do you know how hard it was for me not to take you right there?"

"Demetrius."

"Hush. You are mine. Mine."

"You are mine too."

"Always."

I spread her ass cheeks apart and look at her glistening wet pussy.

"I need you."

"I am going to take you. Right here. Right now. And when we get out of here I am going to fuck you hard. Then I am going to continue fucking you over and over again. You are going to be so sore you will feel me for days. Is that what you want?"

"Oh god, yes."

I slip my cock into her pussy from behind. She is so fucking wet and warm. I can feel how close I am to coming already. I have to hold it together.

"Fuck me. Fuck me."

"You are such a dirty little slut, aren't you? You're daddy's dirty girl. Oh yes, fuck me, baby. Fuck me hard."

"Daddy. Oh fuck yes. Harder."

"Oh, you love it, don't you? You love it when I take you from behind. Daddy's big cock in your pussy. Fuck, you feel so good."

"I'm going to come."

"Come on my cock baby. Come on it."

"Oh.Fuck fuck fuck. Shit."

"You are mine. Only mine. No one will ever have you."

I slap her ass leaving my handprint on her ass. She moans loudly. It looks so perfect there. I rub it soothing the burn.

"Only you. Oh, Daddy. Only you."

She comes screaming and I can't hold it back anymore. My cock pulses inside of her.

"Fuck. I love you."

"I love you."

I slide out of her and pick her up.

"I can stand."

"I know. But I want to hold you. I need to hold you."

She rests her head against my shoulder and wraps her arms around my neck.

"You are the best thing that ever happened to me."

I hold her for a while cradling her against me as we stand under the water. I set her on her feet gently and wash her hair and body. I help scrub the blood stains off of her as much as possible. I wrap her in a towel and dry her off and then put a towel around my waist. I pick her up and carry her to our bed. Placing her down gently I unwrap her like the present she is.

"It's time for me to make you sore angel. Are you ready for me?"

"Yes. Always."

"What is your safe word?"

"Safeword?."

"Yes, angel. In case you don't like what I am doing and need me to stop."

"Oh."

"Yes, angel. Safeword."

"Strawberry."

"OK, Strawberry it is. Now spread your legs for Daddy."

I kneel between her legs and gently kiss her inner thigh.

"Daddy?"

"Yes, baby?"

"Will you please take me hard? I need to feel you."

"Yes, angel."

I grab her legs and push them up and out and wrap my arms around them. Holding her legs and keeping them in place with my shoulders. I push into her fast and hard. My eyes roll back at the sensation as she moans loudly.

"Oh, yes. Yes. Fuck me hard."

"I told you. You are going to be so sore. And I am just getting started."

I thrust into her as fast and hard as I can.

"Oh, God. Oh god. So good. So big."

"You are so tight, baby. I love it."

"Oh, fuck. Fuck me. Fuck me."

"That's it, baby. Take my cock. Take it deep. Take it all. Oh yes."

"Daddy. Daddy. I'm coming. Oh fuck."

"Me too baby. Fuck me. I'm going to come in your tight pussy."

I can feel her pussy start to quiver around my cock.

"Daddy."

"That's it, baby. Come on my cock. Come for Daddy."

"Oh fuck."

Her pussy clamps down on me hard and I have to stop myself from coming as her pussy squeezes me.

"Fuck. Fuck. Fuck. You ready to come again, baby girl."

She nods her head. "Oh yes."

"Fuck. Take it like a good girl."

"Daddy. Daddy. Oh god."

I pull out and push my cock back in her. Her eyes widen and she is trying to move away but I won't let her.

"You are not getting away this time. Not ever. I am going to fill your pussy with my come and that is a promise."

"Oh, my god. Demetrius. Stop."

"No. Shut the fuck up and take this dick like a good girl."

"Please."

"You want me to stop? You want Daddy to stop."

"No. But."

"Then say the magic word."

"Daddy." she moans

"Yes, that's it. Good girl. Good girl."

I start moving in and out of her pussy again.

"Daddy. Daddy."

"That's it, baby. Keep saying it."

"Oh god. Oh god. Oh god."

"That's it. Say it. Say it."

"Oh, Daddy. Daddy. Fuck."

"You are such a good girl. I'm going to make this pussy so sore and then daddy is going to claim your ass. Fuck. You are so tight. Fuck, fuck. Oh god. Come again for me, baby. Come for Daddy. Oh, fuck. Here it comes baby."

I slam into her one last time and I am coming harder than I have ever come before. I shoot into her like a firehose and can't seem to stop.

"Oh, my god. Oh my god."

"Fuck. Fuck. Fuck."

She is thrashing around on the bed and screaming as her pussy pulses around me. Her back is up off of the bed and her whole body is convulsing. She collapses back onto the bed and starts laughing.

"I am never going to be able to sit down."

"Good. I will be able to keep you under my thumb and do whatever I want with you."

"That was. I can't even describe it."

"Do you want me to stop?"

"No. Never."

"Never? What my angel wants she gets."

"Yes. Please. Fuck me."

"I can't say no to that."

I start fucking her again and I know this time when we are done I am going to pass out. It has been a long day. A long and very satisfying day. What better way to end it then fucking my angel senseless.

Marry Me

Luna

A month later

It has been a month since Demetrius used Viktor as an example. He has been keeping me occupied with the club's activities and entrusted me with its day-to-day operations. Now, the Whispering Russian belongs to me.

He told me that the first thing all the men who come through the doors of the club know is that the Russian mob runs this town. True to his word, he takes me to every single meeting he has. He has an office here in the club, so he can always be with me. When he said he would never let me out of his sight, I figured it was just a figure of speech, but nope. He is always close by. I don't know what I did to deserve him, but I am glad he is mine.

I'm currently sitting in my office at the Whispering Russian doing the books. Demetrius and his guys are all stationed outside. Today is a significant day as he's expected to propose to me. However, it's supposed to be a surprise, and I'm not supposed to know about it. But as expected, it's challenging to keep it a secret when everyone knows about it.

"What are you thinking about?"

I look up and smile when Demetrius walks in.

"Oh ... just how much I love my daddy." I jump up and run to him.

"Angel," he growls at me.

I wrap my arms around his neck. He lifts me up and kisses me.

"My angel. I have a surprise for you."

"You do? What is it?"

"If I told you, then it wouldn't be a surprise, baby."

I smile and kiss him one last time before he sets me down and guides me out the door. He has been acting weird all day. I think I know what is coming, but not exactly how he is going to do it.

I climb into the passenger seat of his car and look back at him. "Are going to take me somewhere?"

"Yes, angel." He gets into the driver's side and starts the car. "I am your chauffeur for the night."

"So, what is my surprise?"

"Patience angel." He gives me a sly grin that turns my insides to mush.

He drives us about a mile or two and parks the car. He opens the door and gets out. He comes over to my side of the car and opens my door.

"Where are we?"

"Patience angel."

He holds out his hand to help me from the car.

"You said that already."

"I know. But the answer is still the same patience angel."

"I am so excited. I can't wait."

"I can't wait either."

He extends his hand towards me, signaling me to hold it, and I oblige.

"This way."

"Yes, Daddy," I whisper. I see the smile that makes the corner of his lips move. He places his hand on my lower back and leads me in the direction he wants us to go.

"Close your eyes."

"Why?"

"Trust me, baby girl."

"Ok, daddy."

I close my eyes and let him guide me wherever it is we are going. I can hear music playing.

"Open your eyes."

I open my eyes and discover a massive white tent in front of me. Beneath it, there's a table that he has arranged. It's covered with a lovely white tablecloth and a striking centerpiece featuring a single red rose. A bottle of champagne and two champagne flutes are placed in the center. When I glance over at him, I see that his eyes are brimming with excitement.

"How did you do all of this?"

"I have my ways, angel. Come over here."

He guides me to the table and pulls out my chair, motioning for me to sit. He then takes his seat on the opposite side.

"Champagne?"

"Yes please."

He pours two glasses of champagne and hands one to me.

"To us. To forever. To happily our ever after."

"To us."

We clink our glasses together, and I take a sip.

"Oh. Delicious."

"Yes, it is. And so are you."

He stands up and reaches for me. I stand up and wrap my arms around his neck.

"You are so beautiful."

"Thank you, Daddy."

"I am your daddy and you are my angel."

"Always."

"Always."

I suddenly see him drop down to one knee and reach into his pocket.

"From the first moment, I saw you. I knew you were the one. The one I wanted to spend my life with, the one I wanted to have children with. I saw your innocence right away and knew you needed to be protected. Nothing worked out how I wanted it to. But in the end, I still got what I wanted. You."

I can feel my heart beating in my chest and tears welling up in my eyes. The love I feel for this man is overwhelming.

"I didn't know what love was when you came into my life. I've never been in love before and didn't know how to be. I figured that was for other men. Not men like me. But I do now and I know I am in love with you and have been since the day you drove your beat up truck into Brooklynn. You are my one true love. I will spend the rest of my life making you happy. Because you are my angel."

He reaches into his pocket and pulls out a small box, which he then opens. Overcome with emotion, I cover my mouth with my hand as tears begin to stream down my cheeks.

"Luna Lewis, will you do me the honor of becoming my wife?"

I drop my hands and grab his hand. "Yes, Demetrius. Yes, yes, yes."

He slips the ring on my finger and picks me up, and spins me around. As he sets me down, I feel my heart racing with excitement and joy. My cheeks flush with a warm blush, and tears of happiness begin to well up in my eyes. Demetrius pulls me close and wraps his arms around me, and I bury my head in his chest, feeling overwhelmed with emotion. It's as if my entire body is tingling with the intensity of the moment, and I can hardly believe that I'm about to become his wife. But as I look up into his eyes, I know that this is exactly where I want to be, and I can't wait to start our lives together as a married couple.

"I love you. I love you so much."

"I love you too."

He kisses me, and then slowly moves his lips to my neck. I love this man. I know that the way we met isn't normal, and it's nothing like in the romance books. But I love him and I know he loves me. I will never have to worry about him straying from me.

"I can't wait to make you my wife and my love for the rest of my life. We have so much to talk about. But first, I have a special request."

"Yes?"

"Stop taking your birth control. We have babies to make."

As I beam at him, his grin widens. It's clear that my smile is infectious. I'm eager to start a family with him, my one true love.

"Yes, Daddy."

"Good girl." He kisses me again, and I know tonight will be one to remember.

A Wedding Gift

Demetrius

Today, both of my brothers departed from here. Vlad flew to the Kremlin to complete his work and clarify the change in command. However, he will return soon, as he will be my second in command. On the other hand, Aleksandr is going back to school to complete his degree. Surprisingly, my takeover has been smoother than I anticipated, especially after the dramatic incident with Viktor. I must confess that I had concerns about facing a rebellion after the blood eagle.

No one dares to cross me because they know the consequences. My men are keeping an eye on the Italians in the neighborhood. If they cause any trouble, I'll consider it a direct challenge and make an example out of them. I already have a score to settle with Salvatore.

Luna showed the men to Anton during Viktor's execution, and then they gathered them up one by one and dealt with them. The two men who assaulted her together ran quickly. But I will find them. There is nowhere they could run to that I won't find them. My angel will have her peace. Her revenge. Her justice.

As I step out of my office, I hear a burst of laughter coming from the kitchen area. Curious, I make my way toward the source of the sound and find myself gazing at my future wife, engrossed in a conversation with a few female servers. My heart swells with joy at the sight of her. I never knew I could love anyone as much as I love her.

She looks so content and happy, which fills me with a sense of pride and fulfillment. She used to be scared and abused, but now she is protected and content. She has found her true calling in life and has become a part of my family. Her place is by my side for eternity, and I have complete faith in her. She has never let me down and continues to amaze me every day. She is the most amazing person I have ever met.

I have made a vow to her and I will always stand by it. She will never be alone again as I am always by her side. I am very protective of her and will never let anyone take her away from me. She is my everything and I am hers. However, I need to focus on the task at hand, even though it's difficult. Whenever I think of my beloved, my mind becomes consumed by her.

The club has been doing much better now that Luna runs it. Her employees love her and since I don't allow anyone to touch her, there is security everywhere. Which means everyone is safe here. If she goes out onto the floor, she gets me first and I go with her. I can't even think about someone touching her, much less trying to take her.

Viktor and his men are no longer a problem. Their bodies have been buried where no one will find them. We are also moving into other parts of the city, pushing everyone else out. We already have orders from the Kremlin to take the city under our control. Apparently, Viktor wasn't running the city correctly, and many things were getting out of hand. He was giving the Italians way more leeway than they deserved. They have been a thorn in our side for far too long. But now that the Kremlin is involved, they will have to pay.

The cartel has made a smart decision by pulling their human trafficking rings out of my city. They witnessed how I dealt with my family members who dared to touch what belongs to me and got the hint that it was not safe for them to operate here. Although the Italians are still active, they now acknowledge who's in charge.

Anton approaches me and puts his hand on my shoulder.

"Yes."

"Sorry to interrupt, sir. The Italians are here."

"Thank you."

I turn and see Salvatore and Aldo.

"Gentlemen."

As they turn around, I signal them with a finger and push open the doors to the kitchen. The moment she glances at me, a smile lights up her face, but it quickly fades as she spots Salvatore. Her expression transforms into a stern one, and she averts her gaze back to me.

"Meeting?" She asks. I nod and she walks to me.

As I lead her to my office, I gently place my hand on the small of her back. Salvatore and Aldo, the Don's second in command, follow us in. After settling into my chair, I pull her onto my lap and signal for Aldo and Salvatore to take a seat.

"What's this about?" I ask.

"We need to have a discussion." Aldo starts, "We had business deals with Viktor. Things that were already set in motion. This is a situation that needs to be dealt with."

"The situation is very simple. Forget any business dealings you had with the Bratva. We no longer have any. They will not happen with me. Viktor was in charge of the dealings you had. Those were his issues. Not mine."

"That's not how this works. Pakhan. The deals were already in place. Now you will need to live up to them."

"I told you. No."

"You are not being smart, Demetrius. This would be lucrative for both of us."

I see his eyes flicker to Luna for a moment too long, and my protectiveness goes into overdrive.

"You need to keep your eyes on me and stop looking at my future wife before I pluck your eyes out of your skull, Aldo."

"Is that a threat, Pakhan? I can assure you the Don won't be happy if it is."

I look at him and meet his gaze. "Aldo, I don't care how your Don feels, quite frankly. This is not a threat, it is a promise. Any man who would sell his daughter to this scum," I say, pointing my finger at Salvatore. "gets no respect from me." I look straight at Salvatore and he has the nerve to smirk. I clench my fists. "There will be no human trafficking in my city. The Cartel already got the idea and left. You are free to join them. If I find out, there is any going on, I will make an example out of them. This is your only warning."

"Demetrius. I must insist."

"I don't care what you must do. I don't care what you want. No one will be selling any of the women, girls or boys that call the streets home. I think we are done here."

"So be it."

"Aldo, you know where the door is."

He stands and so does Salvatore.

"Salvatore," I call. He stops and turns around. "Don't think you have escaped my wrath for what you did. I don't care if you become the Don. She will get her revenge."

He smirks. "I look forward to it."

I notice the sudden surge of anger in her eyes and quickly take hold of her hand. She understands the message I am trying to convey.

"Now go."

Aldo leaves first and Salvatore is right behind him. Anton looks at me before closing the door and I nod.

"Are you ok?"

"Yes, Daddy."

"You sure?"

She nods and turns to look at me.

"What was he here for?"

"The Don and Viktor had a deal set up. But that doesn't matter now. There will be none of that in my city." I smooth the hair out of her beautiful face.

"Is the Don really selling his only daughter to Salvatore?"

I nod "He is."

"Why would he do such a thing? That man is a monster."

"It's not our worry, angel. I wanted to talk to you about something."

"Ok."

"When I asked you to marry me. We knew it might take a little while, but I think it is time to make it official. I want to make this a public event. I want you to be my beautiful wife. The mother of my children. I want to everything with you."

"Oh, Demetrius. I would love to be your wife. I want to have your babies so much."

I grab her face and kiss her.

"I love you so much, my angel. Now, what do you say we call the wedding planner and get this show on the road?"

As she jumps off my lap, she lets out a cheerful squeal that warms my heart. Witnessing her happiness brings me immeasurable joy. In the past, I would have gone to great lengths to safeguard her, and I still would without hesitation. However, if she were to ask, I would willingly set the world ablaze just to witness the radiance of her smile.

I reach into my desk and grab a small box. I hold it out to her. "I got you a wedding present."

She looks at me with a furrowed brow. “But we aren’t getting married today.”

"I know, angel. But I am going to give you this gift now and a different wedding present later."

She takes the box and opens it.

"Oh, my god." She pulls out the key to her truck. "You're giving me my truck back?"

"I am. But that isn't the surprise. Come on."

I stand and take her hand, leading her out to the back of the building. What she doesn't know is I had her truck fully restored. I can't wait to see her face. I know how much she loved that old rust bucket. I walk her out the back and stop in front of her truck.

"Demetrius? Is this what I think it is?"

"I had the mechanic bring it back to life. You are now the proud owner of a now nice looking 1970 Chevy K10 instead of the worn out rust bucket it was."

I open the door and help her in.

"I don't know what to say."

"Don't say anything. Just drive."

"Daddy?"

"Yes, baby?"

"Thank you. Thank you so much."

"You are very welcome, angel."

She grabs my hand and squeezes. "Thank you for loving me. For believing in me. For giving me a home. For giving me a family and everything else. But most of all, thank you for always loving me for who I am."

"You are my everything, angel. My everything. Now go."

She starts the truck, and it roars to life. She looks at me and grins.

"I can't believe this. I never thought I would ever get to drive this truck again."

"Well, get out of here. Go have fun. The truck has a tracker on it and the men will be right behind you. I will meet you at home. Be safe baby. Love you."

"Love you too."

Observing her as she leaves the parking lot at a high speed, I can’t help but shake my head. Soon, two cars of guards follow her. I make my way to my car and get inside, reminiscing about how much she cherished that truck. Anton advised me to store it for her. Thankfully, I did, or else it would have been lost forever.

I am happy that she has found her peace and happiness. She is the most important thing in my life and without her; I am nothing.

The Wedding

Luna

3 Months later

The day I have been so excited about is finally here. As I watched the sun drop behind the trees, my excitement grew. The day has finally come that I become Mrs. Demetrius Sokolov. I am half Russian after all. Who would have known? I was so happy when my father agreed to walk me down the aisle. He even moved closer to me so he could be a part of my life now. It's not like he can put me in any more danger than I already am. If anything, it offers even more protection.

My father sticks his head in the door and smiles at me. He walks in and puts his arms out. I move to him and step into his arms as he smiles at me.

"Look at you, my daughter, looking so radiant! It is time. Are you ready?"

"I am so ready." I answer excitedly.

When we step out of the building, the gentle caress of a summer breeze plays with the tendrils of my veil, carrying with it the delicate scent of blooming roses and the distant murmur of excited guests. My heart races in my chest, a symphony of emotions swirling like a tempest as we moved behind the grand archway, hidden from view. This was the culmination of a journey that Demetrius and I had fought tirelessly for, a moment of magic we had dreamt of, and now it was here — our wedding day.

As the opening of the wedding march echoed through the air, a sense of serenity washed over me, a reassuring reminder that I was stepping into a new chapter of my life with the man who has stood beside me through thick and thin. Saved me and loved me regardless of the things that have been done to me. My avenger. My protector. My very own angel of death.

My gown, a masterpiece woven with intricate lace and silk that seemed to shimmer like moonlight, draped around me, trailing behind like a train of stardust. Silver stars adorned my veil, catching the light as if they held secrets of the cosmos.

With each step I took down the aisle, my heart felt like it was beating in time with the rhythm of the universe. I could feel the gazes of our guests upon me, their collective energy a source of strength. The petals underfoot seemed to echo the flutter of my heart, a path that led me towards Demetrius, the man I love more deeply than words could ever convey. A man more precious to me than anything in this world.

As I reached the pavilion, my eyes met his, and all at once, the world around us faded into the background. His eyes held a mixture of emotions, a mirror of my own–the excitement, the anticipation, the journey we had embarked upon. His presence grounded me, anchoring me to the reality that this was no longer a dream, but a beautiful reality we were creating together.

The officiant's voice, a soothing cadence that seemed to blend seamlessly with the rustling leaves, spoke words that resonated with the depths of my soul. Promises were made, vows exchanged, and rings slipped onto our fingers, tangible symbols of the eternity we are pledging to one another. With every word, every touch, the bond between us seemed to grow stronger, an unbreakable thread woven through time and space.

As Demetrius leaned in for our first kiss as husband and wife, time seemed to stand still, and the world around us disappeared. Our lips meet, and in that electrifying moment, I feel the culmination of our love, our struggles, and our unwavering determination. The warmth of his embrace enveloped me, and I knew that together, we had overcome every obstacle to reach this pinnacle of happiness.

As we turned to face our guests, their cheers and applause enveloped us like a wave of love. It was a moment of pure joy, a collective celebration of the love that had brought us here, and the love that would carry us forward. Hand in hand, we walked back down the aisle; the world transformed by the sheer radiance of our union.

Surrounded by the soft flutter of butterflies released by our guests, we entered a realm of revelry and delight. The night sky above was studded with stars, a breathtaking canopy under which we danced, laughed, and shared in the jubilation of our new journey together. With every twirl and every smile, I felt the weight of the world lift from my shoulders, replaced by the weightlessness of love and happiness.

And so, beneath the watchful gaze of the moon and amidst the luminous tapestry of stars, Demetrius and I celebrated our wedding that was not just a ceremony, but a testament to the extraordinary power of love and the indomitable spirit that had guided us to this moment. Our celestial union was a beacon of hope, a reminder that, against all odds, our love story had blossomed, shining brighter than any star in the night sky.

I know that through it all, I will always be

His Everything

The end

Thanks for Reading!

Thank you so much for reading His Everything. I truly hope you enjoyed it. If you love reading it as much as I loved writing it I'd love for you to leave a review. This is an interconnected standalone series and the next one will be in November.

Again thank you for reading!

His Queen

In the heart of Brighton Beach, New York, a chance encounter at a dimly lit bar ignites a passion neither Rose nor Vladimir could have predicted. They succumb to the allure of one another, sharing a passionate night of desire, blissfully unaware of their true identities. She, a Mafia Princess, destined to wed a cruel and heartless man. He, the unyielding second-in-command of the Bratva, the Russian Mafia.

As dawn breaks, their worlds collide, and secrets unravel. Rose finds herself ensnared in a dangerous web of loyalty and obligation, promised to a man who knows no mercy. But Vladimir, driven by an unexplainable connection, is determined to save her from a fate she never chose.

In the shadows of their respective empires, they embark on a treacherous journey to defy destiny, where love and power intersect. Can Vladimir protect his queen without plunging

their worlds into all-out war?

"His Queen" is a sizzling dark romance that delves into the dangerous depths of love, loyalty, and the fine line between desire and destruction.

Warning: This book has dark themes please be sure to read the trigger warnings. If you like a man who knows what he wants and is willing to fight for it this might be the book for you.

Also By: Jenny D

Thank you for reading please rate and comment.
I would love to hear from you!

The Fated Series

The Lycan's Bride – Adra and Damien

The Norse Vampires Bride – Morgan and Axel

The Wolf, The Fae, and The Portal – Zia and Greyson

Bella and Her Twin Beloveds – Bella, Bjorn, and Erik

Forgotten Souls MC

Shep

Tank – Coming Soon

Post Apocalyptic Romance Series

My Three Mates

Winning Shelly's Heart – Planned 2024

The Sokolov Brothers: A Dark Bratva Romance

His Everything- Forced Proximity

His Queen – Forced Marriage – 2023

Her Savior – Taboo Romance – Planned for 2024

His Princess – Friends to Lovers – Planned for 2024

Made in the USA
Monee, IL
06 November 2024